TROJAN
crown

A SINGLE DAD & NANNY ROMANCE

ELEANOR ALDRICK

TROJAN crown

A SINGLE DAD & NANNY ROMANCE

ELEANOR ALDRICK

Trojan Crown
Copyright © 2022 by Eleanor Aldrick
All rights reserved.

Cover Design: Sinfully Seductive Designs
Interior Formatting: Sinfully Seductive Designs
Proof Read by: OnPointeDigitalServices

No part of this book may be reproduced in any form or by any electronic or mechanical means, including information storage and retrieval systems, without written permission from the author, except for the use of brief quotations in a book review.

For more information, address: eleanoraldrick@gmail.com

This is a work of fiction. Names, characters, businesses, places, events, locales, and incidents are either the products of the author's imagination or used in a fictitious manner. Any resemblance to actual persons, living or dead, or actual events is purely coincidental.

ISBN: 9798406195055

FIRST EDITION

10 9 8 7 6 5 4 3 2 1

For all the broken girls who need a little Daddy in their lives.

"There is beauty in the broken."

- Eleanor Aldrick

Playlist
ON REPEAT

Hostage - **Billie Eilish**
Happier Than Ever - Edit - Billie Eilish
Mama Said - **Lukas Graham**
Wildest Dreams - Taylor Swift
Traitor - **Olivia Rodrigo**
Gunpowder & Lead - Miranda Lambert
Nothing Like You - **Nikerryan**
Beggin' - Maneskin
Remember Why You Fell in Love - **Natalie Madigan**
I AM WOMAN - Emmy Meli
Glock - **Dark Polo Gang, Wayne Santana, DrefGold, Giaime**
Madness - Ruelle
Burning - **Ones, Just Lil**

Prologue
ANAX

The mirror mocks me. Freshly showered and naked as the day I was born, there's nowhere to hide.

I just stand there. Assessing. Wondering where my body went wrong.

Like two tiny beacons, the dusky rose of my nipples calls to me, bringing my eyes to the soft mounds that surround them. *Are they big enough?*

Blinking, I let my gaze travel to the undefined stomach below. *Is it firm enough?*

Sucking in a sharp breath, I violently pull my face from the mirror. *Am I not good enough? Is that why he won't touch me?*

The questions are all too much, ripping a choked sob from

my throat and filling the otherwise quiet room.

One after the other, tears escape my glassy blue eyes. And as they fall, I know something needs to change or whatever's left of my heart won't survive this.

Taking a staggering breath, I let my composure crack and my heart breaks right along with it; the fissures reaching into the deepest crevices of my soul.

The pain, *it's so heavy*, I know there's no escaping it.

Wiping the tears that seem to fall steadily now, I wonder how this became my reality? How did I become *that* girl? The one who second guesses her worth, wondering if she's good enough for a man. That's not me, *is it*?

My mind wanders to him. The much older man with his just-fucked hair and stormy eyes that always seem to pull me back in. There was a time he could never get enough of me, when his hands never left my body. He made me feel like I was the most beautiful woman on this earth. Like I was the only thing that mattered.

A groan falls from my lips, wishing I could call someone— *anyone*—and talk to them about this living nightmare.

My stomach turns at the memory of my one and only friend. She warned me this would happen. That he would grow bored. What could a full-grown man want with a then nineteen-year-old?

Foolishly, I ignored her and blamed it on jealousy. Never once giving her words another thought.

On no planet could I think he'd tire of me when he'd made me his world. So, of course, when he asked me to move three-thousand miles away, I did. I left my old life behind and started a new one here with him.

I'm not ashamed to say that I enjoyed a man giving me the attention and structure I lacked all my life. Yes, he was domineering and liked things done a certain way, but that was part of what drew me in.

I shake my head, seriously doubting everything now. *Was it all a lie? Have I been living a farce?*

It's been *months* and not a stolen kiss nor a whispered word of affection. How did my husband of two years turn into a fucking roommate? Was my friend, right? Is he finally bored?

I wrap my silk robe around my still damp body, the black material clinging to my every curve. *Was it our schedules?* I know I'm always at school and he's often out of town for work, so there are days where we don't even see each other. *Is that it? Does he not see enough of me?*

I have to make this better. I have to make this work. I'm about to pull out my makeup bag and start getting ready for my last final when I hear the front door open. Looking up, my face beams back at me in the mirror. *He's home early!* Could it be that he missed me?

Running to the bathroom door, I swing it open, but what I see is not at all what I expected.

My husband is disheveled and upset. "Ray? Is everything okay?"

"Yes," he grumbles, "Nothing I can't sleep off."

He goes to walk past me and I jump to seize the moment. Grabbing onto his wrist, I turn him back toward me. Our eyes clashing—his questioning and mine determined. *Come hell or high water, I'm going to make this work.*

I press my palms to his chest, sliding them down his body as I drop to my knees before him.

"Anaya, stop." Ray's hands fall to my shoulders, trying to push me away, but I'm hell-bent on making him feel good. *Maybe then he'll want me?*

With a speed I didn't know I had, I pull him free, my eyes focused on his as I fist his length. But the cold flint in his eyes is one I don't understand until my lips are wrapped around his girth and I taste it.

As if frozen in time, I *fucking* taste it. The tangy flavor of a woman mixed with his masculine release.

With a horrifying pop, I remove him from my mouth, my eyes still blinking up at him. *He didn't even bother wiping her off... He walked into our home with the evidence of his affair still on his body.*

I can't. I fucking can't.

I rise on bare feet, and before my mind can catch up, I'm running toward the front door.

Out of my periphery I see a hand reach out, but I whirl, missing it as I grab my purse and flee through the door.

I can hear my name being called, but it's so faint compared to the ringing in my ears. It's loud, bouncing around in my head as my lungs catch fire and my feet turn to ice as the soles repeatedly slap against the cold pavement.

I don't know how long I've been running when I come to the big oak tree, my hand falling to the rough bark it's encased in. All I know is that I no longer hear my name being called, and the sharp pain that pierced my chest is now a dull ache.

My breath is coming out hard and rough, the cold air I'm sucking in cooling off the boiling rage I have inside, when I hear it. My phone.

I wasn't thinking when I stepped outside of our home, but I at least had the state of mind to grab my purse. I'm looking down at myself while shaking my head. *I'm still in my damn robe.*

I'm pulling out my phone, mentally registering which hotel I'll be staying at tonight when I see it's my mom. I can't talk to her. *Not now.*

Pushing the call to voicemail, I pull up my browser and start reviewing a three-star motel. But before I can book it, the phone starts ringing again, my mom's name flashing bright across the screen.

My brows furrow as a new worry snakes itself into my chest. This isn't like her. She never calls twice. Fearing the worst, I accept the call and press the phone to my ear. "Mom? Are you okay? Is everything okay?"

"Oh, Anaya. Thank god you answered!" Panic laces her voice, making my entire body turn to ice.

"Mom. Talk to me. What's going on?"

"I need you here, Anaya. The kids, they were kidnapped. I need your help. Mr. Crown said he would pay for everything, but we need you here as soon as possible."

My mind is a whirl of emotions and thoughts. *The kids? What kids?* "I don't know what's going on, but I'll be there."

There's only been one steady constant in my life and that's my mother. There's no way I'm letting her down now, especially not for a worthless marriage I thought was real.

"Thank you, sweetie. I'll arrange for a jet to pick you up. Just head toward the private air space in Jenks and tell them you're with the men of WRATH securities."

I'm nodding as I look down at myself. I don't know who these men of WRATH are, but I bet they won't be impressed by my showing up in nothing but a robe. Yes, I'm definitely making a pit stop at Walmart, but I'll be there. "Okay. I'll be there in an hour."

"Love you, Anaya. I'll see you soon."

"Love you too, momma. See you in a bit." Disconnecting the call, I let it all sink in. I'm leaving. I don't know for how long, but I know it's for the best.

Mom is the house manager for a swanky ranch I visit every summer. The resort is nestled amongst hundreds of acres in beautiful Colorado, the perfect place to clear my head, and whatever it is that Mom needs help with will give me the space and clarity I need.

Sending up a silent prayer to the powers that be, I give my thanks for this wild turn of events. I'm not sure what the future has in store for me, but I know one thing it doesn't... *a lying, cheating, asshole of a husband.*

TROJAN CROWN

Chapter One
AUSTIN

Two weeks ago, Mexico …

The pounding. I feel it everywhere. In my head. In my throat. In my chest. *In my heart*. It's going to give out.

My steps falter as my bare feet dig into the blazing hot sand. *Just a little further.* I'll get out of here if I just keep going.

I'm about to collapse when visions of pigtails and a cocky little grin invade my mind. *My children.* I fucking left them.

Guilt spears me, cutting me right through the bone—and my only solace is that there was no other way. I *had* to get help. I *have* to get help.

The sun's rays are punishing, making my neck blister as I

trek another mile in the Mexican desert, but I can't stop moving. Everything I put my family through, it won't be in vain.

I'm huffing out heavy breaths as my tongue sticks to the roof of my mouth, reminding me I haven't had a drop to drink in God knows how long, but it's what I deserve. Hell on earth.

This is all my fault and I need to make it right.

Should I have stayed? Visions of my wife and children, tied up and on the floor, flash before me. And like a bat to the chest, pain slams into me, seeping into every cell of my body and making me stumble.

No. This had to be done. Staying would have meant certain death for us all. Leaving was the only way of finding help. Our only chance at survival.

I'd do it all again if it gives us the chance of escaping this Hell. One foot in front of the other, I move forward as my head replays the horror of the past few days…

"Enough, Blanca." I glare at my wife, begging her to drop it.

"You won't even notice I'm gone." She bats her long lashes, slowing down her pace and letting our three kids walk in front of us.

We've just left dinner and she thinks now is the perfect time to drop this bomb on me. "No, Blanca. You cannot disappear for a week. Your children need you."

I normally wouldn't be against her taking some time for herself, but this is the third time in two months.

The kids and I barely see her as it is. I swear she spends more time away from the house than I do, and that's saying something.

"They have Pen. She'll be eighteen in less than three months." *She waves a hand toward my stepdaughter, her long dark hair swaying with the breeze as she walks hand in hand with our nine and five-year-old.*

Turning toward her, I suck in a sharp breath and beg for patience. "They need their mother, Blanca—"

Before I can finish my sentence, I'm cut off by screeching tires and our five-year-old's scream. What the fuck?

A blacked-out van has pulled up in front of us, men pouring out of it like a damn clown car. But these aren't clowns. No. I can tell by their tattoos. Jesus Christ.

My feet are already in action, running full speed toward my kids. They can't take them. Over my dead fucking body.

Behind me, I hear Blanca screaming while Penelope is off to the side, fighting off a man with one hand and grabbing a hold of Alex with the other.

I finally reach Amanda just as she's being thrown in the van. Wrapping my arms around her tiny frame, I pull back, but my strength is no match for the three men who've come up behind me.

I try a roundhouse kick in a last-ditch effort, but instead of succeeding, I feel something heavy connect with my head. It's all over. I lose my balance as darkness takes me under. And as black shrouds my vision, I send out one last prayer of hope. My kids. God, please… save my kids.

Light seeps in through my cracked lids as I slowly come to, wincing at the pain that's taking over my body. Damn. It hurts everywhere.

As I blink my eyes open, haunting images resurface. They're memories reminding me of my reality. Horrible visions that will forever be seared into my soul.

I'll never forget Blanca's tear-stained face as they dragged her and our kids away. Helpless is too little of a word to describe what I felt as these fuckers ripped my family apart, pulling me down a long hallway before beating me and leaving me for dead.

I need to find them and get my family out. But these walls, they're stifling, sucking out what little breath I have left and making each pull of air a staggering blow.

Assessing my surroundings, I know time is running out. There are no windows and the stains on the floor let me know this room has a purpose. One I'm not too keen on.

I'm in the middle, sitting on a cold metal chair with both arms bound behind my back.

Working with limited movement, I feel around for anything useful, wincing when my finger slits open against a jagged edge. Jackpot. *If I angle myself just right, maybe I can cut myself free.*

The rope digs into my wrists as I rub up and down against the raw edge of the chair, but I keep working despite the pain.

When the tension on the rope starts to give, my heart fills with hope. I don't know how the chair came to be in this state, but I do know that I'm so damn grateful that it is.

Working my hands faster, I feel the material give. And just in the nick of time, as a man dressed in all black walks in, followed by one of the men I'd seen before.

With a quick glance past him, I can see the hallway is empty. A possible escape. *The asshole from earlier walks toward me, ripping off the gag they'd tied on inside the van. They didn't even bother with a head covering. Not their usual M.O.*

This can only mean one thing… A dead man can't leak coordinates, and they have no plans of my ever leaving.

Well, too bad. I'm not on the same page. "Where's my family?"

A fist flies toward me, knocking my face back and

sending the chair rocking, making it difficult to conceal the fact that my hands are no longer bound. Somehow, I keep both behind me, using my legs which are free to stabilize myself once more.

"Don't talk unless I ask you to, you fucking rat." The man in all black spits out, his eyes narrowing, assessing. "You're going to tell me exactly where you hid it. If you don't, Marco here is going to show you just how we treat those who betray the cartel."

The man next to him grins as he traces a finger across his throat, no doubt fantasizing about decapitation. El Jefe and his men are known for their gruesome punishment, something I knew about going into this but never expected to be a part of.

My stomach rolls, fear turning my body to ice. I'm not worried about myself, but for my kids. They don't deserve this.

"You better start talking. The boss doesn't like waiting for information." The man in black raises a brow, an evil smirk playing on his lips.

I lift my chin defiantly, unwilling to let him see me cower. "I'll tell you what you want if you let my family go."

"No deal." The man in black turns toward the door. "Marco, rough him up. Maybe when I come back, he'll be in more of a talking mood." He's about to walk out when he turns back to me. "Mr. Crown, if you don't tell me what I want to hear, I'll force you to *watch as my men rape and torture your family. One by one, we'll take them from you until you break."*

The door closes with a thud, and my heartbeat jacks up tenfold. This is it. My odds of fighting off two men at once weren't great, but one I could manage. Especially if there aren't any guards outside this door.

Marco walks over to a table, pulling open a drawer and running his fingers along a selection of surgical instruments. "What will it be, hermano?"

"I'm not your brother," I spit back, unwilling to make this any more enjoyable for him.

"That's not what you had us believing. Negotiating with the boss, just like your viejo."

My eyes narrow, the topic of my dad hitting me where it hurts. Anger burns through me, making my breath come out in short, shallow breaths. "Stop talking and get on with your plans. Nothing you say or do will make me give up the information el Jefe wants."

"You think you're this big tough guy. But you'll crack. They all do." Marco's lips peel back, exposing his yellowing teeth as he walks toward me with a scalpel. "Oh, I'm going to have so much fun making you beg."

Not if I can help it.

As soon as he's within reach, I kick out my leg, swiping it under his and making him fall on his ass—the scalpel flying up before coming back down and impaling itself on his face.

"Pinche pendejo!" He groans on the ground as his hands reach for the blade, but I'm already on my feet, hand reaching for the handle of the scalpel and digging it in further.

I've never killed a man, but it's not beyond me. This is him or me. My family or his sick and twisted soul. The choice is clear. He needs to go.

His yells of sheer horror bounce off the walls, and thankfully, his crew was expecting torture to be had... they just didn't know it'd be on one of their own.

Wanting to end this shit as quickly as possible, I flip this asshole onto his stomach, pinning him down with my weight as my arms go around his head in a choke hold. Acting on instinct, my hands go to his head, and with a sick crack, his head twists, his entire body going limp in my arms.

It's done. Now, how in the hell am I going to get out of here without alerting everyone that I've escaped. If they find his body, they'll kill my family without a second thought.

My eyes are lingering on Marco's prone form when the answer hits me. **Shit.** *I don't want to do this, but will it buy me enough time?*

The answer to that has me walking toward the table where Marco had pulled the scalpel from. I open the deeper drawer and find what I'm looking for.

I pick up the machete, my stomach rolling with the

knowledge of what I'm about to do. This has to be done.

Switch clothes, decapitate him, and hide the evidence.

This should get me enough time to find my family and get us the fuck out of here.

As soon as I've switched clothes, I position him for the infamous cartel welcome. Fuck. *Sucking in a massive breath, I lift the machete and swing down. The sound of metal connecting with bone forever embedding itself into my soul. There's no coming back from this.*

My chest heaves from the effort as my stomach rolls. For my family. For my kids. *I repeat the mantra over and over as the blood pools and splatters.* For my kids.

In a daze, I finish the task at hand, shoving his head into a bag I pulled from the torture table.

With a few tentative steps forward, I press my ear to the door and listen. Quiet. Taking a chance, I crack the door open and peer out. Just as before, the hallway is empty.

It's now or never, Austin. *Stepping into the hall, I take in my surroundings. I'm in a long corridor, and if my memory serves me, they brought me in from the left.*

Walking on the balls of my feet, I ditch the head inside the first flowerpot I see and pray that this takes me to my family.

I'm about to turn left when I hear men talking. "The cunt is saying she has ties to the leader of the Cárdenas Cartel."

They're talking about my wife Blanca. I discovered her well-kept secret when I started on this fucked up journey. My eyes briefly close as I take in a quiet breath. Lies, deceit, and death. That's all that surrounds me.

After a beat, another man speaks up, his words coming out with a thick accent. "If she's speaking the truth, el Jefe will want to keep them alive. Use them for leverage."

Hope sparks in my heart. God. Maybe Blanca's past will be the ticket to our escape.

"You're right. We're in deep with their jefe. You know what that means, right?"

"Yeah." I hear a deep exhale. "No playing with our catch."

"Especially not the girl. If she's Cárdenas' daughter, she'll be worth a pretty penny."

Footsteps take over their conversation, the sound drawing nearer. Damnit! I have nowhere to hide. If they find me, it's over, and how will I save my family then?

My eyes fall to a window, and I know I have to jump out. It's a matter of seconds before they find me.

Knowing that my family is relatively safe for now, I take the leap of faith and crack the large window open, sliding out just in time. Thankfully, we're on the ground floor and I crouch down as soon as my feet hit the gravel.

"How long 'til the boss is back?" The words float out of the small opening as the men walk by.

"A week. He's got business in the states."

Their conversation trails off and I'm left with nothing but silence and a choice to make.

This new revelation has given me an opportunity.

Stay and try to sneak my family out, battling countless men at the same time and exposing my family to more danger... or take a chance that they will be safe for at least a week, giving me enough time to find help and come back with a team to wipe these sick bastards out.

With my heart in my throat, I make the hardest decision of my life. Though the latter separates me from my kids, I know it's the lesser of two evils. They're relatively safe for now. I just need to get my ass in gear and get back to them as soon as possible.

If any of them die, I won't survive it. Nor should I.

My face contorts as visions of my lifeless children float inside my head. *My kids.* They're so young, so full of life. *This can't be their end.*

I'm too lost in gruesome thoughts, I don't see it until it's too late.

My foot sinks into something sharp, the jagged material

sending shooting pain up my leg and making me tumble to the ground.

Fuck.

My vision blurs as it focuses in and out on the cut. Glass. I stepped on a broken beer bottle.

Glass... Glass... Glass! People! Glass means people!

I squeeze my eyes shut, a choked sob ripping from my throat as my eyes tingle with impending tears that never come, my body too dehydrated to offer a drop. No matter. This isn't the time for tears. I'll save those for when I'm holding my babies once more.

God. Will they ever forgive me? If they only knew. I'm the reason they're in this mess.

It's okay. It'll be okay. I'll make things right if it's the last thing I do.

With my renewed determination, I walk on, praying against all odds that I find people and make it out of Satan's sweltering asshole alive.

TROJAN CROWN

Chapter Two
ANAYA

"I know I've said this before, but thank you." Mom's soft voice is like balm to my aching heart. I can't help but cling to it as I unpack my bag.

"There's no need to thank me, Mom. You've been there for me too many times to count. Of course I'd come and help you."

I'm putting a pack of nightshirts into a drawer when Mom's hand stops me. "Anaya, where are your things?"

"What do you mean? These are my things." Unable to look her in the eyes, I keep unloading my stuff and shoving it into drawers, hoping she'll drop it. I really don't want to talk about my dumpster fire of a life, and I don't want to tell her I belonged in one of those *People of Walmart* books, walking into the store in just a damn robe and a bag.

"None of these items have been worn, Anaya. These are all new. Even the toothbrush. It's still in its original packaging." She picks it up and waves it in my face, the bright blue encasing taunting me with the truth.

I ignore her, snatching the offending toothbrush before I shove it into the nightstand—as if placing it out of sight will make it any less obvious that all of this is new.

Not wanting to address the elephant in the room, I continue with my task. One by one I hang up the sun dresses I'd purchased, not once lifting my gaze from the fabric.

Just when I thought I was in the clear, Mom hisses my name. "Anaya Marie. Sit and start talking."

Her command has me halting my movements and finally looking up. With a deep sigh, I let my eyes focus on the skin bunching between her brows and let her in on a little of the truth. "When you called, I was sort of in the middle of something. I couldn't go home to get stuff, so I just stopped by Walmart and picked up essentials. No big deal."

There. That wasn't an outright lie. Just a little omission.

Mom raises a brow and sits on the edge of the bed, patting the spot right next to her. "Child. I'm your mother. I know when you're hiding something. And you know I'm not letting this go until you've told me what's really going on, right?"

I huff my way to the bed, groaning as I plop down next to her. I know she's right. She's like a dog with a bone. The sooner I spit this out, the faster she'll drop it. "I caught Ray cheating. I'd just walked out of the house after finding out... and I couldn't bring myself to go back. Not for all the money in the world." My lip wobbles and voice cracks as I bring my hands to my face. "I couldn't do it, Momma. I just couldn't."

"Oh, Anaya." Her arms wrap around me, trying to squeeze my pain away. But she can't. Nobody can.

This ache lives deep inside me and I don't know how I'll get rid of it. Sobbing into her chest, I let her soothing embrace pull the words that are carved into my soul. "I'm so stupid, Momma. How didn't I see? How was I so blind?"

"Don't. Do not blame yourself for something that wasn't under your control. You can't control another person's actions. What he did, that's his cross to bear." She pulls away, her hands finding my face as her eyes search mine. "The only thing you need to do is worry about what you're going to do now that you know who he really is… a weak and foolish man. Only a foolish man would cheat on my beautiful daughter."

A small smile plays on her lips as her thumbs wipe away my tears. "Well, whatever I do, I'm not going back."

She gives me a sad smile and I know I won't like what she says next. "We can't run away from our problems, sweetie. You don't have to get back with him, but you will have to face him at some point. Even if it's just to pick up your stuff and officially end things."

Sniffling, I give her a small nod. "Okay. But I don't have to do that right this second, so how about you fill me in on whatever's going on here. Tell me about the kids I'll be watching." She seems unsure, and that won't do. I know if we keep talking about me, I'll just melt into a useless puddle.

"Please, Mom. I can't talk about me right now."

Mom nods, her face going from sad to sadder, if that's even possible. "You already know Mr. Crown."

"Yes, of course. He's always been so kind. I've been here every summer for the past four years and I've never had a negative thing to say about him."

She nods, but her somber expression doesn't lift. "He has four brothers. One of them had two small children and a stepdaughter. Well that brother, Austin, was in Mexico with his wife and kids when they were all kidnapped, but only the children survived."

My mouth is hanging wide open as I take this all in. *Who would do this to them?*

"Yes. I know. It's tragic." Mom continues as if I'd vocalized my thoughts. "And if all that wasn't enough trauma for those poor kids, they go and get kidnapped again!"

Gasping, I reach for her shoulders. "Oh my god! Tell me they're okay."

"The eldest is still missing, but they found the two younger kids in an abandoned church." She presses the pads of her fingers to her lips. "That's where Jack is right now. He's with the children and the social worker. Last I'd heard, they'd be arriving home sometime this evening."

I'm staring at her wide eyed and in shock. "How is this real life? How does this happen?"

"That's something you'll have to ask Mr. Crown. I'm just the house manager." She smooths down the fabric across her lap even though there isn't a wrinkle to be seen. "You should've seen him, Anaya. The man went absolutely mad when they took those kids." Her voice cracks and eyes water. I know she's putting on a front, but it's clear as day she was worried too.

"So, where is the eldest? The stepdaughter?"

Her glassy eyes meet mine and she nods. "That's why Mr. Crown asked you to come help with the kids. They're still searching for her and he's going to need all the help he can get with Amanda and Alex."

I'm still trying to process everything she's said when her latest words sink in. "Hold on. I don't have any real childcare experience other than watching Doña Flora's daughter growing up. Why me? Why did he ask for me?"

"The family has been through so much. They don't trust any outsiders, and to be honest, I wouldn't either. So, even though you aren't a professional nanny, Mr. Crown pleaded you come help with the kids. He knows you and knows you come from honest stock." Mom pats my hand and smiles, knowing full well she's the stock he's referring to. "He trusts you, and that alone is worth more than any world-acclaimed nanny ever could."

"Makes sense. I'd be weary of outsiders too if I were him."

"Yes, it's one less thing to worry about. The kids have their own security detail, but they aren't nanny material. Those children need love and warmth. Something I'm sure you'll give to them in spades."

"Of course. You know I will."

Mom nods. "Good. Those kids already lost their parents, and now with the possibility of losing Pen too, I'm not sure they'll survive it." She shakes her head as if clearing it of any negative thoughts. "But anyway, Jack won't stop searching until he finds Austin's stepdaughter. In the meantime though, we'll need to help them deal with her absence. They're bound to have big emotions, and rightfully so."

I feel my brows furrow. "Surely Mr. Crown could afford a therapist for the two."

Mom's face goes stark white. "No therapists." She clears her throat and her face regains a little bit of its color. "Their last therapist was the one who helped in their kidnapping. It's no surprise Mr. Crown isn't champing at the bit to find them a new one."

"Wow. You weren't kidding about not trusting outsiders. Alright then. No therapists for now." I roll in my lips and give her a jerky nod. "How old are they?"

"Alex is nine and Amanda is five. Amanda is a sweetheart and Alex is a little old man trapped in a kid's body." She chuckles while pressing a hand to her chest. "They're wonderful kids. All of them. They're full of so much love, even after all that they've been through. Jack has to find Pen. He just has to."

"He will. We have to keep the faith." I bring my hands to her face, and now it's my turn to wipe away her tears. "How about you help me finish unpacking and then we can make some of your famous hot chocolate so we can have it ready for the kids. It's the only thing that ever made my world right when I was little."

"Yes. That's a good idea, baby. I'm so glad you're here. I

have a feeling you're going to be good for this family."

I smile and hope she's right, because with all my inner turmoil, I'll just be thankful if I don't end up bringing more drama to their doorstep.

"Stop fidgeting, Anaya. They're going to love you." Mom raises a brow, knowing full well what's going on in my head.

We're both standing by the front door and the sheer opulence of the room is enough to make me feel inadequate. Yes, it's a modern farmhouse, but the casual nature of the style doesn't mean they spared any expense.

This home really is lovely, and the foyer we're standing in is grand, with double doors leading out to a large wraparound deck complete with rocking chairs. It's the type of home you see in movies, where you'd expect a happily ever after.

The irony is real. This home has seen anything but happy as of late.

The kids will be here any minute with the Crown brothers... Well, all except for Austin. My stomach goes in knots at the thought. I'd never met the middle Crown brother, but just thinking of the way he left this earth turns me inside out.

I'm about to pry Mom for more details when the rumble of an SUV pulls my attention to the door. Thanks to the wall of windows, I can see the sadness pouring out of the large vehicle.

One by one, a parade of somber men unloads—each one as handsome as the last. *Jesus. What do they put in the water here?*

The men are all well over six feet and as broad as a wall. *Oof.* My lady bits clench, thinking of the poor mother who birthed them.

Jack finally steps out, the only man I recognize, his frame and stature so similar to that of the others before him. He stops to open the back door and two seconds later, a little girl with blond pigtails pops out looking so damn sad.

I'm so focused on her, I almost miss the little boy. He too has a matching sadness that's palpable even from where I stand.

"God," Mom whispers beside me, urging me to grab hold of her hand and squeeze.

"It's okay. It's going to be okay," I utter the words and I pray that my speaking them out loud brings them to fruition. No child deserves this much tragedy in their lives.

The door swings open and all eyes fall on us.

"Gamma Mary!" The two children run toward my mom, the relief in their voice resonating deep within me. It must be a small semblance of normalcy, seeing her.

"Hey kiddos." She crouches down, pulling both into an embrace. "Guess what? I have someone special here to meet you."

Both faces blink up at her before they turn to look at me, apprehension heavy in their eyes.

"Hi." I give them a small wave as I too crouch down to their level. "My name is Anaya. Mary is my mom."

This revelation brings a smile to their face, and they excitedly turn back to Jack. "Is that true, Uncle Jack?"

He chuckles, "Yes, but that's something you should ask

Mary, not me. All this time, I thought Anaya was Mary's granddaughter, not her daughter. It wasn't until recently that they'd both set me straight." Jack rubs at the back of his neck awkwardly, only continuing after he's let out a long breath. "Aside from that, I can tell you I know Anaya personally. She's been coming here for the past four summers, and this year she's agreed to come spend it with you two."

At this news, the kids' eyes go wide. Alex grabs a hold of Amanda's hand and pulls her toward him in a protective stance. *Oh boy.* I have my work cut out for me when it comes to earning their trust, but really, I wouldn't have expected any different.

"Do you have any questions for me?" I smile wide, letting them know I'm happy to spend my time with them.

Alex gives me a curt nod. "Can you play Minecraft?"

And just like that, the room erupts into laughter. Here I was expecting him to grill me on my credentials, but like a true nine-year-old, he asks about a video game. Ray might be a massive shithead, but at least I learned a lot about gaming from him.

"Yes. I sure can." Standing up, I outstretch both hands. "How about you two come help with dinner and then, when we're done, we'll have some of Mom's hot chocolate while we play."

Their faces light up as soon as the words hot chocolate come out of my mouth and their tiny hands slip into mine.

I know I should probably stick around for introductions with the other brothers, but I can see that these kids are hanging on by a very thin emotional thread. If my bypassing formalities will help them settle back into their home, then I can deal with being perceived as rude. They're the reason I was brought here, and keeping them happy and sane is my priority.

With a smile and a nod to the other brothers, I head toward the kitchen with my new charges, excited to see how they take to being my little sous chefs.

TROJAN CROWN

Chapter Three
ANAYA

Two weeks later…

"The kids have really taken to you," Mom whispers as we watch Amanda and Alex play in the creek.

The weather is nice and we've brought the kids for a swim, taking advantage of how beautiful the property is.

"Well, I can say that I've taken to them too." I'm about to call them back in for some more sunscreen when the whir of an engine has me turning. Off in the distance I see Jack approaching with Matt, the brother that lives south from here.

I've had a chance to meet the other Crown brothers over the past two weeks. Matt owns a whiskey distillery and visits often.

Hunter is a brooding silent type who lives in his secluded cabin up the mountain but has been on the property until searching for the missing stepdaughter ends.

A shiver runs through me as I wonder what that poor girl is going through.

As the Polaris gets closer, I see that Jace, the youngest of the brothers, is sitting in the back along with Hunter. *Wow.* My stomach knots at this realization. There must be something serious going on if all four brothers have come to collect us.

Mom must have the same thinking because she's already getting up and calling the children. I quickly follow, gathering our things and placing them back into the basket I had packed.

I'm just finishing up when the men reach us and first to speak is Jack. "Anaya, we have to get back to the house. There's a surprise for the kids."

His words come out choked and I know whatever it is must be big. These men are as tough as nails and seeing them all glassy eyed has me unnerved.

They'd been gone overnight. From what Mom said, they had some business down in Texas, but she didn't elaborate. A quick glance over and I see that she's just as clueless as I am.

Not wanting to take longer than necessary, I walk with the basket to our side-by-side, but Jace cuts in and takes it before I can reach it. "Here, let me help."

"Thank you, Jace." He's the youngest and most playful of the bunch, so I decide to probe him for answers. "Any hints as to what this big surprise is?"

His eyes twinkle, and this small reaction brings some peace

to my heart. There's no way bad news could follow that full-bodied smile. And lord knows the kids have had enough of that. "Now, what kind of surprise would it be if I spoiled it?"

"Between you and me, I don't like surprises." I smirk, giving him side-eye. "I'm the girl who looks up a movie ending while watching a movie. It's *that* bad."

Jace throws his head back and cackles. "Oh, that's too funny! Well, little Anaya, I can assure you that it's nothing but a happy ending from here on out."

I might be younger than all the Crown brothers, at only twenty-one, but I've lived enough to know that life doesn't offer any guarantees and that the promise of a happily ever after isn't real.

Call me an escapist, but that's why I love reading so much. *Reading.* It's the only place in the world you can get away from it all, diving deep into a story where you lose yourself, forgetting all your problems. Only there, can you find a true happily ever after, hidden in the pages of your imagination.

"Ready?" Jack calls from buckling in Amanda, pulling me from my thoughts. He seems antsy, and a mixture of joy and sorrow is splashed across his face, further fueling my curiosity.

Knowing it's not my place to ask again, I crawl into the driver's seat and answer, "Ready."

I'm all jitters as the men load back up into their vehicle, my hand turning the ignition as I steer behind them.

Never has the path back to the house seemed this long. It feels like ages before we're standing in front of the massive wraparound porch, complete with white rocking chairs.

Jack is taking the kids, one in each hand as Matt walks in front of them, opening the door and leading everyone inside.

I'm last in line to enter, my foot stepping onto the porch steps when I hear it.

"¡*Papito*!" Amanda squeals before breaking down into hysterical sobbing.

Could it be?

"Da-ad!" Alex's shouting comes out strangled, his voice thick with emotion.

Oh my god. Their dad. Austin. He's here!

Mom's profile lets me see the tears streaming down her face, and following her line of sight, I see it and freeze—my whole body unable to move.

Amanda and Alex are crowded around a man in a wheelchair as tears flow down his face. *His breathtakingly handsome face.* The slope of his strong nose and chiseled jaw are like something straight out of a movie. *He's unreal.*

Even though he's sitting, I can tell that he's tall, his large frame dwarfing the chair he's in.

Caught in the moment, my eyes continue to take him in. He's wearing jeans and a dress shirt, the fabric tightening around his thick biceps as he holds on to the children, hanging on to them for dear life. All three of them are now openly sobbing, lost in their own world where finally—*finally*—there's a little happy.

As if he couldn't get any more perfect, masculine hands pull the kids toward him and I'm transfixed, watching his strong fingers swipe away the children's tears—the entire situation makes my chest squeeze with so much joy.

In this bitterly sweet moment, I am overflowing with emotions of happiness for the children. I'm so happy that they've reconnected with their father, a father they love very much and who seems to love them right back.

But as my eyes linger on all three, pain hits me square in the chest, my heart cracking open, letting the sadness and resentment towards my own father come to the surface. Why couldn't all dads love their kids like this? God, what this man must've gone through to find his way back to his babies.

He was thought dead, yet here he is, clearly willing to fight the Grim Reaper himself to return to his family.

"Gentle, kids. Your dad is still recovering." Matt calls from somewhere off to my right. I'm unsure of his location because my eyes are still glued to the trio huddled together.

That's when Austin lifts his head from the top of Amanda's little head. "Let an old man enjoy his kids. A little cracked rib won't—" his words die in his mouth as his eyes fall to mine, his forest green meeting with my watery blue. "Who's she?"

Gone is the softness from his voice, replaced with nothing but steel and barbed wire. I'm about to answer when Amanda jumps from his lap and runs toward me, placing her hand in mine and dragging me forward.

"*Papito*, this is Anaya. She's our very own Mary Poppins." Her smile beams up at me, pushing out the cold draft Austin's glare sent rushing in.

"Is that so?" Austin's narrowed gaze pierces right through me, threatening to make me break and run out the door.

What's his problem? Whatever. I'm here for the kids, not him. Remembering who I am, I cock a brow and stare him back down, answering with a simple, "That's so."

There's an awkward pause before Jack clears his throat. "We talked about this. Anaya is Mary's daughter and I've known her for years. She's good."

Nothing. No response from Austin.

The steely man just sits there, his eyes never leaving my face. As the silence stretches, threatening to swallow us whole, we all wait for someone to cry uncle. *It won't be me.*

"She's awesome, *apá*. She even knows how to play Minecraft." Alex's sweet voice cuts through the tension, clearly understanding something isn't right, and my heart breaks. He shouldn't have to take up for his nanny.

"And she makes the best pancakes, too," Amanda adds in my defense.

Sheesh. His distaste for me must be so obvious that even the five-year-old senses it. I can't let them feel this added discomfort, not on my behalf. It's the opposite of what I'm supposed to be doing here. Making things easier for them.

Wanting to ease the tension, I put on a smile and say, "If you're up for eating, I can whip us up breakfast for dinner so you can try the pancakes yourself."

I'm met with more silence, so I wait. And wait. And wait.

Mom takes pity on me and speaks up. "Right. Well, you probably want to get settled, Austin. How about we let you get to your room, and we'll be waiting in the kitchen with the kids when you're ready?"

Immediately, the whaling begins. Alex's face has gone ghostly and Amanda is visibly shaking with how upset she is.

"We just got him back! He can't leave. He just can't!" Amanda protests as big fat tears stream down her trembling face.

"Shhh." Austin presses both kids into a firm embrace, all while cooing and placing soft kisses on Amanda's head.

Feeling helpless at the pain I'm witnessing, I move forward, my feet moving of their own volition. Before I know it, I've crouched down next to the wheelchair and my hand is rubbing slow circles on Amanda's back.

My spirit may be battered, but this is one thing my past trauma will never allow. I won't sit back and let another father break his daughter's heart. Regardless of what he's gone through, the kids are my priority, and if he fails them, I'll be the first one to give him hell.

"Sweetie, he isn't going anywhere." My eyes flit up, issuing a silent warning to their father. "Right, Daddy?"

Austin raises a brow, his steely eyes turning molten and sending heat coursing through me. But with a clearing of his throat, it's gone just as quickly as it appeared. "That's right, pumpkin. I'm right here."

Taking him at his word, I continue with my reassurance. "He'll only be a few rooms away, and if your heart gets to hurting too much, then I promise I'll take you to see him myself."

I'm about to withdraw my hand when Austin's fingers brush against mine, the simple contact making me suck in a sharp breath. His touch, it's electric, causing my entire body to react. Never in my life have I felt anything like it. How can something so small make my body overheat?

As if unfazed, Austin continues to stroke down Amanda's back, but his narrowed eyes never leave mine. "I'm not going anywhere, baby. I promise."

A shiver racks me at his words, his gaze making me feel as if the promise were directed at me. But that's absurd, isn't it?

Amanda finally lifts her head from Austin's chest, her head bobbing up and down in a small nod. "Okay... But hurry, *papito*."

Austin's stoic face does a one-eighty at his daughter's term of endearment, the action making his dimples come out to play. *Lord help me, those dimples.* "I'll be quick, baby. Nothing could keep me away from you two."

With another quick hug, the kids finally release their dad and follow mom and me into the kitchen. As we're stepping into the hall, I hear Jack's low gravelly voice. "What the hell was *that*?"

So it wasn't all in my head. The man really has something against me. Well, screw him. Jack's the one who asked me to come here, not him.

But the farther we get from the conversation, the more my mind whirls.

Even though I don't care what Austin thinks, I don't want him to keep me from the children. I've gotten attached and think we've made significant progress with their anxiety. Tearing yet another person away from their lives would only do more harm to their fragile emotional state. Surely he wouldn't ask me to leave, would he?

With a deep sigh, I vow to play nice, shoving my pride aside. It'll be worth it if I can help the kids.

Austin

"What the hell was *that*?" Jack hisses as he gets behind me, wheeling my chair down the hallway opposite from the kitchen.

"You don't need to do that. I can walk, you know." I look toward Matt and Jace for help. "Come on, guys. Tell him it's a couple of broken ribs, not legs."

They both lift their hands up, palms exposed, not wanting any part of this conversation. Hunter was the smartest, slipping out before the tough conversations were to be had.

"Don't look at me bro, I'm the biggest baby. I'd be milking it if I were you. Asking for room service and the whole nine. Maybe even asking the nanny for a foot rub."

The thought of that woman putting her hands on Jace has my blood boiling, a small growl erupting in my chest and catching me off guard. Before I can analyze it any further, Jack cuts in.

"Stop trying to rope the guys in and tell me what's your problem with the nanny." He ignores my claim of self-sufficiency and continues to push me toward my room.

"She's just a little thing. Way too young to care for my kids. And besides, she's a stranger." Even as I spit the words out, I know that's not why.

Despite her youth, she seemed to know what she was doing with my daughter. Amanda even called her Mary Poppins. *Yeah right.* She's no Mary—she's nothing but a Monroe, with her blonde hair and luscious curves, the thoughts she elicits are nothing short of inappropriate.

Her full lips calling me *Daddy* comes to mind and I do everything I can to shove that shit right down. I've never been into Daddy kink, but when she uttered the word, it was as if she'd given my dick the green light. Everything I'd just been through went out the window, leaving no room for anything but the heat she stirred inside. It was fucking terrifying.

In all my years, I've never reacted to a woman the way I did her. My cock stirred the moment I saw her, the fucker acting like it found its new home. *Not okay.* Not only is she supposed to be watching my kids, but I just put my family through hell—a hell that cost Blanca her life. What kind of sick fuck gets aroused by another woman so soon after losing his wife?

Jack cuts into my thoughts of self-loathing. "Anaya is twenty-one, the typical age of an *au pair*. And I told you, she's fully vetted and I know her. She's been coming to the ranch for the past four years."

Doubling down on my reasoning, I add credence to my argument. "Yeah. And wasn't that psychologist fully vetted too? Didn't stop the cartel from paying him off to take the kids."

"You know this is different. She's Mary's daughter, not some cartel princess."

Jack's words make me shudder, remembering my

stepdaughter. "Speaking of cartels, any word on Penelope?"

We're inside my room now, all present brothers freezing at hearing her name. It's a blow to all of them that they took her right from under their noses, but the bigger blow is to my conscience. She never would've been in that position had it not been for my meddling.

If I just would've let sleeping dogs lie, her father would've never known she existed. *Hell,* her mother would still be alive if it weren't for me.

Guilt seeps in, a deep rage rolling over me, making my chest rattle as I take in a ragged breath.

"The men of WRATH securities think they have a lead. As soon as it's confirmed, we're moving in and bringing her home."

Hope blooms in my chest. "I'm going with you."

"You can barely walk, brother," Matt speaks up, always trying to be the voice of reason.

"I can walk well enough. Besides, it's my fault she's in this mess." I press my lips into a thin line and suck in a sharp breath through my nose before continuing. "I did this to her. I need to get her out."

Jack lets out a sound of frustration while running a hand over his face. "It's not all on you, Austin. I should've vetted the doctor better. Kept a closer eye on his activities while on the ranch."

My eyes narrow as I focus on his words. He's leaving out a big piece of information. I have no doubt that his emotional entanglement with my stepdaughter clouded his judgment too.

When my brothers first broke the news that Jack had been

intimate with Penelope, I just about lost what was left of my mind. To be frank, the only reason I'm not ripping his head off for making a move on my stepdaughter is because I fucked up too.

Those in glass houses shouldn't throw stones and all that shit. But that doesn't mean I'll be okay with it once we get her back.

I rub my temples and sigh. *One day at a time. One fucked up crisis at a time.*

"What matters is that there's progress and we're getting her back." Jace, the optimistic of our bunch, cuts into the thick tension of the room.

"Yes. That's true." I tear my gaze from Jack and look at our youngest brother. "I still want to come along on the rescue mission. They're not making a move right away. That should give me enough time to heal." I rise from the wheelchair, the pain in my chest making me wince. "The chair is just a safety precaution because my balance isn't the best, but with therapy and a crutch, I'll be back to normal in no time."

They all nod, though the doubt is clear in their eyes. Doesn't matter. I don't need to prove myself to them. I just need to get well enough to get Pen back, and get her back I will, even if it costs me my life.

TROJAN CROWN

Chapter Four
ANAYA

"**W**hat did those eggs ever do to you?" Mom raises a brow over her shoulder as she loads up the air fryer with bacon.

"Me? What about you? That's enough bacon to feed a small army!"

"The Crown men love bacon, and so do the kids. Even so, you don't see me abusing the strips of meat before I cook them." She's pursing her lips now, suppressing a laugh. "Don't worry, Anaya. Austin will come around. He's just been through a lot."

"So, you caught that, huh?" I glance over at the kids, making sure they're still occupied with the activity books I gave them. "The man clearly doesn't like me, and I don't think it has anything to do with his time in Mexico."

"Child, he just went through some traumatic things. Cut him a break." Mom sighs, exasperated with me, but I know this is more than just his recent trauma. I feel it in my bones.

From the moment I saw him, it's like the air shifted—my chest tightened and breathing halted. Something in him called to me, and I'd be willing to bet the whole kit & caboodle that his attitude with me has something to do with that. Did he feel it too?

"Something smells good in here!" Jace's cheery voice interrupts my thoughts as the Crown brothers all walk into the kitchen. Without delay, Amanda and Alex run toward their father, almost bringing him to the ground.

"Easy, easy. Dad's balance isn't the greatest right now." He's doing his best to stay upright, but it's clear he was in the wheelchair for a reason and that walking is his own doing. *Stubborn man.*

"Maybe we should bring the wheelchair in," Matt murmurs, more like in thought to himself, but it doesn't go unnoticed by the cranky Crown.

"I said I was fine." Austin spits out with so much venom you'd think Matt had suggested he go back to Mexico.

"Boys, settle down. First batch of bacon and pancakes are on the table." Mom's walking over to them with both trays, paying the glaring brothers no mind. "Anaya is almost done with the eggs, so take a seat and dig in."

"Yes, ma'am. You don't have to tell me twice." Jace's stomach grumbles as he sits down. "If Anaya's cooking is anything like yours, I might just have to marry her."

A low penetrating sound comes from somewhere to the left, and my eyes find Austin growling at his brother. Outright growling. *What in the world?*

My brows are still pulled together when I realize one of the brothers is missing. "Where's Hunter?"

This makes Austin's eyes snap to mine, the chill in them cold enough to freeze me on impact. "Why? Gonna make him want to marry you too?"

What the fuck? A beat passes where I'm just standing there, staring at this beastly man.

"Hunter stepped out after the kids said hello to their dad. He's not one for emotional anything, so I bet he's out chopping wood, or doing something else just as manly," Matt answers, eating up the awkward silence that had descended upon the room.

That's pretty much all I've been running into with the newest Crown brother. Silence that's awkward.

Not wanting to give him any more attention, lest we fall into another uncomfortable moment, I plate up the eggs and bring them to the table. "Hope y'all like 'em scrambled."

I set down the massive skillet with the eggs, complete with more bacon, cheese, green onions, and tomatoes. My mouth waters and I'm dying for a taste, but you won't catch me eating at the table with Austin.

"This smells amazing, Anaya." Jack offers praise, serving himself as I walk out of the kitchen.

"Enjoy! Just holler at me when the kids are done eating."

Turning toward Amanda and Alex, I give them my biggest smile. "We can hit up the game room before bedtime."

"Stay." Austin's gravelly demand has me freezing in place before I can leave.

Slowly, I turn to face him, only to be blown away by his rugged beauty. Deep green eyes bore into me, his brows pushing together. Seems he's just as surprised by his request as I am.

Licking my suddenly dry lips, I take a second to gather my composure. I'm shell shocked, and apparently so is the rest of the room as everyone has fallen silent—even the kids.

Stay. It was a demand, not a request.

My chest is vibrating with rage, pushing me closer to giving him a piece of my mind. *Behave, Anaya.* I remind myself that I want this job. Not only because I've grown attached to the kids, but because I'm not ready to go back home.

Slowly trekking to the open seat across from his, I place both hands on the backrest and bite my tongue before answering. I need to give myself a second because all of the words that I'm thinking are definitely not kid friendly. *Be nice, Anaya.*

I'm still fuming when I pull out my seat. *Who does he think he is, my father?* And because I have no filter, my mouth reiterates what I was just thinking, letting the words out on a breathy hitch. "Yes, *Daddy*."

Mortification sets in and I wish I could take it all back. *Damn it.* What was meant to sound sarcastic ended up sounding completely inappropriate.

I'm mortified, trying to keep my eyes lowered out of embarrassment when a strangled sound has me looking up. My eyes clash with Austin's and I see something akin to pain flashing before his eyes, guilt hitting me straight in the chest. This man has been through so much, the last thing I want to do is bring him any more pain.

"He isn't Daddy, silly. He's *papito*!" Amanda's cheery little voice breaks into my thoughts and I just about fall out of my seat.

To make matters worse, Alex puts in his two cents. "Technically, it's *Papa*, or *Apa* for short, but Amanda has always called him *papito*."

I'm choking on air as the rest of the table snickers. Thank God the kids are oblivious to my major fuck up. I try to bury my face behind my hands as a full-bodied flush takes me over. God, I hope my mom didn't hear that. "Um…Right. I'll remember that for next time."

"It's okay kids." Austin releases a low chuckle, the sound resonating deep in my belly. "She can call me *Daddy* if she wants to."

Ground, please swallow me whole. If I wasn't beet red before, I most certainly am now.

Yup. I'm never living this down.

Just then, Mom places food and water in front of me and softly pats my shoulder. "Drink, Anaya."

I do as I'm told because my brain can't handle thinking on its own right now. *Gah.* I'm on autopilot as I bring the glass to my lips, my hand trembling with embarrassment.

Mom definitely heard my wanna-be sarcastic comment, and if anyone can read me like a book, it's my mom. I just pray that she doesn't dig further and leaves well enough alone.

I honestly don't know what's about to come out of my mouth if pushed, and the last thing I need is to mess this all up, putting me on a one-way ticket back home.

An involuntary shudder racks me as I think of Ray.

It's been two weeks and I haven't heard a word from him. Yes, I've turned off my cell, so he doesn't have a way of reaching me, but he knows where my mom works and lives. I figure it's a matter of time before he tries his luck here.

I need to call him, if only so he doesn't come out here looking for me. That's the last thing I want for this family. Tacking on my drama to theirs. They're already going through a lot, and if this stunt doesn't send me on a jet back home, then that certainly will.

Huffing out a breath, I poke at the food in front of me and shove a fork full of pancakes into my mouth. I'm going to make this work, even if it means biting my tongue and playing nice with the cranky Crown.

Austin

Dinner is winding down and the tightness in my pants has yet to go away. *'Yes, Daddy.'* Anaya's words are in a loop in my head.

The way she said them takes me back to earlier in the day,

making me wonder if she has a submissive kink. *Damn it.* What the fuck am I thinking? That's the last thing that should cross my mind. Yes, it's been a long while since I've played in the bedroom—Blanca never being one who enjoyed the same things I did—but that's no excuse.

My family is in shambles because of me. Hell, Penelope is still missing and my wife is dead. All because of me.

A silent rage battles within me as I try to temper my emotions. There's no need to let my children see this ugly side of me. They've already been through so much. The last thing they need is a mean father on top of all that.

My thoughts drift back to my dad. The reason I went down the rabbit hole in the first place.

I need to tell my brothers what I found and offload this knowledge that's weighing down on me like a ton of bricks. A weight that almost dragged me down and buried me alive, costing me everything.

Knowledge is dangerous, though. I have to make sure none of them will do as I did. I need to keep them safe.

I'm lost in my thoughts when a chair scraping against the hardwood floors gets my attention.

"May we be excused?" Alex asks while Amanda practically bounces in her seat.

I blink, realizing that I don't know what their routine is here. I've been gone from their lives for a few short weeks, yet it feels like years. "It's seven. What time do you go to bed?"

A melodic voice answers, "They're both in bed by eight, but Alex gets an extra thirty minutes until lights out."

My eyes are focused on Anaya's beautiful mouth, her rosebud lips slightly parted as she awaits my response. I don't have one. My mind is too busy chastising itself for the images her pouty mouth elicits.

Right on cue, visions of my fat cock sliding inch by inch into her wet hole flash before me. I shudder, imagining her warm little tongue pressing up against my heated flesh and sucking. *Fucking hell, what I'd give to have her on her knees.*

This is so damn wrong. She's young, the nanny, and to top it all off, I'm basically the one who signed my wife's death warrant. *What the hell is wrong with me?* I'm breathless, battling to push these selfish thoughts out of my head, when Anaya clears her throat.

"*Right.*" Unwilling to wait any longer, she turns to the kids without my input. "You have thirty minutes in the game room before I come and collect you for bed."

Both kids come over, giving me another crushing hug I willingly accept before they're flying out of the room and heading toward video games and dolls. If that's still what they play with. They're both in higher spirits than before and I'm positive the new nanny has something to do with it.

Making a mental note, I decide to find out what it is and what the kids are into now. Yes, I'm still recovering, but this brush with death has taught me that every day is a gift, and I sure as hell won't waste a second of it.

"What's their bedtime routine?" Anaya was getting up from her chair but my question stops her, leaving her slightly bent over the table, her ample cleavage on full display. *Jesus Christ.*

Is there *any* part of her that isn't edible?

Anaya blinks up at me. "Um, Alex showers and changes on his own while I bathe Amanda and get her ready for bed. Once I'm done with her, we have a joint story time. We alternate and take turns on who gets to pick the book for the night."

I nod, warmth filling me as I picture her in a role that Blanca never fulfilled, even as the kids' biological mother. The only thing that woman did right was take time to teach them her native tongue. Other than that, she was always ready and willing to pawn off her motherly duties.

Thankfully, we always had help from Pen. She cared for the kids when Blanca was inevitably off at some charity or meeting. And sad to say, most of my days were spent late at the office. Having been the only brother to follow in our father's footsteps, I had a lot on my plate with the family business.

Rubbing my temples, I let the realization sink in. How screwed up is it that I didn't see how dysfunctional it had all been for the children? Absentee parents and being raised by their half-sister.

"Are you okay?" Anaya's soft voice has my gaze lifting to hers. Worry mars her pretty face and I'm instantly hit with the need to make it go away.

"Yes. I'm good." I attempt a smile that comes out more of a grimace based on her deepening concern. "But I'd like to be present during story time from now on."

She swallows, her delicate throat working up and down, sending more inappropriate images flying into my head. *Lord help me. I'm going to Hell.*

Anaya nods, but I don't answer, just mentally will my dick to get the memo as she gets up from her chair and walks away. It gives me a perfect picture of the nanny's tight little ass. *Fuck, it's beautiful.*

I'm so lost in the way the globes move—lifting and falling with every step—that it's not until a firm hand lands on my shoulder that I stop, finally pulling my eyes away from Anaya's body.

"Office. Now." Jack's voice cuts through my mental haze and I see that he's peering down at me, a mixture of confusion and concern painting his face.

I let his words sink in and I know that it's time. Our talk is long past due, and we've been skirting around the obvious since they picked me up in Dallas. Nothing we're about to talk about is good, but it all needs to be said.

I nod and push my seat back, rising with a deep inhale. Like it or not, it's time to face the music.

TROJAN CROWN

Chapter Five
AUSTIN

Jack hands me a tumbler with amber liquid. "God, how I've missed this. Is it yours Matt?"

My brother nods from across the study, always modest about his private label. He may not have followed in the family business, but it's for the best. His whiskey competes with some of the top labels from around the world. "Best batch we've had to date."

"As much as I'd like to sit here and talk about liquor, we've got pressing matters to address." Jack takes a seat in one of the wingback chairs next to the fireplace, his eyes landing on mine before he starts again. "Look, I know this is going to be hard, and

I didn't ask you down in Texas because I wanted to give you some time, but I just need to know…"

"Spit it out," I urge our eldest brother on. Whatever it is, I rather get it out of the way as quickly as possible.

"We thought you were dead. The men of WRATH told us they'd seen a decapitated body wearing your clothing. Under the circumstances. They couldn't stay and take prints, but we assumed it was you. What happened?"

"I had to do it." My stomach rolls, the memory of what I did haunting me every time I close my eyes. A man just doesn't come back from something as brutal as that. It stains your soul, forever embedding the gruesome details into the registry of your mind. "I needed enough time to find Blanca and the kids. If they found my torturer on the ground, then they'd immediately be on high alert. So I did what I had to do. Switched clothes, took off his head and hid it. It wasn't pretty, and I never in a million years thought I'd do something like that, but when it came to my family or him, the choice was easy."

Jack nods as Hunter makes a noise of agreement. Jace and Matt, however, just stare at me—both in various stages of disbelief and horror.

"What I'm about to ask is meant in no way as disrespect. We just want to know… You decapitated the sicario, but then you left the compound. Why?"

"It's a decision I didn't make lightly, one that still cuts deep to this day." I take a sip of whiskey, letting the liquid burn, embracing the sting before I lay it all out there. "I'd overheard the men guarding my family talking about Blanca. How she'd told them that Penelope was an heir to the Cárdenas Cartel. They wanted to use her as barter, but because *el Jefe* was out of town, they had to wait to make that decision. It gave Blanca and the kids a tiny window of safety, but it was there. I had to decide whether to fight numerous men on my own or leave them and find help. Leaving was the lesser of two evils."

At some point during my speaking, Jack had gotten up and is now at his desk. "I need to tell the men of WRATH what you just said. They had eyes on her at Cárdenas' villa but didn't know under what capacity she was there. This is huge."

I nod, glad to find out that the same men who pulled me from the desert are the same ones on the job for extracting Penelope. By the time I reached civilization, they had already pulled my kids out of the hell they'd been enduring for an entire week.

Unfortunately, Blanca didn't make it. By the time the rescue came, they'd already killed her. Decapitated and laid to rest next to the body of my would-be torturer.

A soul searing guilt claws its way through my body, making my skin uncomfortably tight. I want to rid myself of it, set myself on fire and burn until the guilt of Blanca's death floats away. But that's impossible and incredibly selfish. I don't deserve absolution of this fault, and the children don't deserve to lose another parent.

A hand on my shoulder squeezes and my eyes drift up to find Hunter standing next to me. "You did what you had to do, brother. Nobody faults you."

God. His words are like a flaming knife to the heart. It is my fault. This is all my fault. Squeezing my eyes shut, I let him know just that. "I'm the reason we were in Mexico. I'm the one who had business with the Las Cruces cartel."

The room grows silent and the air shifts, the tension palpable. First to speak is Jack. "Why?"

One word. One word with a ton of weight.

"Dad." I sit there debating whether to elaborate, knowing that this information has the power to send one or all of them down the same rabbit hole I went on. Ultimately, I conclude they deserve to know. What they do with it is up to them. "We all know that our parents' death wasn't an accident."

All Crown brothers murmur in agreement. Four years ago, our parents were driven off the road after a night at the theatre. The coroner's report showed an insane blood alcohol level for our father, suggesting that he'd been drunk when he got behind the wheel that night.

Nothing could have been a brighter red flag for our family. Our father never drank. He was vehemently against it and even went as far as threatening to remove Matt from his will when he started his own distillery. Clearly, the story being painted wasn't the real one.

"I thought we all agreed to leave it alone once we uncovered who Dad's silent partner was." Matt raises a brow, wondering why I'd deviated from our plan, which wasn't really a plan at all.

"Feigning ignorance wasn't jiving with me," I retort, quickly dialing back the fire in my tone. It's that very attitude that put my family in danger in the first place. "I reached out to

Dad's partner with the excuse that I'd be taking over the reins and that I wanted to keep our relationship moving forward."

Jack slams his fist onto his desk, the sound bouncing off the walls and making his glass rattle. "Damn it, Austin. You knew his ties to the Las Cruces cartel. Why on earth would you want to stay in touch?"

Matt cuts in. "He's right. As tragic as Dad's death was, this was your ticket out. You could have used this as a way of severing ties, but you strengthened them instead. Why?"

"I had to know. I just had to know." My hands are in my hair, pulling at the strands as I try to will a time machine to life. What I would give to take it all back.

"What's done is done." Jace surprises us with his levelheaded wisdom, making us all look up and stare at the youngest Crown brother. "Curiosity killed the cat, and in this case, Blanca."

Aaaaand he's back, saying the most inappropriate but accurate shit. It sucks the air right out of my lungs.

"Yes. I agree that this can't happen again, but blood needs to be had." Hunter speaks up, the air around him crackling with his palpable rage. "These fuckers have cost our family far too much. Everyone involved must pay."

Matt nods. "It's what we decided last week. Before we had the information you just dropped on us."

I feel a twitch in my eye as I hear this. "Before you make any decisions, you have to know what I found."

This gets their attention, all the brothers remaining quiet as I drop the biggest bomb of all.

"Dad was being blackmailed. He didn't want to have anything to do with the Las Cruces cartel, but they'd threaten his family. Specifically, Blanca and Penelope."

Jack sucks in a sharp breath while the rest of the room murmurs various curse words.

"But why?" Jack asks, his eyes wild with a multitude of emotions.

"At first, I didn't know. I'd been digging for two years when I'd discovered that bit of information. Blanca was married to the head of the Cárdenas cartel before he became *Jefe*. She'd been an accomplice to a multitude of crimes, and only broke free once she was pregnant with Penelope." I get up and approach the bar. I'm going to need more of the hard stuff to keep going. Pouring myself another healthy serving, I blow out a breath and continue. "Apparently, some wrongs Blanca committed were against the head of the Las Cruces Cartel, and once he'd found her location and who she had financial ties to… let's just say he wanted reparations."

"Jesus. Why didn't dad say anything?" Jace looks about as shocked as I was when I first found out.

Shrugging my shoulders, I answer, "My guess is he didn't want to worry us with it. Wanted to handle it all himself so it didn't touch his family. Instead, he just cut the cartel into the business and kept up pretenses, as if everything was fine."

Hunter paces back and forth in front of the fireplace. "But then what went wrong? This had presumably been going on for years. Why did they decide to end Dad's life, and along with it, Mom's?"

"That, I don't know. I never got around to meeting with *el Jefe*. I'd been working my way up to that point, but it all went to shit in Mexico. They thought I'd hidden something. What, I have no fucking clue."

"This is all too crazy." Jace is now up from his chair, pacing back and forth in front of Jack's desk.

"Pen…" My stepdaughter's name leave's Jack's lips in a whisper. "Our priority is getting her back. Just because the head of the Cárdenas cartel is her dad doesn't mean he doesn't have any ill will toward her. He could be angry at Blanca for keeping her from him all these years."

"Agreed." I nod as I approach his desk. "Call back the men of WRATH securities and tell them we need to get all the info we can on Cárdenas. See if he has any business ties to Las Cruces or the Crown Enterprise. We don't want any surprises."

"Also, find out if they have any more info on the jefe for the Las Cruces cartel. Last we heard; they'd all gone into hiding after our raid. They're one of the largest runners in the country. It seems strange that all the key players have vanished off the grid. Something just doesn't sound right." Hunter's words have me taking a step back.

"They all just disappeared?"

"Yup. Like a man-whore ghosting last night's lay." Jace's analogy has me shaking my head while huffing out a half-hearted chuckle.

"You have a way with words, brother."

"It's a gift. What can I say?" Jace gives me his signature grin. One I'm sure gets him his way with the ladies, but does nothing but make me laugh.

"It's a gift, alright. The gift of bullshit," Matt ribs.

It's the last bit of lightness before the men of WRATH pick up our call and reality sets in once more. We have a long and dark path back to normal, if that's even possible. But one way or another, I'll get us there.

TROJAN CROWN

Chapter Six
ANAYA

"**B**ut we did that book last time," Alex whines from his perch at the foot of the bed as I tuck Amanda in.

"Rules are rules." I remind them with a smile on my face, though I wouldn't mind hearing something other than Rumpelstiltskin. It's creepy as hell, but the little girl loves it.

"Yeah. Rules are rules," Amanda sing-songs, making me hold back a giggle.

I'm about to suggest something a little more Disney and a little less Brothers Grimm when a deep masculine voice has my entire body tingling.

"Isn't that a little too dark for her?" Austin's green eyes are focused on mine, threatening to dig up all of my hidden secrets, airing them one by one as I'm rendered helpless and watching.

Snap. The. Fuck. Out. Blinking myself free from the fog this man puts me in, I find my words and use them. "For your information, she'd already read it before my arrival. Who was I to deny her a perfectly appropriate bedtime story?"

I'm hearing myself speak, but even as the words come out, I know they're bullshit. The story at the end is especially gruesome, but she swore up and down Pen read it to her on the regular, and Alex confirmed.

Internally cringing, I doubt my skills as a nanny. Maybe the story *is* too much for a girl who's been through so much trauma like she has. *Gah, have I been damaging her tiny mental psyche with my story time?*

If Austin agrees with my internal struggle, he doesn't comment. He simply walks to the other side of the bed and sits, making the queen-sized mattress feel infinitely smaller. Pulling an arm behind Amanda's back, he lowers down and places a kiss on the crown of her head. "How about Daddy tells you a story of a beautiful princess. One who lived on a very beautiful ranch."

Amanda rolls her eyes as she scoffs, the action pulling a giggle from my lips. "Daddy, you're talking about me, aren't you?"

Austin is visibly trying to hold back from laughing, but it doesn't stop his shoulders from shaking. "Of course not, sweetie."

With a raised brow, Amanda pulls the large book from my hands and deftly opens it to the right page before shoving it onto her dad's lap, putting him on the spot. "I still want Rumpelstiltskin."

Oh my god, I'm internally laughing my ass off. *Let's see you deny her the story, mister. Not so easy, is it?*

I have the biggest smile on my face as I turn to leave. "I'll give y'all some privacy since you have story time covered."

Taking this as my cue to exit, I turn my body, but my feet haven't even fully hit the floor when Austin's demand has me halting in place.

"Stay." One word. It's all it takes, and my body complies.

Slowly turning back, I pin him with my covert death glare, trying not to frighten the kids but wanting to let him know he needs to back the fuck off with those commands.

I'm not one who takes kindly to being bossed around, but for some reason, his one-word commands have me heeling like Lassie. Something I don't like or need.

A man who can pull that sort of visceral reaction from me is a man I can't be around. I'm about to tell him as much when he cuts me off with the unexpected.

"Please, Anaya. Stay."

Lord Jesus, Mary, and Joseph. My ovaries just exploded. This man that's all hard edges and steel is looking at me with so much vulnerability, it's making my insides flutter. How can he melt me into a puddle of goo with just three little words?

Instead of verbally responding—because let's be honest, I don't trust myself with full sentences—I simply nod and turn back toward the center of the bed.

Just then, Amanda makes a noise of contentment as she snuggles into the crook of her dad's embrace, pulling my attention to what really matters. The kids.

Austin clears his throat and is about to read when Amanda reaches over and pulls my hand into hers, bringing me a fraction closer and causing my arm to rest next to her father's.

This brief touch sends shivers up my arm and butterflies fluttering in my chest, enveloping me in warmth. Though soon enough, the pang of reality douses that kindling.

I'm a thief. This moment doesn't belong to me, it belongs to their mother. It should be her in this room with these beautiful children and this beautiful man.

But does this realization stop me from wanting it? *Hell no.*

As Austin's words fill the room, I let myself soak in this stolen moment. Maybe it's selfish, but I want it and I'm going to let myself have it—even if just this once.

Lost in the feeling, I let myself freefall into this simple pleasure, committing every second to memory and enjoying it for what it is, fleeting.

"Done," I whisper as I click the send button on Mom's computer.

I'm in her office, submitting my very last final, making it so that I'm now officially done with my undergraduate career. Luckily, I only had one exam to go when I left Ray in the dust, meaning I only had one professor to persuade into letting me submit my exam online.

Not only was he understanding, but he also gave me an extension. I'm shutting down the computer, ready to celebrate with a latte when the door swings open and Jack's towering frame walks through.

"Anaya. Mary said I would find you here. Can I have a moment?"

"Yes. Of course." I nervously sit back down, hoping he isn't mad that I'd let mom watch the kids while I sent my email.

"Wipe that look off your face. This isn't that serious."

I let out a small breath of relief, but don't let my guard down completely. "What is this about, then?"

"As you saw, Austin is home and back in the picture. Typically, it's the children's parents that would arrange for childcare, but since I'm still technically their guardian, the decision is still mine. At least until we get the legalities all worked out with Austin's estate."

"Okay. What does that mean for me?" I blink, my chest heating and stomach churning. It's no secret that Austin isn't my biggest fan.

"Well, initially we'd discussed you staying until we brought Pen home, but that hadn't factored in Austin's presence or his state of mind. He's not usually so…"

"Cranky?" I offer, the secret moniker rolling off my tongue like second nature.

Jack chuckles while his long fingers absently rub at his stubble. "That's one word for it. Anyway, I don't want to put you out, and I know that he's going to be difficult, but it would mean a lot if you could stick around until we get Pen home and guardianship transferred. Is that something you'd be willing to do still?"

I know what I want to say, but something holds me back, my brain wandering to how deep Austin's trauma goes. "What exactly did he go through? I mean, I know it's probably not my place to ask, but I'd like to know what I'd be facing."

Jack lets out a long breath before tilting his head back and facing the ceiling. "A lot. He's been through a lot." Finally dropping his face to mine, he stares me dead in the eyes. "To summarize it, he's seen and done things no man should ever do. And to make matters worse, he had to spend two weeks wandering the Mexican desert without food and water, injured as all get out."

My mouth is hanging open now, no words escaping it. I'm stunned into silence. I mean, I knew they'd been kidnapped, but what does he mean with '*done things no man should do*'?

"Anaya. I know that's a lot to take in, but I need an answer. If you're not okay with that, then I need to make plans for a replacement."

His words bring me back to the here and now, sending a lead ball straight to my stomach. Replacement? Yeah, no. That's not going to happen. Not if I can help it.

I've grown attached to the kids. There's no way I'd let this take me from them. Besides, I'm not ready to face Ray.

A wave of nausea hits me and nodding is all I can do to answer, staving off the urge to hurl all over the desk.

"Does that nod mean you'll stay?" Jack raises a brow, the curiosity in his eyes evident.

"Yes. That's a yes, I'll stay." I smile and push back the bile that's threatening to destroy Mom's desk.

No matter what Austin has done in the past, I'm pretty damn sure it was warranted. And now that I've talked to Jack, I can understand a little more of the *why* behind his crabby behavior.

I still don't like it, but at least now I know enough to empathize a little. Hopefully that's enough to keep me from strangling him to death.

"Okay. Great. That's great news. I'll get out of your hair." Jack claps his hands together once, a huge smile gracing his ruggedly handsome face. "Oh, and congrats on your last final. Your mom told me you're now officially done with school."

I smile and nod as the eldest Crown walks through the threshold, his backside just as pretty as the front.

There's no denying that all of the Crown men are drop dead gorgeous. But there's just something different about Austin. The rest of the brothers have a light complexion and dirty blond hair, but Austin has this deep tan and dark hair that makes me swoon every time I see him. Unfortunately for me, the hottest brother is also the crankiest. And if that weren't enough, he's the father to the kids under my care.

Chapter Seven
AUSTIN

A piercing scream has me ripping out of bed like a bat out of hell. *Amanda.*

God, please let her be okay. I run toward her, my feet not carrying me fast enough. That sound. I've heard it before on the night we were all taken.

Fear courses through me as I reach the hallway, only for it to be thwarted on the spot by the vision that lies before me.

Anaya is holding Amanda to her chest, gently rocking back and forth while she quietly sings her a lullaby.

"Sleep, my heart's darling, in slumber repose. Let the fair lid o'er those blue eyes now close…"

My heart pounds hard in my chest, the sound threatening to drown out the heavenly song. *Breathtaking.* This woman holding my little girl, giving her comfort, has stolen the air right from my very lungs.

I turn to leave, not wanting to break this tender moment, but I'm halted by a small voice.

"*Papito.*" Amanda's one word is shaky, and the reality that I did that to her cuts me to the core.

Fuck. My poor child. This is my fault. "I'm here, pumpkin."

Taking two steps at a time, I bridge the distance between us, only to realize the bed seems miniscule with Anaya here. There's a pause where our eyes clash, a myriad of unspoken emotions flying back and forth, none of which I dare say out loud. Finally settling on the tamest, I attempt a smile and open my mouth. "Thank you."

Those words feel so inadequate when there is so much to say.

Thank you for being here, for comforting my child. Thank you for being the light in the dark, the joy in this never-ending cave of sorrow.

Anaya clears her throat, the tension heavy in the room, and I wonder if she could hear what I was thinking.

"There's no reason to thank me." She places a kiss atop Amanda's head and goes to move her off her lap, but my daughter clings to her like a spider monkey. I don't blame her one bit. I would too if I were in her shoes.

"Sweetie, your dad is here now. He can stay with you,

maybe even read you another story." Her tone is gentle, with only a hint of indecision shining through. She isn't sure if she should stay, but I've never been surer of anything in my life. Like a bone deep truth, I know this is where she belongs.

I'm about to tell her to stay, but my daughter cuts me off and does it for me. "Why can't you both stay? He can read and you can scratch my head." She looks up between us, her glistening eyes big and wide, and I know there's no denying her.

Anaya must feel the same because she laughs, making no move to go. Instead, she lays Amanda back down and lays sideways behind her, her hand going up to the crown of my girl's head, her fingers gently scratching away just as she'd been requested to.

I'm standing there, gawking at the two when Anaya speaks up. "Well, Daddy. Are you just going to stand there or are you going to read us a story?"

Lord Jesus. I bite my tongue and fight a groan. I may be the kids' father, but my body wants to be her Daddy.

My dick jumps in my pants, oblivious to the fact that I'm going straight to hell. There's no reason this woman calling me daddy should stir the kind of emotions it does. *It's beyond wrong. It's obscene.* But here I am, my cock at the ready, knowing I'd love nothing more than to spank her ass red and spoil her rotten.

Closing my eyes, I try to mentally will my dick down. I know she meant nothing by it, but my body couldn't give two fucks. It still liked what it heard.

Needing to hide the growing bulge in my pants, I make

myself useful and walk toward Amanda's bookshelf, pulling out the enormous book of Brothers Grimm. Thankfully, I'm relatively back to normal when I lower myself onto the bed, taking the opposite of Anaya, and I'm able to get through the entire story without another incident.

But as soon as Amanda's eyes have closed and the horrid little tale of Rumpelstiltskin is through, I pounce, needing an answer to a question that's been plaguing me since I walked in. "How long has this been happening?"

Anaya lifts herself on her forearm, her clear blue eyes blinking up at me in the dim light. "The nightmares? Oh, for as long as I've been here. We've had plenty of sleepless nights. This is sort of the routine. She either makes it into my room or I come barreling in when I hear her crying out and upset."

My heart cracks, pain pouring out of it like a burst dam. God. Will I ever rectify the hurt I've caused?

With a stone lodged in my throat, I give this angel my gratitude. "Thank you, again. Your being here for her means a lot to my daughter."

It means a lot to me too, but I don't dare say it.

"Oh, it's nothing. Just my job," she whispers, her eyes unable to meet mine.

I know she's lying. This is much more than just a job to her. I can see it as clear as day, even here in the cloak of darkness.

Moments pass where I'm simply taking her in, memorizing the curves of her beautiful face, when she finally decides to rise. "I should probably get going. She'll be good for the night, but I'm right down the hall in case she isn't."

I press a kiss to Amanda's forehead and rise with her, following her small but curvaceous frame to the door. I wish I were a better man. That I could keep my eyes from that tight ass, but I can't, and in that moment, I know her getting up was for the best.

There's no telling what I would have done had we lingered any longer. Just as I think that, images dance before me, teasing me with what could never be—me pulling the nanny to her feet before yanking her into the *en suite*, ripping her clothes off and fucking her hard against the wall. *Shit.* I have to stop. Sleep pants aren't the most forgiving, and if she were to turn around, she'd see as clear as day that I'm hard and aching.

As if I'd conjured it, Anaya suddenly stops, the action causing us to collide, bringing her luscious backside onto my lap. *Fuuuck.* My dick is nestled perfectly between her ass. It would take no effort to lift her nightgown and plunge into her warmth.

Our heavy breathing fills the space, but neither of us is willing to acknowledge the contact because doing so would break the spell.

We're stuck in this moment, clearly aware of the situation but refusing to change it. For fuck's sake, I'm at full mast with my cock twitching against her softness, yet she isn't moving an inch.

Inwardly groaning, I remind myself of all the reasons this is wrong. She's young, married, and the nanny. Not to mention I'm a fucking widower.

"Goodnight." Anaya's voice is shaky as she steps out of our

bubble, making the right call and breaking a moment that spelled disaster.

What I'd give for things to be different, to take this woman in my arms and carry her back to my bed. But they're not, and we can't. That's not how real life works. The monster doesn't get a happily ever after.

"Goodnight," I whisper behind her, the one word coming out thick and heavy with the desire that surrounds us. There's no doubt she feels it too. Not with how she licked her lips just now.

It doesn't matter. As I turn and walk back toward my room, I know that's a line I could never cross. She's amazing with the children, helping soothe whatever pain I've caused. The least I could do is keep it in my pants and not assault the nanny. I need to make sure she stays right here, where she belongs.

Anaya

Two weeks. Two weeks of bedtime stories, picnics by the creek, and horseback rides. All filled with stolen glances and accidental caresses, each one driving me mad.

I'm a married woman and Austin is a widower, making the thoughts that fill my head so very wrong. He's completely off-limits, so why does my body react to his the way it does? Like a magnet being pulled every time he's in the room, I can't help but gravitate toward the cranky Crown who drives me crazy.

And he isn't even nice to me. Quite the opposite. It's like

he finds it necessary to be extra cold and distant with me, but it's the way he's with his kids that melts me every time.

It may be my childhood issues, but there's something about a man who isn't afraid to show his kids love and support that I find so damn appealing.

Like now, we're out in the field flying kites with the kids. Amanda just had a meltdown because she couldn't get hers to stay up in the air, and Austin instead of belittling her feelings, he's down at her level talking her through her frustration all while reeling the kite back in and teaching her about never giving up.

"You'll see, pumpkin. When you actually get it up in the air it will feel all that more exciting. We enjoy things more when we've worked hard for them." Just then, Austin's eyes fall to mine and my treacherous heart wishes it was me he was trying to earn.

Gah. Get it together, Anaya. You're still married.

My stomach lurches, knowing I have to deal with Ray at some point—sooner rather than later.

It's either that or risk his showing up here at the ranch. I'm playing with fire, pushing the limits, knowing it's just a matter of time.

Ray isn't one to let things fester and even if it's just to officially end things between us, he'll be rearing his evil head soon.

I'm looking down at the gold band around my finger, twisting it to the point where the skin underneath is turning pink, when a deep masculine voice pulls me from my thoughts.

"Where is he?"

I'm blinking, looking into the dark green pools of his eyes. "What?"

"Your husband. Where is he?"

"I—I don't know."

Austin's eyes narrow into thin slits, trying to assess what my words even mean. What wife doesn't know where her husband is? Surely that's not a normal response.

The last words I expected to hear tumble out of his mouth. "He's a fucking idiot."

My mouth drops open in surprise, but before I can ask him to elaborate, he's turning away and walking toward Alex. Do I dare follow him and demand an explanation?

I know it should offend a typical wife, but it's no secret I wholeheartedly agree with his assessment of Ray, though I doubt his reason for feeling that way is the same as mine.

I'm about to go pry the answer out of him when I hear a vehicle approaching. Turning to the horizon, I see Jack and Matt in the Polaris.

"Kids, let's pick up our supplies." I'd made us kite making kits, the materials of which are strewn about the field, but if Jack's face is any indication, I think today's outdoor activities are about to come to an end.

I'm just adding the last ball of string to the basket when Jack's booming voice has a ball of lead forming in my stomach.

"It's time. We're heading to Mexico!"

I'm frozen in place as the kids start their protest, Amanda's wailing the loudest of all. "You can't go, *papito*! You just can't!"

Austin picks her up, pressing her tiny head to his chest while glaring at his brother.

"Jack, maybe try a little more tact next time," Matt mumbles loud enough for me to hear.

"Why do you have to go too, Dad?" Alex's eyes are welling up with tears as his tiny hands clench into tight fists.

"I have to. It's my fault Pen is where she is, and it's my responsibility to get her back." Austin crouches down to Alex while still holding Amanda in his arms. "Actions have consequences, something you're already learning. This is just like that. What kind of man would I be if I didn't own up to my mistakes and try to rectify them?"

Slayed. My heart is slayed right then and there. This brooding man, despite the shit he's been through, he still holds tight to his honor, fighting for those he loves and not being too proud to admit whatever faults he thinks are his.

I don't know why he thinks the tragedy that fell upon his family is his fault, but whatever it is, it couldn't be that bad... *could it?*

"We're leaving in an hour." Jack cuts into Austin's moment with the kids and I want to knee him in the balls for it. Can't he see this is hard for the children?

With another scathing glare, Austin rises and walks toward our vehicle. "Don't push me, Jack. I know you're eager to see Penelope, but don't fucking push me."

I feel my brows practically hit my hairline at this statement. Am I missing something here?

Matt catches my facial expression and shakes his head. "Don't ask."

Well, that makes me want to know even more. I make a mental note to grill Mom about this. She's got to know what's going on.

I'm loading the basket into the side-by-side when Austin's hand presses against my lower back, his body leaning in as his lips hover over the shell of my ear. "We need a moment before I leave."

My body is rigid, frozen as a statue, but somehow I manage to give him a small nod.

He accepts my response and moves his hand into mine, pulling me a good distance away from the others.

My chest is a flutter and my head is filled with all sorts of incoherent thoughts, none of which offers an answer as to what he could possibly want from me.

Once we're out of earshot, he turns me toward him, my back toward the children. I don't know what I was expecting, but it sure as hell wasn't this.

"I don't know if I'll make it back."

"What?" My lips part and a strangled noise comes from somewhere deep in my throat.

"I've set up a trust account for you and the children. I want you to stay on with them and Jack if I don't return. There's enough to pay you through Amanda turning eighteen."

I'm blinking, shocked at what's coming out of this man's mouth. "But you barely know me?"

It's the only sentence I can manage because what I really

want to say can't ever come out. *Stay. Don't leave the kids. Don't leave me.*

"I know Mary, I know my brother, and I know my kids. They all adore you. Tell me you'll be there for them if I can't… please."

I'm choked up, my eyes leaking and face heating. This is an immense honor, this man trusting me with what he loves most. Unable to form words, I simply nod while letting out a shaky breath.

Before I know what's happening, Austin's hands are on my face, pulling me toward him as his lips land on my forehead.

I'm stunned into silence as his mouth hovers, issuing the softest of kisses before he whispers, '*thank you.*'

And just as quickly as it all happened, the moment is gone. Austin walks past me, leaving me in the wake of all this emotion.

It's all too much. His trust in me, the kiss, his leaving. I'm on the verge of unravelling when I remember where I am. In a field with the others waiting for me to return.

Not wanting to hold back the rescue mission, I pull myself together, vowing to put my big girl pants on and handle this like the bad bitch I know I need to be.

Even though at this moment, I feel anything but.

Chapter Eight
AUSTIN

"I still think you aren't physically ready," Matt grumbles from across the jet.

We're on our way to Texas, where we're meeting up with the men of WRATH before heading to Mexico.

"Yeah, well, good thing it wasn't up to you." Laying back on the leather headrest, I take in a centering breath, preparing myself for whatever lies up ahead.

"Want to talk about the nanny?" Jack's words cut in, interrupting my mental pep talk like a needle scratching a record player.

"No." It's all I give him, my eyes remaining closed.

"Okay. Let me rephrase this. Let's talk about the nanny. I'll go first." He doesn't wait for me to respond, just trudges right on. "She's married. Did you know that?"

This has my eyes opening and head whipping toward him. "Yes, I fucking know she's married. What does it even matter, anyway?"

Jack raises a brow, unfazed by the bite in my tone. "Just wanted to make sure you knew, because the way you held her out in the field... it didn't seem at all the way an employer should hold an employee."

I scoff, bitterness flowing through me like a lifeblood. "Isn't that rich. The uncle who usurps his relationship with his niece, giving me a reminder on what's appropriate."

Out of my periphery, I see Jace snort, a little of his whiskey spraying out. "He's got you there."

"Nobody asked you," Jack bites back.

"In all fairness, you can't get on your high and mighty morality horse when you skirted that shit with Pen." Matt is giving Jack side-eye, making me wish I'd been here to see how that situation went down.

I know I wouldn't have let them get close that way. Hell, I'm not even sure how I'm going to handle it when we get her back. *If* we get her back.

I run a hand over my face. "Fuck, we have to get her home."

Hunter raises his glass. "To getting Penelope back and watching you tear out Jack's throat when you see them together."

Jace snickers, Matt shakes his head and Jack shoots imaginary daggers at Hunter—but me? I'm just praying Hunter's prediction isn't an omen of what's to come.

More blood on my hands, all from this blind rage that consumes me every second of every day, eating away at what little of a soul I have left.

I'm tired as hell, having seen enough bloodshed to last me a lifetime. But as our plane descends into Dallas, I suspect that this is just the beginning and that I should brace myself for the war that lies ahead.

Nobody said dealing with cartels was going to be sunshine and rainbows, something I should have thought of before thrusting myself into this world.

There's no going back now, and for better or worse, I know this violence will forever be a part of my life.

"We haven't been able to get eyes on anyone from the Las Cruces cartel." Aiden, the former Navy SEAL who's leading this recovery, is talking. All eyes focused on the screen splayed front and center of the conference room we're in.

"What were their last known coordinates?" My brows push together, wondering how one of Mexico's largest cartels just up and vanishes.

"We think they were the ones who emptied the gas tanks up at Hunter's cabin a week before your retrieval."

"I bet they're the fuckers who gutted our horses, too."

Aiden's words had my brows pushing up, but it's Jack's words that have fury raging through me.

"What?! Why didn't anyone tell me about this? Are the horses up at the ranch all new?"

Hunter nods while Jack clearly can't answer, his jaw clenching so hard I can hear something cracking.

"Jesus. These are fucking monsters."

"Understatement of the century," Jace mutters.

"Yes. We think it was their sicarios who were responsible for the horses." Aiden walks over to his computer and presses some buttons, making images of four men pop up on the screen behind him. "They were last seen by a park ranger, Ericson. According to him, they'd been trekking through his territory. Something he found odd since the area was still heavily covered in snow and that part of the mountain rarely sees visitors this time of year."

"Is Ericson okay?" Hunter speaks up, probably wondering whether his old friend held his own against these savages.

"Yes. We spoke with him yesterday, wanting to make sure he hadn't seen them again." William, one of the other men on the recovery mission, answers. "He said that all's been quiet up there."

"Where the hell did they all go? I doubt they'd just give up on Penelope. From what we've been briefed on, it wasn't even their cartel who arranged the kidnapping of Pen and the kids." I dig my fingers into my hair, resting my elbows on the table and trying to make sense of it all.

"Correct," Aiden answers. "The therapist Jack had hired

was paid off by the Cárdenas cartel, all in an effort to get his sole heir home."

The hair on my neck raises. "What do you mean *sole heir*?"

Aiden rolls in his lips and looks toward William. There seems to be a non-verbal exchange before Aiden finally answers. "Word is he wants Penelope to take over the cartel in the event of his untimely passing."

"Over my fucking dead body!" Jack slams his palms down on the table, making the whole thing shake. "She's coming home with me, even if I have to kill every last one of them with my own fucking hands."

William walks over to Jack, placing a hand on his shoulder. "I understand, brother. Trust me. I understand. We'll do everything in our power to get her back safely and with as little bloodshed as possible. But if it comes down to it, we're prepared to do whatever's necessary."

Aiden is looking back and forth between Jack and me, and I can tell there's something he wants to say.

"Go on. Spit it out." I raise a brow, begging him to tell me I'm wrong and that there's nothing that's eating at him.

"Look, I don't like surprises. Especially on a mission that's as delicate as this one." Aidan waits for my response.

"And?" I answer, not understanding where he's going with this.

"Jack's relationship with Penelope. I want to make sure you're aware." Aiden raises a brow, waiting for me to confirm or deny.

"What? Do I know that my brother went after my

stepdaughter when he thought I was dead?"

Jack makes a noise, something between a growl and a gargle. "It wasn't like that, Austin, and you fucking know it."

"No. I don't know it. And to be honest, I don't want to fucking know it. I just want to get Penelope home and we can worry about the logistics of what happens later."

William cuts into our stare-off. "I think what Aiden was asking was whether you'll feel the sudden need to throttle Jack when you see him and Pen in the same room. We can't have you finding out halfway through our mission and jeopardizing our safety."

"And trust me, nobody understands your position better than I do. I practically murdered William when I found out he'd been seeing my daughter behind my back." Aiden waives a hand over at William, his eyes narrowed and brows furrowed. "You want to take it out on Jack? Be my guest. We just ask that you hold off until the mission is complete."

"Hey, I'm not paying you to give my brother ideas," Jack huffs, but the rest of the room erupts into much needed laughter.

"Yes. I give you my word that I'll be on my best behavior." Raising a brow, I look toward Jack. "Although, all bets are off as soon as we land back on American soil."

"Good. Now that we've addressed the elephant in the room, we can finally get back to the matter at hand, bringing your stepdaughter home." Aiden goes back to his computer, clicking buttons and pulling up a floor plan of Cárdenas' villa.

Regardless of what's transpired between Penelope and Jack, I just want to make sure she's where she belongs—with her family. Everything else can be figured out later. Preferably without my actually seeing it.

I'd rather maim and decapitate a thousand men than deal with my barely eighteen-year-old daughter shacking up with Jack. Nope. Lord knows I'm not ready for that shit.

Chapter Nine
ANAYA

My eyes search the horizon for a sign, anything that tells me they're okay.

It's been a week since Austin left and saying that I wasn't worried would be an outright lie. Not a second goes by that I don't think about those pools of emerald and the cranky Crown they belong to.

Is he okay? Is he coming back?

Giggles in the distance have me pulling away from the window. Both kids are with Mom in the kitchen and I'm about to give up and join them when a cloud of dust in the distance catches my eye. Could it be?

Without thinking, I step outside, not even bothering with putting on shoes. It's early morning and the road leading up to the house is thick with fog, obstructing my vision.

It's not until the vehicle gets closer that I see that it's a black SUV, but not one I've seen any of the brothers drive. Feeling my brows push together, I stare on and hope that it's not bad news.

Walking out further, I let the dirt and rocks dig up into the soles of my feet. Finally, after what feels like an eternity, the SUV stops in front of the house.

But as the dark head of hair becomes visible, all blood drains from my body. *Ray*. He's here.

Stupid girl. I knew it was only a matter of time.

I take a stumbling step back, needing more space from the asshole in front of me.

"Anaya." His voice, one I once thought brought comfort, now brings nothing but pain.

"What are you doing here, Ray? Don't you have some home-wrecker to be with?"

"Stop, Anaya. That was a mistake. She meant nothing to me." He steps closer, despite my retreating form. Can't he see I don't want him anywhere near me? "Why don't we go inside and talk. Something we should've done a long time ago."

"No! Stay back, Ray. I mean it. I'm not ready to talk to you. Didn't you get the hint? I ran as far away from you as possible. Even turned off my phone so I didn't have to deal with your cheating ass." He's advancing even as I get closer to the front door. "Stop, Ray. I'm not ready to talk. You need to give me more time."

"Time?" Ray sneers, his face contorting into one of disgust. "I've given you plenty of time. You need to get over it and come home."

He's on me now, a breath away when his hands clamp down on my biceps, his fingers squeezing to where I know they'll bruise.

I know I should probably be scared, but right now all I feel is a blinding rage.

A cackle born from fury and sarcasm erupts from deep within me as he holds me. "Home? You're not my home. You're nothing but a mistake. And if you don't want to give me time, then I'll tell you right here and now. I want a divorce, and I never want to see you again."

"Shut up. Shut that stupid mouth. You have no idea what you're talking about, Anaya. You are mine. You promised to be mine the day you married me and that's the way it's going to stay until the day you *die*." His fingers dig in even deeper with that last word, something dark crossing over his face like the promise of the devil hidden inside.

Rearing my head back, I spit in his face. "I'd rather die than go back with you."

His face twists into something unrecognizable and I think he's about to strike me when the loud cocking of a shotgun reverberates behind us. "Ray. Take a step away from my daughter and get your ass back in your car. Don't come back here. Ever. Or I won't hesitate to put a hole into that empty head of yours, you hear?"

"Momma Mary." Ray drops his hold, raising both palms toward my mom, but she isn't having any of it.

"Don't you 'Momma Mary' me. You lost that right when you dipped your wick in another woman. Now do as I say or find out how good of a shot I am." Mom raises a brow, still aiming the shotgun at Ray.

Seeing she's not letting up, he gives her a small nod before turning to me while walking backward toward his car. "Anaya, this isn't over. I'm not giving up on us. I promise I'll make things right. I'll show you where you belong."

His words are meant to be sweet, but they bring me nothing but uncomfortable terror. Like some ominous cloud hanging over me.

I want nothing to do with him, and this encounter has made it all that much clearer. He was the biggest mistake of my life; one I have to rectify immediately. I make a mental note to get divorce papers filed ASAP.

As soon as he's back in his SUV I let out a breath of relief, finally letting myself go up onto the porch with Mom.

"Where are the kids?" I whisper as we both watch the taillights disappear into the morning fog.

"I told them to lock themselves in the study and call for the ranch hand." Mom is finally lowering the shotgun when another set of headlights approaches the house. A ball of lead forms in my stomach, thinking Ray changed his mind and is coming back. It's not until the car reaches the big clearing that I see the familiar outline of the SUV and let out a breath of relief.

"They're home!" I squeal, rushing to open the door. "I'll go get the kids. I know they won't want to miss the homecoming."

"Anaya," Mom calls from the porch. "Give us a minute to make sure everything's okay."

Her words have me slowing my run. *Oh my god.* I didn't even think of the possibility that not everyone would be returning.

Turning back toward Mom, I nod. "Okay. I'll go wait with the kids. You can get us when you know everyone is okay."

"Breathe, Anaya. Everything is going to be okay."

I roll in my lips and attempt a closed-mouth smile, though it's forced. These kids have been through so much. I just pray that today is another happy memory instead of a tragic one.

I'm in the study with both kids when there's a knock at the door. With a lump in my throat, I crack it open and peer out. *This is it. The moment of truth.* Mom is standing there with a huge smile on her face, making my body release all the tension it'd been holding onto.

Finally, turning toward the children, I let them in on the good news. "Daddy's home."

Before I've finished the sentence, they're zooming past me and heading into the hallway.

My cheeks hurt from how hard I'm smiling as I turn to face Mom, wanting to give the kids a little space so they can reconnect with their dad and their sister. "Did you see them?"

"I did. Penelope is glowing despite the recent events and all the boys look good and healthy."

I'd been chewing on my bottom lip, but at her confirmation I let it go, releasing the poor battered flesh that's probably blood red at this point. "Thank god. I don't know what I would've done had they not all returned."

I say *all,* but one set of deep emerald eyes flitter before my mind's eye.

"Come. Let's go join them. I'm not sure if Austin or Penelope will be ready to entertain the children just yet." Mom weaves her arm through mine, walking me out into the hallway and toward the homecoming.

As soon as we reach the foyer, I see her, Penelope. She's stunning. With long brown hair and big hazel eyes that are now full of so much love as she hugs her brother and sister.

"Careful," Jack's voice cuts into the moment, his hands steadying Penelope. "Your sister is carrying precious cargo."

My eyes go wide at his statement… *is she pregnant*? I shoot a look to Mom whose eyes are just as big as mine. I guess this is news to her too.

Just then Jack's step-niece looks back at him, staring death darts straight at him. *Interesting.*

"Cargo?" Alex cuts into the staring match, making Penelope's facial expression falter.

She lowers herself down to Alex, whispering, "It's a secret I'll tell you about later. For now, how about you give me a great big hug? I've missed you two so much."

"We missed you too, Pen." Both kids are tearing up now, sniffling as they squeeze their sister.

"Shhh. Dry those eyes. Everything is going to be okay." Her eyes come up over their head, landing on a black SUV just outside the window. "Look who's here."

"Dad!" Both kids beeline it to the door and I take it as my cue to step out of the shadows and finally introduce myself to the newest arrival.

Jack speaks up before I can say anything. "Pen, this is Mary's daughter, Anaya. She's been helping with the kids while we handled things in Mexico."

Penelope's expression shifts from one of apprehension to one of gratitude in a matter of seconds. She extends her hand to me, a soft smile playing on her lips. "So nice to meet you, Anaya. Thank you so much for all that you've done. I honestly couldn't thank you enough."

My cheeks heat at her words. The kids adore Penelope, and her acceptance means the world to me. "No worries, miss. It's been a pleasure. Those two have the biggest heart."

"I'm glad you like your job because I'll be asking you to stay on. Austin will be staying here at the ranch while he undergoes therapy and once finished, he'll be helping take over the business." Jack speaks beside Penelope, his words making me freeze in place.

My head is a jumbled mess, unsure if this is what I should be doing. I thought that this was a temporary job. A favor until Penelope was home and able to care for the kids.

I'm lost in thoughts when Austin walks in with the children, his eyes landing on mine and changing from a serene green to a murky emerald. "Anaya. Hello."

His words come out choppy and forced, like he had to have a cattle prod to his ass in order to say them. *Great. He still hates me.* "*Sir.* Welcome home."

Austin clears his throat, uncomfortable with the words I used to address him. Over the past month, I've realized his aversion to terms of dominance such as master, sir, or my favorite—*Daddy.* He becomes flustered every time, but that last one puts him in a special kind of tizzy. So of course, I use it to make him turn red, irritating him whenever I can.

Heat washes over me at the memory of the last time I called him *Daddy*. Yes, he was bothered. But if I were being honest with myself, so was I.

It stirred something deep inside me. Something I'm not really sure I'm ready to acknowledge.

Oblivious to my inner monolog, Austin turns toward Amanda and Alex. "Kids, why don't you show me what you've been up to while I've been away?"

Amanda hops up and down while Alex's face splits into a wide grin. "Yes, dad. You have to see the model airplane I've been working on with Anaya."

"And my dolly. I cut her hair and made her all pretty." Amanda squeals, not wanting to be left behind.

With both kids in hand and a wide smile, Austin heads out of the foyer. "I'll see y'all for dinner. I'm off to spend some time with my kids."

My heart squeezes at his words. God knows what this man has been through this past week yet here he is, not wasting a second of time without his children. Despite his being an asshole boss, he's an amazing father and my heart soars for the kids. They deserve it. They deserve to have someone making them a priority.

I'm still staring off at Austin's retreating frame when I hear a slap.

"Don't touch me." Penelope hisses at Jack, drawing my eyes to the pair who are still lingering by the door.

"What are you talking about? I touched you in Mexico, in front of a freaking cartel boss, risking my life by showing his only heir affection. And now? Now you deny me a simple touch?"

My eyes are widening at what's transpiring before me. It's clearly a private moment that has me feeling like an interloper.

Mom must have the same thought because I feel her hand in mine, dragging me away from the two and toward the kitchen.

Well, she can drag me as far away as she wants, but she can bet her favorite china that once we get there, I'm grilling her about this. There's no way I'm being left out of the loop.

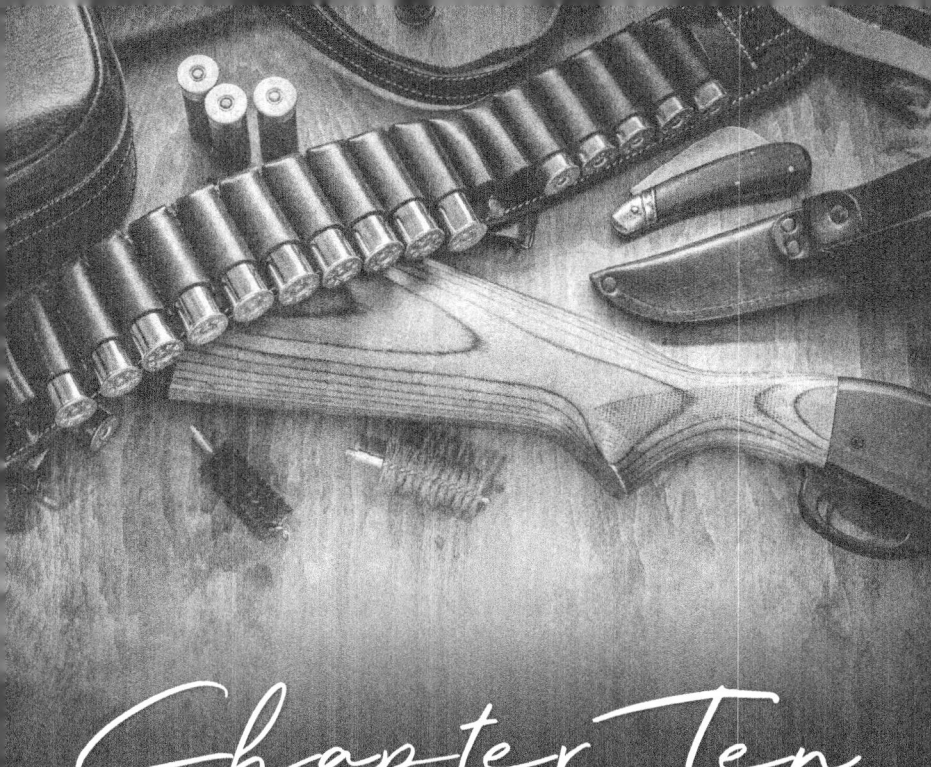

Chapter Ten
ANAYA

"Sooo… what was that all about?" I start prying as soon as I'm through the kitchen threshold, not giving her a second to forget what we just witnessed.

"I don't know what you're talking about, Anaya." Mom walks toward her home office, hidden right through the pantry. It's a convenient location which gives her privacy and allows her to stay near her favorite room in the house—the kitchen.

This is her domain, but even here she can't hide from me. I follow her through the ample butler's pantry and through the secret sliding door. "Oh, no. You're not running away from this."

At this, she turns. "I'm not running, Anaya. That's the private family business of Mr. Crown and Pen."

I purse my lips and give her side-eye. "If Mr. Crown wants me to stay on, I need to know what's going on between him and his step-niece. Either that or I walk. I can't blindly care for kids, not anticipating what type of support they might need in the event of more drama. Besides, Penelope is home, and I was only supposed to stay on until she returned."

I'm totally bluffing. There's no way I would abandon the kids, but I'm nosy as hell, so I'm banking on my mom not knowing that. She's always been able to read me, but after this morning's dramatic events, I'm hoping she thinks I've had my share of drama to last me all year.

"Anaya, that isn't fair to the children. They need you."

"Life isn't fair, and you know that." I'm staring straight at her, unflinching, praying she buys what I'm selling—even if it makes me seem coldhearted. Truth be told, this is more than just my being nosy. It involves the children too. I need to know how to tread around the situation and if I need to prepare them for more of a shift in their surrounding relationships.

I see her wall crumble as she plops down into her chair. "Fine. But not a word of this gets out. Especially to the children. This is their family business and I'm only telling you in the event the kids don't take the news well. This way, you're not blindsided and don't know what to say or do."

She's raising a brow, waiting for me to agree. Of course, I do. I'm no snitch and I'm definitely no gossip. "Yes, Mom. You have my word."

"I noticed the spark between Pen and Jack as soon as she arrived at the ranch. But it wasn't until I'd caught her on Jack's lap, practically grinding on him, that I realized there was something more going on."

My mouth is hanging wide open. What in the world? "But she's seventeen, isn't she? And his *niece*?!"

"Technically, she's not anymore since her mother passed away and she never was blood related to Jack since Austin was her stepfather. As for the age, yes. She was seventeen when I caught them in a compromising position, but she's since turned eighteen. Unfortunately, she spent her birthday while down in Mexico." She powers up her computer, turning away from me. "Which reminds me, we need to rectify that and you're helping me plan her a proper birthday party."

I'm still floored by all of this information when something else hits me... "Wait, so if she's *with* Jack, then... the baby? Is it his?"

A whoosh of air escapes Mom's lips. "Christ. I hadn't thought of that. I was too wrapped up in the homecoming."

I'm nodding at her, my fingertips pressed to my lips as my eyes go wide as saucers. "Does Austin know any of this?"

Mom shakes her head. "This I don't know. You'll have to ask Austin yourself."

I'm nodding when a voice I know all too well speaks from behind me. "Ask me what?"

Shit. How much did he hear?

Amanda and Alex come to either side of me, pressing themselves into me with hugs. "Anaya, can you help us get our puzzle from your room? Dad wouldn't let us go in there without your permission."

I turn and see his narrowed eyes and frown. Why is he upset?

"Should I be questioning why the kids were working on a puzzle in your room?"

Wow. Just wow. What exactly is he accusing me of?

I rear my head back, eyes blinking in disbelief. "For your information, it was a puzzle I was working on myself. One night the kids came in, restless and unable to sleep." I glare at him, willing him to know that he was the reason they couldn't sleep. "So I suggested we work on my puzzle. It's been the perfect remedy for insomnia."

Austin's eyes soften, though he doesn't reply. He just stares. And stares. Finally giving up on an apology for his assumptions, I take both kids in hand. "How about we go see if we can find cardboard or something similar to put under the puzzle. Maybe that way we can move it into the game room so your daddy can help with it, too."

Both kids smile up at me, eager to help with the task. And with a nod and a smile back at Mom, I head out of the room, leaving the cranky Crown behind.

Austin

That woman drives me fucking insane.

I knew there was no nefarious reason behind the puzzle

being in her room, but did that stop me from asking and accusing her of something?

No. It sure as hell didn't.

I'm rubbing a hand over my face and letting out a breath when I see it. *What the hell?*

"Mary, why is a shotgun on your desk?" I pick it up and open the barrel. Loaded. "Let me rephrase… why is a *loaded* shotgun on your desk?"

Her face heats, and just then our ranch hand enters. "Ma'am, you called?"

Mary looks even more flustered now, something I rarely see. "It's no worry, Sam. I've handled the matter, though I'd appreciate it if you'd be a little quicker next time."

Sam tips his hat. "Sorry, ma'am. We had a situation with a birthing cow. The vet had me step in and my hands were a little occupied."

She nods, dismissing him. But I'm not done with either of them. "Sam, please stay. Mary, why did you call the ranch hand? Would it have anything to do with the shotgun on your desk?"

Mary's cheeks flush red as she nods. "We had a situation at the front of the house, but I took care of it."

Sam makes a noise of distress at Mary's words. "I'm so sorry. I would've dropped everything had I known."

I address Sam without taking my eyes off Mary. "Please be sure to treat every request from Mary as an emergency. We've had a rough couple of months, and we can't take any chances."

"Yes, sir."

Deciding now is as good a time as any to call an all-hands

meeting, I turn toward Sam and clap a hand on his shoulder. "I need you to round up all the men. Tell them to meet Jack and me in his office in about an hour."

Sam nods, his eyes apologetic. But I don't want apologies. I want actions, and after our meeting I'll make sure everyone is on the same page.

As soon as Sam has cleared the office door, I lay into Mary. "I need you to tell me everything. How many? What did they look like? Did they have any distinguishing tattoos? Did they say what they wanted?"

Mary presses herself further back into her seat. "Austin, please." She's pressing her hand to her chest, clearly overwhelmed with everything I just laid on her.

"I'm sorry, Mary, but I need to know. Our family has made enemies with one of the most notorious cartels in Mexico. In order to keep us safe, I need you to tell me every last detail."

She blows out a breath before covering her face with her hands. "It wasn't a cartel."

My brows drop and pull together. "How could you be so sure? Is that what they told you?"

She clears her throat while straightening her already immaculate dress. "I know, because it was Anaya's husband."

My entire body clenches at her words, a fire lighting somewhere in my chest as I process what she just said. "Excuse me?"

"Yes. But it's okay. He won't be coming back anymore." She still isn't looking at me, her hands clamped together on her lap.

"Is that so? Can I ask why your daughter's husband was welcomed with a shotgun instead of a hug? Last I checked, that's not a typical greeting for someone you're married to?" I feel my cheek jump with the restraint I'm having to show.

So many questions are running through my mind. *Did he hurt her? Is that why she left? Is she running away? Away from him?*

"The details are not mine to tell, Austin. But since you are the ranch owner's brother, I'll tell you that he will no longer be coming around. Anything else needs to be learned from Anaya herself."

This makes my blood boil for more reasons than one, and I really try to rein myself in, but I feel myself explode before I can properly temper my emotions. "Mary, I really do care and respect you. That's why I'm going to let you in on a secret. This ranch is as good as mine. Jack is taking on *family business* and the ranch will be in my care. Every single person on here is under my protection. *Including the nanny*. So, when I ask you something, I expect you to answer."

She's clenching her jaw now, eyes shooting daggers into mine. *I see where Anaya gets her fire.* "I understand, Mr. Crown. But what happens between Anaya and her husband is still her business, and none of yours."

My ire hits new levels, and the cheek jumping turns into eye twitching.

Thoughts of Anaya in the arms of another man, a man who was terrifying enough to merit a damn gun, sends nothing but homicidal rage running through me.

"Clearly she was in some sort of danger." I wave at the shotgun still on display. "That means my children were in danger too. Everyone here on the ranch was in danger. Damn it, Mary. I deserve to know what in the hell happened."

Her audible swallow fills the room before she gives me the same answer as before. "I understand, but it's still not my place. This is a conversation you need to have with Anaya."

I feel the corner of my mouth turn up as the anger ebbs with the realization of what she is. "You're loyal, Mary. Something I value and the only reason I'm allowing your insubordination."

She nods, her features softening with my reprimand laced with praise. "Loyalty is everything, sir."

An involuntary shudder hits me, and not the good kind. "Please, just call me Austin."

There's only one woman in this home that can get away with calling me sir, and it definitely isn't Mary.

"Yes, Austin." She raises a knowing brow, and I wonder if she can read my thoughts.

Doesn't matter. It won't deter me from finding out what in the hell happened here. "I'm going in search of your daughter, and I better get answers."

"Please." Mary's face scrunches. "Be gentle. She's been through a lot."

I make a non-committal sound, unwilling to promise something I'm not sure I can deliver. The things I'm feeling are anything but gentle as my mind races with all the scenarios that asshole of a husband put her through, each new scene renewing my ire. I'm about to walk out when I remember, "Please put that back in its safe. We don't want the kids getting a hold of it."

"Definitely." Mary gets up, picking up the firearm before walking it over to her closet.

"Oh, and Mary. If you're ever faced with an unwanted intruder, call me. Night or day. I'll be there."

She smiles at me then, the skin around her eyes crinkling. "I will, Austin. Promise."

Her assurance brings me little comfort and I know I won't rest easy until I get the full story from Anaya.

With each step toward my nanny, my fury reaches new heights, sending my breathing into a rapid-fire staccato. This man needs to go, but I can't quash a threat I don't know about, and I intend to know every single thing about Anaya's other half. Starting with his intention.

Chapter Eleven
ANAYA

I'm minding my own business, walking back to the game room, when a hand grips me by the wrist, the force whirling me around and pushing me up against the wall.

"Why was he here?" Austin's hard body is pressed against mine, the contact knocking all air from my lungs.

"What? What are you talking about?" His words don't make sense. I'm gone, lost in vivid pools of emerald as his strong hands hold mine above my head.

"Your *husband*," he snarls, spitting out the last word as if it personally offended him.

I'm blinking, my mouth suddenly as dry as the Sahara. *This is so wrong*—his muscular body is flush against mine, his hard breathing sending his chest into mine with every exhale. God, it's so wrong. But it feels so good.

It takes everything in me not to moan out in pleasure, my starved body craving his touch. I should push him off. Tell him this is inappropriate. But I don't. Instead, I just play dumb. "I don't know what you're talking about, Austin."

His grip around my wrists squeezes, but I stare on, unwilling to elaborate.

Just when I thought I had no breath left, the man presses his body harder into mine. "Talk."

Damn him and his one word commands. Who does he think he is?

Out of sheer stubbornness, I hold out, refusing to answer.

Austin clenches his jaw, the tension making his cheek jump. "Answer me, Anaya."

Unable to look him in the eye, I turn my face, his warm breath tickling my neck and making me shiver in his hold. It's clear he's not dropping this, so I finally sigh and give him a little of my truth.

"He came to take me home."

I'm thinking that my answer will appease him, but it seems to have the opposite effect. He's visibly angry, pulling something akin to a growl out of his chest, the hard expanse reverberating against my body.

Austin's possessive eyes narrow before he leans in, his warm breath dancing across my lips. "No, baby. *This* is your home."

My head whips back as much as the space and his embrace allows. *Is he serious right now?*

Blinking up at him, I try to make sense of what's happening. This entire time, he's been nothing but silent and cold, so at odds with the look in his eyes and the fire in his tone. It all screams ownership with one little word—*baby.* The term of endearment wasn't lost on me, and I'd be lying if I said it didn't threaten to take my knees out. It's only because he's holding me upright that I didn't fall.

I respond after finally recovering my wherewithal. "I was only supposed to stay until Penelope came back."

Austin opens his mouth, his jaw shifting from left to right before he takes in a deep breath and finally releases me. I know it should relieve me, but the lack of his warmth has me feeling bereft.

He's pacing now, both hands in his hair, looking every bit unhinged as I feel. "About that. Penelope and Jack…"

His words hang in the air, the pained look on his face palpable, as if it hurts too much to finish that sentence.

Oh, God. This poor man.

Not wanting to make this any harder for him, I reach my hand out and grab a hold of his, trying to bring him some semblance of comfort in what can only be an uncomfortable situation. "It's okay. I know."

He pulls away, his eyes sharpening. "*What* do you know?"

"That Jack and Penelope are a thing."

His face contorts into one of disgust before he gives me his back. "How long have you known?"

"A couple of hours." I swallow hard, deciding to give him a pass on the accusatory tone. The man went through literal hell on earth to get back to his kids, only to find out his family was the real-life version of a taboo love story.

"Right. Well, I don't know if Jack already told you, but we're going to need you to stay on a bit longer. The situation is a little tense now and I don't know how things will play out. Don't think Pen would be up for babysitting if I suddenly castrated my brother." He's turned back toward me, letting me see his eyes, all wild and full of violence.

His words should scare me, give me pause, but they don't. Now that his body is fully facing mine, I can see past the anger and through to the hurt and what he really is. *A brother who feels betrayed.*

My eyes greedily take him in, allowing me the pleasure of cataloging all of his features.

His dark brown hair is disheveled, a few strands reaching forward toward his breathtaking eyes and strong nose. As if all that weren't enough, the gods deemed him worthy of full lips and a chiseled jaw—my fucking downfall.

My vision is trained on his stubble when a hint of green catches my eye.

A design is peeking out from his collar, the vivid jade contrasting against the crispness of his white dress shirt. *Oh my god... he has tattoos?*

"Anaya," Austin says my name and I realize I've been caught ogling.

"Y-yes?"

The corner of his mouth twitches, but it was so fast I doubt my vision. "I know my brother hired you, but *I* need you to stay on. Say you'll stay."

My breathing picks up and my heart pounds heavily in my chest. Not because I don't know how to answer, but because I'm afraid of what my answer will bring.

I've been at the ranch for a little over a month, and a great part of that time has been spent having inappropriate thoughts toward this cranky Crown. Saying yes can only lead me further down this path of temptation and sin. Dare I let myself?

"Enough." The indecision must show on my face because a resolve settles over Austin, his large frame stepping toward me before his hand lifts toward my face. There's a loud sigh and I'm unsure who it came from. Before I can figure it out, Austin makes a statement that has my heart doing the two-step. "You're staying. This is your home now."

The vehemence in his voice has my brows lifting. "Oh, and why is that?"

"Besides the fact that you're amazing with the kids and that they love you, you're safe here. Nothing will hurt you. *I promise*." His words come out choked, the pain evident on his face.

My chest squeezes, feeling the magnitude of his statement but not fully understanding it. Why is it so important to keep me safe? He barely knows me.

Austin takes another step forward, his hands wrapping around each of my biceps, his fingers lightly squeezing. "I don't know what he's done to you in the past, but I know what he won't be doing in the future." His words stop, but his thumbs keep stroking my exposed flesh, the pads rubbing and making my skin tingle from his touch. "As long as I'm alive, that man will never lay a hand on you."

He sounds so sure, his statement leaving no room for doubt. It makes me shiver as I take in his promise, letting it envelop me like a warm blanket on a chilly night. *It feels so good to finally feel safe, that I never want to leave this embrace.*

Austin's eyes bounce back and forth between mine, searching for an answer. Something must click because his face becomes fierce, his hold on me tightening further. "Fuck. He hurt you, didn't he? He's a dead man."

This shakes me out of my stupor. "No. No. He didn't hurt me like that."

Austin is staring into my eyes, the orbs I love so much narrowing into tiny slits. "How did he hurt you?"

"Just my ego. No big deal." *God.* I really don't want to talk about this. "Anyway. I'll think about it. Staying on, that is." Wiggling out of his hold, I slide off to the right. "Better get back to the kids. Last time I left them alone, Alex was trying to get Amanda to glue her hands to the table."

His eyes go wide at that, and I realize I'm not doing a very good job of painting myself as a capable caretaker.

Nervous Chatter 1- Nanny 0.

I've started walking, but his words halt me. "Anaya, his name. What is it?"

Chewing on my lip, I slowly turn back, debating whether I

should tell him.

He sees the warring thoughts on my face, turning his own a bright shade of red. "Don't be stubborn. It's not just your safety I'm worried about."

The kids. Of course he'd want to keep a potential threat on his radar. Letting out a small breath, I tell him, "Ray Garcia."

Austin bristles, his face flashing with shock before he quickly schools his features. *What was that about?*

Doesn't matter. I high-tail it out of there, practically running out of the hallway. This brief encounter has left me all out of sorts. Lord knows I can't handle any more broody alpha energy.

"Anaya!" Amanda gets up from in front of her dollhouse and runs toward me. "You have to play with Pen and me."

I look behind the little blonde ball of energy, seeing her big sister. She must've snuck in when I was in the hall with Austin. *Oh damn. Did she see anything?*

I'm mortified! God. That's her *stepdad*. Her dead mom's husband! She basically saw him pinning me to the wall and if my panties are any indication, a very willing me panting beneath him.

"Hey." Her warm eyes reach mine, a small smile playing on her lips, not giving anything away. "Alex is working on his next airplane model and Amanda has just been showing me the dresses you've made for her dolls. I've got things covered here in case you have some business to handle... you know... with Austin."

My face flushes red and I'm pretty sure I resemble a damn tomato. So much for her not seeing anything. Lord, she must hate me. I know I would if I were in her shoes. *The nanny home wrecker. Such a cliché.*

Clearing my throat, I step forward, unwilling to let this stop me from doing my job. "No business to handle. He just had some questions for me. They've been answered. We're all good."

She smirks. "If you say so."

I lower myself between her and Amanda, leaning slightly so I can whisper, "Penelope, I'm so sorry. It isn't what it looks like. Promise."

Her smirk turns into a genuine smile. "First, call me Pen. Second, I don't know what you're talking about. I didn't see a thing."

Pen's words bring me peace. With all the drama we have going on, the last thing I need is rumors spreading about me and the much older cranky Crown.

My thoughts float back to my friend who'd warned me about Ray. *'Older men are nothing but heartache. You'd do best to stay away.'* She was right about my soon-to-be ex, and I'm sure her warning would apply to Austin too. Not only is he broody as hell, but he's got so much emotional baggage it makes mine look like a small pocketbook.

I'm about to pull out the box containing all the doll clothing when the door to the game room flings open.

"I told you to leave her alone, *brother*." Austin is trailing a wild looking Jack, his eyes immediately falling on Pen.

"Pen. My study. Now," Jack booms, rendering the entire room speechless. Seems like these one-word commands run in the family.

Austin steps in front of Jack. "She's not going anywhere with you until I've talked to her. I gave you fair warning. As soon as we stepped foot on American soil, all assurances were off."

"God, Austin. You're making it sound like this is something I forced on her. Like she doesn't want to be with me."

I feel Pen bristle next to me as my eyes seek out the children, their small faces in clear distress. Standing up, I approach Austin and place my hand on his forearm. "Perhaps this is something that can be discussed outside?"

I make a face, shifting my eyes toward the kids, trying to get my point across. This isn't a kid friendly conversation.

Austin's eyes look panicked for a second before he clears his throat. "Pen, can I have a word with you?"

She'd been frozen in place as soon as they arrived, but Austin's words move her into action. "Um, sure. Of course, Austin."

"Over my dead body," Jack growls, but his words stop as soon as Pen is next to him, shooting what are clearly mental death darts.

"I think this is a conversation that needs to be had, Jack." Pen raises a brow, daring him to argue.

Jack releases a strangled noise, but nods. "Fine. But I'm

going to be present." He turns to me before his eyes flit to the children. "You good here, Anaya?"

"Of course she is. Haven't you heard? Monroe is the next Mary Poppins." Austin rolls his eyes before heading into the hallway, giving his back to the room.

Monroe? What the—?

My mind is a jumbled mess, eyes still trained on the trio heading toward Jack's study, when a small hand fits into mine.

Amanda's big eyes are looking up at me, worry riddling her pretty little face. "Is *papito* mad at Pen?"

Crouching down, I look her in the eye. "No sweetheart. He's just being a good dad and watching out for her. It's nothing you need to worry your pretty little head over. Promise."

She nods, her face settling into one of peace. In that moment I'm so grateful to have known what's really going on behind the scenes, because lord knows what I would've said had I been clueless.

I give Alex a reassuring smile as we head back to the dollhouse, but he doesn't seem at all bothered by what's just transpired. Either he already knows, or he's just that lost in his project.

Either way, that's something I'll tackle when he asks. I'm sure there'll be more if Austin's face was any indication.

I just hope he doesn't follow through with his threat from earlier. I really don't think Pen will take it well if he castrates her future baby daddy.

TROJAN CROWN

Chapter Twelve
AUSTIN

I whirl on Jack as soon as the door shuts, landing a blow straight across his traitorous face, the force making his head swing back.

"Stop! Austin, please!" Penelope screeches as she flings herself on my back, but her tiny frame is no obstacle for what I want. *My brother's annihilation.*

I was able to hold back, pushing reality out of my mind enough to retrieve my stepdaughter and bring her back home—but all that went out the window when I saw her up in his arms, his hands on her ass.

I had to do a double take as I walked past the study,

unbelieving what my eyes were seeing. We hadn't even been back twenty-four hours and he was already disrespecting me under the same roof.

"Austin, stop." Jack's words come out garbled as I grip both hands around his neck when I realize it. He isn't fighting me back. *Motherfucker.*

"Fight me, damnit!" I growl in his face, refusing to weaken the hold I have, all while Pen pounds her fists into my back.

"No. I deserve it..." His red face is turning blue now, the discoloration surrounding his lips a warning sign. "But if you don't stop... I'll die."

A ragged sob reverberates against my back, and I know I can't do this. Kill my own brother. *Not in front of Pen, at least.*

Reluctantly, I drop my hands, but not before shoving Jack against a wall—*hard*. "Fine. I'm stopping, but that doesn't mean this is over. I expect answers."

Pen's tear-streaked face comes into view as she grabs my hand, pulling me down into a chair. "Sit. Please. I promise I'll answer whatever you ask. Just please, don't take it out on Jack. This isn't his fault."

My lips pull back and I sneer at my brother, "What? You going to say something or just let my stepdaughter do all the work and defend you?"

Jack shakes his head, walking toward the bar. "I'm just trying to get my wind back."

He pours two rocks glasses, bringing one to me before sitting himself across from mine, Pen walking to his side, standing there like some sort of guardian angel.

I snort, supposing she is because if it weren't for her, Jack would be six feet under.

"Look, I never intended this to happen. For the love of my life to come in such a forbidden package." His face turns toward Pen and I can see it, the adoration in his eyes. It makes me sick.

"Why? Why her, Jack? Out of everyone in this entire fucking world, why did it have to be Blanca's daughter?"

His face whips back toward mine, a fire I recognize all too well lighting his eyes. "It's not a choice, Austin. When it happens to you, you'll fucking know. It's like an indiscernible pull, a driving force that drags you like a damn magnet toward your other half. Hell, I still don't fully understand it. All I know is that I can't live without her in my life."

Pen scoffs, "Is that why you sent me away?"

Jack reaches for her arm, yanking and pulling her down into his lap, the vision sending me reeling. "Princess, you know why I did that."

My eyes narrow, trying to understand what he's saying. "You sent her away? When? After you had your way with her?"

"Yes." "No."

Pen and Jack answer simultaneously, but Jack is the only one who elaborates. "I thought I knew what was best for Pen. Letting her go was my way of letting her live her life, not letting her tie herself down to an older man, so that she could experience life on her own terms."

Pen smacks Jack on the chest. "You were wrong. I'm not like other girls and you knew that, but you still did it anyway."

God. I'm in the middle of a damn lover's quarrel. "Both of you, stop. I don't want to hear any of this shit. All I need to know is that Pen isn't being manipulated or forced. Now that she's eighteen, there's nothing I can legally do, but so help me, if I so much as get a whiff of her being coerced, I'll have your head on a spike, *brother*."

Pen shakes her head vehemently. "No. He didn't force me. He's the one that's always pushed me away."

"Never again, baby." Jack squeezes her tiny frame to his body, making me want to hurl something until the vision before me shatters.

"Enough!" I press the pads of my fingers into my lids, wanting to erase what I've seen. "I can't handle seeing you two like this. It's too much."

I hear some shuffling, and when I open my eyes, I see Pen is standing next to Jack again and no longer on his lap. *Thank God*.

"I figured this would happen." Jack stands from his chair and heads toward his desk. "I'm calling Sam and seeing if your cabin is ready."

My brows push together as my eyes narrow. "My cabin?"

"Yes. I knew this would be a little awkward."

"A little!?" My brows shoot up at his words.

"Yeah, well, my point is that I expected this, so I had one of the resort cabins set up for you. There's more than enough room for you, the kids, and Anaya."

His words have my stomach tightening. "Anaya? Why is she coming with us?"

"She's the nanny, Austin. She's always been just down the

hall from the kids in case they've needed her. It would be cruel to separate them."

I nod, though I don't like the idea of this one bit. "Look, I agree that us all being under the same roof right now is a little intense, but can't you two just keep to yourselves? Keep the PDA to a minimum and I promise to keep my homicidal thoughts to myself."

Jack laughs, though there's no humor in his tone. "We both know that's a disaster waiting to happen. We're already going to have enough close contact now that you're taking over the ranch and I'm handling the family business."

Pen's eyes nervously flit between Jack and me. "Is that set in stone?"

She's worried, and I don't blame her. Pen's biological father, a very powerful cartel leader, *allowed* us to bring her home with the promise that Jack would be the head of his *familia* in the event of his untimely death.

That means' he'll be under his tutelage soon, giving us a very small window for me to take the reins over the ranch.

Jack sighs, his eyes heavy with this burden. "You know it was the only way."

"Yes. The only way without bloodshed, anyway," I add, regretting my words as soon as they've left me.

Pen's face has soured further, her hand drifting to her abdomen where life is growing within her.

My chest tightens, the sudden urge to vomit hitting me hard and knocking all the air out of me. *She's pregnant. With my brother's child.*

With a hard thrust, I push out of my chair. Maybe living under a separate roof *is* necessary. There's no telling what the constant reminder of their relationship will do to me once she starts showing.

"I'll go pack our things. Let me know when Sam's here." Without another glance back, I leave, knowing there's not much more I can take before I have Jack back in my grasp, his face turning a pretty shade of blue.

TROJAN CROWN

Chapter Thirteen
ANAYA

I'm in my new room, tucking panties into a drawer when Austin walks in, freezing in place as his gaze zeroes in on the black lace in my hands. I watch as his Adam's apple bobs, his thick swallow audible in the small room.

"Can I help you?" I raise a brow, feigning strength and annoyance, even though my stomach is all a flutter.

Austin clears his throat as his feet bring him deeper into the room, his proximity making me even more nervous.

"Yes. I wanted to talk to you about some changes. As I mentioned before, I wasn't sure how I'd handle Jack and Pen under the same roof." He rubs at his stubble, breathing audibly through his nose. "Well, as you saw in the game room, it isn't going well."

"Is that why we've moved out into one of the cabins on the property?"

"Yes." A shudder washes over him before he continues. "That house... I don't even want to know what's happened or what's going to happen in it. That's why I'm having a home built about ten acres west of the main house, but we'll be staying here in the meantime."

I'm nodding, wondering where I fit in. "Okay. Does this mean you still want me to stay on?"

"That's what I wanted to talk to you about. I asked you earlier today if you could stay on, and you said you'd think about it, but I need to know." Austin pins me with an intense stare I can't discern. "Things are clearly changing, which means I'll be cutting your checks instead of Jack. The terms under which my brother hired you will no longer apply and there'll be changes to the conditions surrounding your *employment*."

It's my turn to swallow back the lump in my throat. The way he said that last word has me feeling all kinds of filthy. "Okay. Have my duties changed?"

His face transforms as his eyes fill with heat, but he quickly blinks it away. "No. That's not it." He leans back on the dresser and crosses his arms in front of his broad chest, the new stance letting me perv on his exposed forearms.

Jesus. He's rolled back his button-up shirt—*something he never does*—the change letting me see all the beautiful art he has tracing his bronzed flesh. The intricate designs are all black lines apart from the various pops of green. *So. Damn. Sexy.*

"Anaya, I know my brother hired you, but I'd like to ask you to stay on with me as your direct boss. I'll be the one paying you. The one giving you orders."

My knees wobble and my core clenches. *God. Why did that sound so hot?*

"Yes, sir." I hear it. The shake in my voice, and apparently, so does Austin.

He pushes off the dresser and walks toward me, only stopping once his body is a mere breath from mine. "Is that something you like, Anaya? Taking orders?"

My face heats and I look away, unable to withstand the heat in his eyes. It's like molten lava, searing a path wherever they land, threatening to melt me in place.

"Answer me, Monroe." The pad of his fingers press against my jaw line, coaxing my head to turn toward his.

I blink, letting my eyes settle onto a sliver of his neck because I can't muster enough courage to do more. "Monroe. Why do you keep calling me that?"

His hand leaves my chin, the backs of his fingers caressing my cheek, back and forth. "Because that's what you are. My blue-eyed Monroe, with your blonde hair, endless curves, and bee-stung lips. You're every man's weakness."

My eyes shoot up to his and I see the surprise in his face, like he hadn't expected to tell me all that.

But like a gauntlet being thrown down, he clears his throat and steps back; the moment shattering whatever heat there'd been between us. "It's late. I shouldn't be in here."

He turns and heads toward the door, speaking without turning back. "Let me know if you're not okay with the new terms. I'll give you two weeks to decide."

And just like that, he's gone, leaving me a shaky mess of emotions with a massive need to relieve the deep ache between my thighs.

It's been ages since I've pleasured myself, and the thought of doing it here and now, a door down from his, only gets me wetter.

Shaking my head, I walk toward the door and close it, trying to push out all my sinful thoughts along with it.

Pressing my back to the door, I let myself slide down, groaning as my butt hits the ground.

I'm a married woman and he's a newly widowed man. *What in the hell is wrong with me?*

Austin

I've just closed my bedroom door when my phone lights up. Looking down, I see the number to William from WRATH securities flashing across the screen. Without hesitation, I click the line open and press the phone to my ear. "Talk to me."

"Hello to you too." There's a smile in his voice, which hopefully means good news.

"Hello, William. There, I've greeted you. Is that enough or should I send you flowers and chocolates too? Maybe pen you a sonnet while I'm at it."

Laughter booms through the receiver. "So damn dramatic. Don't get your panties in a wad."

"They aren't. Do you have anything for me, or did you just want to hear my masculine voice—let it remind you of what a real man sounds like?"

"Har. Har. Keep talking and I won't tell you about Anaya's husband, Ray."

With the mere mention of that man's name, my breathing picks up and my cheek starts jumping like a recently acquired tic. "William, you better start talking, or I swear I'll pull my hand through this damn phone and rip the information right from your throat."

More laughter ensues, making my patience wear thin and driving me to the brink of insanity. "Okay. So get this, he's a model citizen. Clean as a whistle. Not even a damn speeding ticket. Mother Teresa wouldn't even come back this clean. Either he's lived the life of a monk, or something's not right."

I feel my face scrunch at his words. *How is that possible?* "Can you send me a copy of his social and driver's license?"

"Already on it. You should have a copy of both in your inbox right now."

I place him on speaker and pull up the email app on my phone. Finding William's message, I tap it open and wait for the images to load.

I'd pictured a million different scenarios in my head when it came to Anaya's husband, but none of them were this.

The guy in the photo looks to be in his early to mid-forties, the date of birth corroborating my assumption. *Anaya is into older men?* I mean, I'm older than her at thirty-three, but only by a decade and a year.

This guy, Ray, seems to have an extra ten years on top of that.

"Austin? You there, brother?"

"Yeah, sorry. It's just sort of a shock."

"What? That he's a saint on paper?"

Of course he didn't catch the massive age gap between Anaya and Ray. He's only looking at it from a security standpoint. *Which is what I should be doing too, isn't it?*

I grunt out a sound, unwilling to come clean with my thoughts.

"Yeah. But we'll get to the bottom of it. It's what we do. It's what we live for." William's too cheery tone has me sighing.

Truth be told, I wish I could be as happy as he is. And for fuck's sake, I should be. Penelope is home and my children are safe. I'm a lucky man.

But nothing I tell myself can shake this immense guilt I carry around my neck like a damn anchor, bringing me down and placing me in a perpetually bad mood. To make matters worse, I know I'm not easy on Anaya.

She makes me feel extra messed up. I look at her and the feelings she elicits have me acting like a damn lecherous thief, stealing moments of joy that I have no business experiencing.

My thoughts drift back to how she looked in her room—her full lips parting when I asked her if she liked taking orders. God. That made my dick so hard, it's a miracle I didn't reach down and give it a squeeze right then and there.

"Austin? You there?" William's voice cuts through the line and it's then I realize I've mentally checked out for the last couple of minutes.

"Yeah, sorry. I'm here."

"Everything okay? I mean, besides the current mystery and the fact that we still don't know what happened to *el Jefe* and his men."

"Speaking of which. What's going on with that, any leads?" Distraction and avoidance are the name of the game. I don't understand what's going on in my head and I'm definitely not ready to delve into that can of worms with William.

"We haven't been able to get anything solid, but something Cárdenas said when we left his villa stuck out. I think he might have something to do with it. If so, then you can count yourself lucky. One less problem to deal with."

"Lucky my ass," I scoff. "Nothing that good comes free. One way or another, that man will come knocking—like the grim reaper, collecting what's owed."

"Amen to that." William lets out a long sigh. "Anyway, that's all I have for now. I'll keep you posted if I get anything else. We'll talk soon."

The line goes dead and I'm both relieved to have his happy ass off the line but also angst ridden, wanting to know more of what they have on Ray. I have no doubt that their file has important details like where he's at right this second.

As if it has a mind of its own, my hand clenches into a tight fist, the skin around my knuckles cracking from the stretch.

Thoughts of Anaya with another man have me vibrating, turning my vision red. What could she want with him? *He's old enough to be her dad.*

Against my better judgment, I open the bedroom door and step into the hall, unwilling to wait for answers. I need them now, and It's a good thing I know where to get them.

TROJAN CROWN

Chapter Fourteen
AUSTIN

I'm about to knock on the door when a small gasp has me freezing, my hand hovering over the door like a game of green light red light.

If I thought I was a mess before, it's nothing compared to the tornado of emotions the half moan half mewl I hear next has me feeling. The sounds coming out of that room have my knees buckling, making me brace both hands on the door frame just to keep myself upright.

There's no question that the woman who's been haunting my dreams is pleasuring herself just a few feet away.

I should be a good man and walk away. *I should.* But I

don't. What's another transgression on my way to hell?

My intention is to listen. That's it. But that shit goes out the window as soon as the next words fall from her mouth in a throaty whisper, "Yes, Daddy."

Faaaaaak. That's it. I'm destroyed. Not only is this woman a godsend to my children, but she's a kinky little thing, sent to torture me into an early grave.

As I stand here letting her words sink in, I've never been more grateful that Blanca had the kids call me *Papa* instead of Daddy—from now on, that name is solely reserved for this woman's lips.

Before I know what's happening, I'm opening the door, stepping into her room with no fucks to give except for one. Give her what she needs.

My eyes land on her body first, the vision making my cock throb. *Holy mother of God.* She's naked, sitting atop her bed like a perfect little offering, waiting to be sacrificed. *Mine.* The one word hits me like a Mack truck to the face. It's violent. Visceral. All consuming.

I need to have her. Taste her.

"Austin!" she whisper-hisses, scrambling back on the bed until her back hits the headboard.

She's about to cover herself with a pillow, but I'm not having any of that. Like a man possessed, I storm forward and my extremities act of their own accord.

"Don't," I grit out through clenched teeth, my hand snapping onto her tiny wrist and pinning it against the headboard.

The angel on my left is yelling at me to stop. This isn't right. I'm her fucking boss. Her *much older* boss. This is inappropriate.

But the devil on my right reminds me I'm damned. Might as well do something good with my life, and by the quake of Anaya's knees, I know exactly where that good lives—right between those thighs.

And that's where I land a knee, right between the legs that'll lead me to the promised land. I'm hovering over her, half of my body on the bed and the other half grounding me to the floor, that half keeping me tethered to the small sense of decency I still possess.

I want to destroy her with pleasure, leaving her nothing more than a puddle of release. But first I need to know she's mine. That her mind and her body are here with me, not with some limp dick who isn't worthy of her.

I may be all sorts of fucked up, but I'm not a damn rapist and I'm no consolation prize. If I take her, she's mine. There'll be no going back to that dipshit. I'm playing for keeps, too far gone to care if I even deserve this precious gift.

With my free hand, I grip her chin and tilt her head up—exposing her glittering, wild eyes. *What's going on in that pretty little head?*

She's yet to say another word besides my name, her breathing now coming out in short little pants. "Talk to me, Monroe."

"It's Anaya. Not Monroe." She juts out her chin in defiance.

Naked and trembling, she's still fierce, giving me the fire I didn't know I needed until now. I *tsk*, moving her face to the left as I lower my mouth to the shell of her ear. "That's no way to talk to your Daddy. Is it?"

A shudder wracks her small frame, and it takes everything in me not to lay her down, fucking her right then and there.

Anaya squeezes her eyes shut, tilting her head away to hide the prettiest blush that's now spreading across her face. "You heard me…" she whispers almost to herself, but I heard her loud and clear.

She's embarrassed by what she wants, and that's something I'll never be okay with.

"Hey…" I grip her chin and turn her back toward me, taking in a deep inhale when our lips are a breath apart, committing her sweet scent to memory. "Don't *ever* be ashamed of what you like. You're fucking perfect the way you are, you hear me?"

She doesn't answer in obvious discomfort, this realization making me beyond mad.

Anaya is fiercely independent outside of the bedroom, and if inside of it she needs the safety and support of a Daddy to feel her best, then who the fuck cares. I'll be more than willing to fit that role and give her what she needs. It'd be my goddamn honor.

"Answer me, Anaya, or I'll be forced to take you over my knee until you tell me what I want to hear. Say it. Say you're perfect."

Her eyes open so wide they almost look comical. "You wouldn't."

"Try me, little girl." I open her legs wide and drop my hand, issuing a quick slap to her swollen pussy. "Now, say it."

Anaya whimpers, her lower body jerking from my touch, but my little thing does as she's told. "I'm-I'm perfect."

"Good girl."

Her big doe eyes blink up at me in a daze. It's clear by her blown out pupils that she likes the way I manhandle her. I'm practically roaring with this knowledge, realizing my instincts about her being submissive in bed were right.

Grabbing her jaw, I bring her mouth to mine, devouring it whole. There's no need to ask permission. This beautiful flower blooms before me, opening up and letting me inside.

I take, take, take because she was made for me. *My pretty little thing.*

I'm lost in the push and pull of our tongues, our heavy breathing, and the brush of her erect nipples against my hard chest when it hits me. *She's still married.*

"Anaya, I need to ask you something."

"Okay... Yes." She lets out a shaky breath, our eyes never straying from each other's.

"Yes what, baby?"

She bites her plump bottom lip, the corner of her mouth tilting up in an almost smile. "Yes, Daddy."

My cock pulses in response and it takes everything in me not to lunge forward, taking that dirty little mouth with mine. *She's fucking perfect.*

"Good girl." I stroke her bruised lip with the pad of my thumb before letting my hand trail down her luscious body, slowly caressing every curve on my way to the junction of her thighs. "Tell me. Does this little pussy need her Daddy? Does she need attention?"

Anaya mewls, my words making her back arch and sending her full breasts thrusting toward my face.

Unwilling to pass this up, my hand abandons its journey south and cups the peak, directing the pebbled nipple straight into my mouth. *Fuuuuuuck.* She's delicious. "These tits, baby. They're my new drug." I whisper onto the tender flesh, taking the bud between my teeth and rolling it left to right.

Anaya lets out a noise of despair, "Austin. Please."

I pull back, looking at the wanton mess writhing before me. If I were being honest, I'm not sure how much more I can take of this torture either.

Needing more, I release my grip before slapping the fleshy side of her tit, making it jiggle. *Beautiful.* Nothing short of it.

But like a dark cloud, visions of Ray's driver's license flashes before me, the memory threatening to rip this precious angel away from me. *Fuck that.* The last thing I want to be doing right now is bringing up that asshole, but it's a necessary evil, so I do.

"Tell me, precious." My hand trails to her lower back, making her arch toward me and sending her breasts pressing against my chest. "Ray is in his forties. Is that what you like? Older men?"

She shudders, but I don't think it's from pleasure. Anaya buries her head into my chest, refusing to answer, but I know I won't move forward without knowing.

Both of my hands hold her to me, traveling up her smooth back and reveling in its softness. "Answer me, Monroe. I need to know if that's all this is. You looking for me to fill the role of your missing Daddy?"

She sucks in a sharp breath, her small hands coming to my chest before giving me a hard shove. The unexpected action loosens my grip, giving Anaya enough room to rear her hand back before her palm slaps against my cheek, the sound echoing off the walls in the small room.

"How dare you?" Her wild hair matches the glint in her eyes, feral and chaotic. "Get. Out. Right now!"

She's fuming and I swear I've never seen a more beautiful sight. *Okay.* So maybe I could've worded that better, but I'm not about to apologize. I need to know.

"No. I'm not leaving until I get my answer."

She's openly glaring now, and if looks could kill, I'd be a goner. "You get one answer, but then you're leaving."

A dark rumble resembling a laugh falls from my lips. "Oh, baby. I'm getting much more than that."

She narrows her eyes, little nostrils flaring with indignation. "One. Answer."

"Do you love him?" My chest squeezes as the words slip out, making me realize how vulnerable this question has made me.

How could this little thing have the power to destroy me with her response? In such a short time, she's embedded herself into my heart, digging her tiny claws into me. And worst of all, I'm afraid the hold she has on me is permanent.

Anaya cackles, her laughter sending a wave of unease running through me. That is until I hear what she has to say. "Hell-to-the-no. That ship sailed when I tasted another woman on him."

Rage. Nothing but blind fury fills me, demanding blood as retribution. *He did what?* No matter. He won't live long enough to regret it.

"Austin?" Anaya is looking up at me, her anger nowhere to be seen. Instead, concern mars her pretty face. "You're shaking and your face is all red."

I take in a deep breath, trying to slow my racing heart. *Is she afraid of me? If she saw the thoughts running through my head, she definitely would be.*

Her slender fingers reach up and caress the cheek she'd just slapped minutes ago. "Are you okay?"

Wow. My heart stops in the wake of her kindness. Here I am, barging into her room, homicidal thoughts now invading my head and she's worried... *about me.* Damn, if I weren't already falling for the nanny, this is where I'd start.

Guilt hits me straight in the gut. She's perfect. Too damn perfect for me. I need to let her go.

"I'm okay, baby." I cup her face and bring her forehead to my lips before pressing a hard kiss to the damp skin. She deserves so much better than this—the monster I am. With a strength I didn't know I possessed, I release my hold, ripping myself away and stepping off the bed.

"Austin?" Anaya's confusion is evident, but this is for the best. I never should have crossed that threshold. I had no right.

Needing to rectify this, I walk away, lead weighing down each one of my steps the closer I get to the door. I'm leaving behind perfection incarnate because it doesn't belong to me. It never could.

With one last glance back, I give her the only thing I can. My protection. "He won't hurt you, Anaya. Never again."

I close the door before she can say anything, knowing that my willpower is waning and it won't take much to send me back in, taking her in my arms and having my way with her.

But that's not what she needs. She doesn't need my scars which far outweigh her own.

From this day forward, I vow to keep her safe. Something I failed to do with my own wife, the guilt of which still bears down on my soul, but I'll be damned if I let that happen again. No, I'll rip through heaven and hell just to keep Anaya safe. Even if that means keeping her safe from me.

Chapter Fifteen
ANAYA

What just happened?

I'm sitting on my bed, naked and panting, wondering what-in-the-actual hell just happened.

I'm too shocked to let the embarrassment of being caught touching myself set in. I should be mortified, but instead, I'm pissed.

This infuriating man just came in here, practically promised to rock my world with his possessive touches and demanding words, only to walk away from me at the very last minute.

What changed? My mind replays our exchange and I know it's something having to do with Ray. Just now, the thought of him makes me want to vomit, my stomach contracting with the distaste his memory conjures.

I shiver, praying the lawyer I hired files the divorce papers soon. I can't be rid of the man fast enough. For all I care, he can keep everything in the home we shared. Some might think me a coward, refusing to face him, but I don't care. I'd rather put him behind me and move on—I just hope he lets me.

It doesn't matter if I'll be alone again. I'd let loneliness swallow me whole before I'd get back with that asshole.

Getting under the covers, Austin's words replay in my mind *'You looking for me to fill the role of your missing Daddy?'*

Ugh. The memory makes me vibrate with indignation. I'm strong. I've survived worse and I'll survive this too. Yes, I may have a type—older with a penchant for control—and he definitely fits the role. But for fuck's sake, the only reason he caught me calling out for *Daddy* was because he'd been the one I'd been thinking of, imagining the last time I said it making him all red and heated. Still, just because I was fantasizing about him doesn't mean I'll let him walk all over me.

There's only one man I let destroy me, and that was my father. Never again will I let that happen. I walked away from Ray, and I'll walk away from anyone after him, refusing to let anyone hurt me the way my dad did.

Rolling onto my side, I let the memory of the last time I saw him replay in my head; the pain serving as a reminder that

I'm a survivor and that this too shall pass.

Anaya, age ten

"Stay, *Andres*. At least for the baby." Mom's choked sob cuts through the sleepy fog I'm in. It's definitely past my bedtime, but the familiar sounds of my parents fighting have woken me up.

Our house is small, just a one-bedroom apartment I share with both my mom and dad. The space is little, which means I should be used to hearing them fight, but it still makes me sick every time.

I sit up, rubbing my eyes and wishing this pain in my stomach would go away. It happens every time the fighting starts. My tummy gets all heavy and I want to throw up. It's no different this time.

"She's not a baby anymore, Mary. She'll survive." Dad's words come out a little slurred and I know he's been drinking. He says it makes the pain go away and right now I wonder if it will make mine go away too.

Even though my dad is mean sometimes, saying things that hurt, I still love him. Getting out of my little cot, I tiptoe to the door, wondering what he's going to say about me now. *Did I disappoint him?*

"She may not be a baby anymore, but she's still *your* baby. Don't you think your leaving is going to hurt her?" Mom's strangled words have me stumbling backward, my eyes stinging before they fill with tears.

Leaving? Is he leaving? No. That can't be true.

Before I know what I'm doing, I'm ripping the door open only to freeze in place at what I see.

Dad is standing by the door, his hand gripping onto a tattered suitcase. *God. He's really leaving.*

"No!" I run as fast as my little legs can carry me, my arms wrapping around one of my dad's legs. Sobbing into his pant leg, I beg with all that I have, "Please don't go Dad! I-I need you."

To my utter horror, he shakes his leg, like he's trying to throw off a stray dog and not his daughter. "Anaya. You're ten now. You're a big girl. You don't need me."

My chest hurts so much I feel like it's going to fall into itself, leaving nothing but a hole where my heart was. That's what he's doing. His words are ripping my heart out.

Looking up into Dad's eyes, I see they're hazy—maybe he's just had too much to drink? "You don't mean that, Dad. You can't. I'm your little girl."

"My little girl." He makes a sound, something between a scoff and a splutter. "I wanted a boy, and you're what I got stuck with. But no more. A nagging wife and a whiny little girl will not chain me down." He gives his leg one more hard shake before turning his attention to my mom who has been loudly crying this entire time. "Mary, do something good for once and get your daughter off my leg. I've got a train to catch."

I shriek as Mom puts her hands on my shoulders, trying to pry me away from my dad. "No! Please, Momma. Don't!"

Despite my protests, Mom keeps pulling at my arms, finally untangling me from Dad's pant leg. As soon as my feet slip past his own, the man I've loved my entire life walks out the door without so much as a glance back or a goodbye.

I'm broken. Sitting on the floor while my mom comes up behind me, her own cries mixing with my own. *How could he do this? Didn't he love us? Were we not enough?*

"Shhh. Baby. Momma's got you." Mom picks up and places me on her lap, one of her hands pressing my head into her chest as she rocks us back and forth. "Everything's going to be alright. I promise. We're strong. We'll get through this. You'll see."

Her tears roll onto my cheek as the two of us just sit there on the floor, crying until we can't cry no more. Hours upon hours must pass because the dark turns to dawn and the birds begin to chirp, singing a cheerful tune I want no part of.

My heart is gone, and in its place lives nothing but a hole. One I'll never let another man through for as long as I live.

Chapter Sixteen
AUSTIN

"Care to tell us why we're here?" Matt's raised brow resembles the look on the rest of my brothers' faces.

We're at the main house, inside of Jack's study. "Yes. Anaya's husband. I have William running a background check, and so far, it's come out clean, but something doesn't feel right. For starters, his surname is Garcia."

Jack sucks in a sharp breath. "As in your late wife's maiden name, Garcia?"

"That'd be the one." I'm standing in front of the fireplace, pacing back and forth. It's been days since Anaya's revelation, but with the move to the new cabin and then the incident in her bedroom, I'd all but forgotten.

"There could be a reasonable explanation. It's a very common last name." Jace spits out this fact as though I hadn't thought about it.

"Yes, it's very common. But what are the odds?" I raise both brows, begging him to add anything more of value.

"What are you thinking? That he's her brother? We already know she'd been with Cárdenas, and Garcia is the name she received at birth." Hunter lays out the facts, trying to make sense of this new bit of info.

"Brother or cousin. He'd be too young to have been her father. He's only a decade or so older than she would be." I finally stop, taking in all of their expressions. They're just as surprised as I am.

"Okay, so let's say he's somehow related. What does it matter? How is it tied to us, if at all?" Jace makes a valid point, Matt later adding to this train of thought.

"Exactly. If they were related, wouldn't we have seen him by now? I mean, the guy has been married to Anaya for some time now, right? He could've paid us all a visit, but he hadn't."

Matt's words have a growl ripping from my throat. "He hadn't until this week. The fucker was here, and Mary had to chase him off with a shotgun."

My brothers let out various curses, all eyes on me.

"What the fuck? Why didn't I know about this?" Jack asks, fury painting his face.

"Maybe if you hadn't been too preoccupied with my

daughter, you would've heard."

"Bullshit! I had every right to know!" Jack is now standing in front of me, his face an inch from mine.

"Want seconds, big brother? I don't have any qualms with throwing some punches right now."

"Both of you. Enough!" Matt steps between us, putting some much needed space between Jack and me. Lord knows if another second had passed, he'd be laid out on the floor. "We need to figure this out, and both of you squabbling like a pair of old bitties isn't helping."

He's right. "Fine. But that doesn't mean I'm suddenly okay with this."

The *this* being Jack and Pen. But I'm willing to put it aside for now, at least until we get everything figured out.

"I want to know why the guy was greeted with a shotgun. Isn't he Anaya's husband?" Jace asks the very same question that plagued me.

"It seems they're on the outs because of some stunt he pulled." I say nothing further, thinking his indiscretion isn't something Anaya would like for me to share.

"So, is she getting back with him, or are they getting a divorce?" Jack asks from behind the safety of his desk.

Divorce. My heart clenches, wanting nothing more than to have Anaya be free of that man. "I don't know. She hasn't said, but she needs to leave his ass for good."

Right then, I vow to make it my mission. She deserves so much better than that jack-off who did her wrong.

"Unless the men of WRATH find anything, I say we wait it

out." Hunter, who's been awfully quiet, finally speaks.

"Oh yeah? Why's that?" I sit back on the chesterfield, letting my arms splay along the back of the sofa.

"He's never bothered paying us a visit until now, the only draw to our family being his hold on Anaya. Either he takes the hint the shotgun provided, or he comes back. If he comes back, then we deal with him. But if he stays away, there's no point in wasting our time. No sense in making waves when there's no need. We have enough on our plate with the missing cartel members and Jack going into business with Cárdenas."

"I'm not taking any chances on the shotgun getting the message across." I rub at my mouth, already thinking of all the things I want to do to that man.

"Austin?" Matt pulls me out of my darkness and I'm met with his eyes, holding nothing but concern.

"What?"

"Maybe you just let it be until he comes to us." He's talking to me like I'm a damn child. Like he knows better. But he doesn't. Not when it comes to Anaya. Only I know what she needs, and it definitely isn't some cheating son-of-a-bitch.

"Maybe you just keep that thought to yourself. Like I said, I'm not taking any chances. I'm keeping Anaya safe, and that means going on the offensive." I get up, ready to leave my brothers behind when Hunter's words stop me cold.

"Be careful, brother. Hold on too tightly to that little bird and you might just snap its neck."

What the fuck?

Matt lets out a sigh, and out of my periphery I see he's

rubbing a hand over his face. "I think what our dear brother is trying to say is, if you do something too rash, it might push Anaya away."

Now I'm really confused. I'm stumbling back, looking at them as if they're all crazy. "I don't know what you're talking about. All I know is that keeping that girl safe is my priority."

They all exchange glances, as if they're all in on some secret conversation, their reaction making my blood boil. "What? What the fuck is the problem here? Care to let me in on whatever the hell this is?" My hands are waving between them, equal parts frantic and furious.

Hunter takes a step toward me, his hand landing on my shoulder and squeezing. "It's not your job to keep everyone safe, brother. What happened to Blanca wasn't your fault. None of it was your fault."

My forehead creases as my brows push together. "Despite that being completely wrong, what does that have to do with Anaya?"

Matt comes closer, his words coming out hushed. "Austin, we all would've done the same had we been in your shoes. You need to stop blaming yourself, and trying to gain redemption through Anaya isn't going to help you. She isn't Blanca, and you going all caveman on her will only serve to drive her away."

Redemption. That's not what this is... is it? No. There's more to it than that. Maybe a small bit of me is hanging on to the fact that I let Blanca down, but that has nothing to do with how the nanny makes me feel.

Protecting her is a primal need, something in me refusing to let anything harm her. I'd even go as far as cutting off my own arm if it threatened her in any way.

That's all this is. That's all it could ever be. "I appreciate everyone trying to absolve me of my fault with Blanca, but no amount of psycho-babble bullshit will ever hide the fact that I fucked up. I shouldn't have brought them to Mexico. That's on me." I step toward the door, giving them all my back. "But that fault has nothing to do with the nanny. She's under my care, just as everyone on this ranch will be. It's my job to keep her safe, and if any of you dare get in my way, expect to get the shit knocked out of you, because I'm not backing down."

Not giving anyone a chance to answer, I leave, closing the door behind me and heading toward my cabin. There's some business I need to handle, and it's not going to wait until morning.

I've made it two steps down the hallway when Penelope's hesitant voice stops me. "Austin?"

Looking up I see the anguish strewn across her face, the vision making my brows drop instantly. "What is it?"

Before she utters another word, she's thrusting a leather book into my hand, urging me to take it. I do, opening it up and seeing swirls and lines I know all too well. Blanca's penmanship is scribbled throughout this massive journal.

"It's Mom's." Pen's words break me out of the mental tornado I'd been under, a million-and-one questions zooming by my head at warp speed.

"Okay. But why are you giving this to me now?"

She's shifting on her feet, unwilling to look me in the eye as she answers. "It came in the boxes Jack shipped from our old house. They must've packed up mom's things too, and it all ended up here."

"But why are you handing it to me now? Don't you want to keep it?"

"Not really. There's stuff in there I'd rather forget." She finally looks up at me, her eyes glassy and red. "Look, I saw you and Anaya earlier."

Her words suck the air out of me like a sucker punch to the gut. "God. Pen, I'm so sorry you saw that. That it possibly tarnished the image of your mother and me, but it's not what it looked like."

"Stop. You don't have to explain." She holds up a palm. "I'm giving you the journal because there are things in here that might make what you're battling a little easier."

I rub at my scruff. She couldn't possibly know the thoughts of guilt that plague me, could she? "Okay. I'll take it."

"Good. You might want to start where the feather is." She rolls in her lips, her eyes welling with tears until a big fat drop escapes, the lone bead rolling down her flushed cheek. Pen goes to turn but looks back at the last minute. "And Austin, thank you."

"For what?" I'm truly confused, wondering what she has to thank me for.

"For being the family rock. I never thanked you before, but

it doesn't mean I didn't appreciate everything you did for me, even though I was never your flesh and blood. It didn't matter what I was going through, I knew I could always count on you."

I'm at a loss for words, taken aback by what she's saying. If anything, I'd thought she'd resent me for working so much and never spending enough time at home. Funny how fresh eyes paint a completely different picture. "There's no need to thank me, Pen. I'll always be here for you. No matter what, we're family. Never forget that."

She fully turns to me now, getting on her tiptoes as she gives me a hug. "I know. And you never forget that you deserve to be happy too."

Her words further surprise me, but she doesn't elaborate. And with a quick peck on the cheek and a smile, she's turning and walking, leaving me holding Blanca's book of untold secrets.

With a deep sigh, I continue down my original path, making my way back to the cabin and dreading what I'll find inside. Whatever it is, I hope it eases some of the remorse that's weighing me down.

TROJAN CROWN

Chapter Seventeen
AUSTIN

Off in the distance, birds chirp, their cheery song making me want to hurl this journal at them. I'm sitting in the living room of our cabin, my head whirring with everything I've learned over the past couple of hours.

I mean, I knew Blanca had her secrets, but this is all too much.

Not only was she hiding the fact that Cárdenas was Penelope's father, making her a cartel Princess if there ever was one. But she'd been stepping out on me this entire time. A mystery man she never named in her journal, but he was there nonetheless.

This entry in particular, I've been going over and over in my head. How did I not see it? Yes, she'd been taking frequent trips away from the kids and me, and yes, we hadn't been intimate in ages—but I thought it was the supposed stress she was under. She blamed her mood on the responsibilities she took on as the leader of her women's league.

What a crock of shit. My eyes scan the passage one more time. Maybe if I read it again it'll all make sense.

> Fraud. I feel like it.
>
> Day after day, I lay in our bed, knowing he's not what I want. Not what makes me happy. But the kids. They're what keep me here. They're still so little, and I see the damage leaving Cárdenas did to Penelope. I don't want that for Amanda and Alex.
>
> Right now, he sleeps. His breathing annoying the-ever-shit out of me. Ugh. What I would give to be with Him again.
>
> Last week in the Riviera was amazing. My pussy is still sore from all the damage he did. Delicious damage.
>
> Time. I'll give myself a little more time with Austin. Enough so that it won't be too traumatic for the kids when I leave. It's not like my husband will miss me, anyway. I barely see him with how much he works.
>
> It's for the best. Every time he tries to be intimate, it sends my skin crawling.
>
> Time. Just a little bit more. Right here, right now, I promise myself. Life is too short not to live it doing what and who you love.

A sardonic laugh breaks past my lips. Karma is real. The mother of my children never got to live her life doing who she loved—at least not on the regular.

The journal is heavy in my hand, weighing more than is humanly possible. I can't stand it. Gathering up the festering hate I've manifested the past couple of hours, I do what I wanted earlier and hurl the fucking thing clear across the room. The force of it makes it whoosh through the air before it makes a loud thud, the leather and paper slamming against the wall but remaining the pile of shit that it is.

"Did that make you feel better?" A sweet voice breaks through the all-consuming rage, abating the deep ache and replacing it with peace.

"No. But hearing your voice did." There's no humor in my tone. I'm dead fucking serious.

Staring at her parted mouth, it seems my honesty has left her speechless.

Can't say that I blame her. Complimentary is the last word that comes to mind when I think of how I've treated her all this time. But it's because of what she stirs inside.

Even now, her parted lips have my dick going hard and my breath turning ragged. It's like they're an open invitation to slide inside, pumping myself in and out of that warm, wet mouth. *Would she take me in deep, or would she be a shy little thing, barely licking the tip?*

We're lost in this silent stare off, both of our chests rising and falling to the same beat. There's a heavy tension in the air and I have no doubt she feels it too. *Jesus*. My heart feels like it's going to implode if I don't touch her.

How could I not? She's standing there in a white cotton

nightgown held up by thin little straps, the fabric doing nothing to hide her nipples pebbling and begging to be sucked.

That's the last straw, making my feet move despite the alarms going off in my head and telling me that this is all kinds of wrong. *She's so young. She's the nanny. She's still married.* None of it matters as I inch toward her delectable body.

I've had enough of my guilt to serve me an eternity and it's time I go after what *I* want. Fuck the memory of Blanca and the bullshit image she left behind. Fuck the wasted years, all shrouded in deceit. Taking my dead wife's advice, I plan on living my life doing what and who I love.

Not hesitating, I tightly grip her jaw and press my hard body into hers. She's perfect, fitting me like she was meant to be there all along.

"Austin?" Anaya's brows furrow. She's breathing fast and heavy as I grab her thigh and hike it up onto my hip.

Despite her question, she's opening for me, her heat pressing against my length and making the fucker twitch against her core.

"Yes, baby?" She's mewling and I can't help but grind my aching cock into her. *Fucking hell.* Even this brief moment of friction has me threatening to spill into my slacks. My need for Anaya is unbearable. *I need inside her. Now.*

"What are you doing?" Her lips speak of confusion, but her actions speak of lust.

Like a horny teenager, the nanny's pussy grinds into my weeping cock, humping me on every upward thrust.

"What we both *need*." Lowering my head to the crook of

her neck, I latch on and suck. *Damn, she's delicious.*

Anaya hisses, but her hips never stop their movement. "You plan on leaving me high and dry again? Because if that's the game you're playing, I'm not interested."

I chuckle, her words making my chest rumble as it fills with warmth. "You're a feisty little brat, aren't you?"

I slide a hand between us and gently slap her pussy. Heaven on earth, that's what she is.

Never has carnal pleasure brought me to my knees, but as I stare at the soaked lace clinging to her puffy lips, I just know that this will be the Woman that changes it all.

Unable to hold back any longer, I push the tiny triangle of fabric to the side, sliding a thick finger through her silky folds. "*Fuck*, baby. You're soaking wet."

Anaya moans, pushing herself into my hand. "I am. What are you going to do about it?" *There it is. That fire I love so much.*

"Keep sassing and find out." With one hard tug, I rip her panties off, dropping the fabric before kicking her legs open wide and slapping her pussy hard. "Be good for Daddy. I don't want to take it out on this sweet little thing before she's ready."

Anaya moans, her back arching and pressing her full tits against my chest. "The kids… they'll be up soon. We can't."

"We can, and we will. It'll have to be quick, but I'm done denying myself." My thumb hones in on her little nub, swirling around the hard pearl over and over again until her breath and whining are at a fever pitch. "You're mine now, baby. Mine to pleasure. Mine to protect."

Anaya mewls, her hips bucking into my hand as heavy-lidded eyes stare back into mine, but she doesn't answer.

"Tell me you want this, Anaya. Tell me you need your daddy."

"Yes. Yes, please. I need you, Daddy." She's panting, using her legs around as leverage to ride my hand as much as her position allows.

That's it, the only thread that was holding me back. Her consent. Now that I have it, not even God himself could hold me back.

She's slick and warm as I insert three fingers at once, groaning at the tightness that surrounds them. *Holy shit*, she's fucking tight. A kinder man would've started with one, eased her into this, but I'm not kind and she needs to get used to my girth.

I pump into her with hard, long strokes, pressing up into her inner wall and making her cry out in pleasure.

"God, Austin." She's digging into my shoulders so tightly, I'm sure she's drawing blood. "More. I need more."

Her words demolish me. She needs me, and that knowledge sends my primal instincts into overdrive.

I undo my pants with eager fingers and my throbbing cock breaks free, pulsing so hard the tip slaps against Anaya's stomach. The action brings her eyes to my manhood, and I can't deny that the look of awe in her eyes makes me grow even harder.

"You're so *big*."

Grabbing her by the ass, I lift her against the wall and wrap her long legs around my waist. "What's wrong, baby? Worried it won't fit?"

She gives me a nervous nod as the column of her delicate throat undulates, the vision filling me with nothing but filthy thoughts. *God, I can't wait to slide up in there.*

"Don't worry, baby. Daddy promises to make it feel good." I grind my bare cock against her, letting my length glide between her folds and making her whimper.

She's coming alive under my touch, a feral look taking her over as the fat head of my cock rubs against her clit. *Oh, yes.* My baby likes how we fit and I'm not even inside. I need to give her more.

Anaya gasps on an upward stroke, giving me the opening to take her mouth and taste the sweetest lips on this earth.

She's moaning into me as I guide her toward my needy tip, her legs shaking around me as I lower her wet little hole ever so slowly onto my pulsing length.

Shit. All coherent thought leaves me as her walls hug me tight, that first moment of sliding into her instantly becoming my favorite thing in life.

"*Christ.* You're so tight. My sweet little thing." I'm vibrating, my whole body trembling from the most exquisite sensation. Never in my life has any woman felt this good. Not my wife, and not anyone before her.

Who knew my nanny would be the key to unlocking unworldly pleasures? Certainly not me. But now that I do, I'm not letting go.

"Mmmmph. You feel sooo good." Anaya writhes against

me, the bottom of her feet pressing against the back of my thighs as she rises and falls on my aching cock.

"Baby girl, keep squeezing me like that and I won't last."

Her blue eyes fall to mine, a wicked grin spreading across her full lips. "Challenge accepted."

Goddamn. Anaya throws herself into our fucking, arching her back on every downward stroke, only to grind her hot pussy at my base before every retreat. She's going to kill me, right here and now.

Needing to regain control, I leverage her weight against the wall, lifting her nightgown so her gorgeous tits are exposed, the two mounds bouncing up with every upward thrust. My eyes trail down from her perky breasts down to where our bodies are joined, the sight making my knees weak. "So. Damn. Perfect."

Seeing us connected like this—my hard, pulsating length coated in her sweetness as it disappears into her soft pink folds—it's my everything. She's my everything.

With a guttural roar, I pound into her soft flesh, bringing a hand to a bouncing tit before slapping it, making the pale flesh turn pink. I growl through gritted teeth. "Mine. Every fucking inch of you is mine."

Anaya says nothing, just stares at me through hooded eyes, her mouth hanging open and panting.

"Say it, Anaya. Say you're mine and I'll give you what you need." Letting my hand drop to her heat, I hover my thumb over her clit.

With a moan and a snarl, my sweet girl slaps me clear across the face, her pussy strangling me as she grinds down.

"Yours. I'm fucking yours, you asshole."

I bite back a grin, loving the fire she unleashes. "It's okay, baby. Because I'm yours too. I'm your fucking Daddy, and don't you forget it."

I push into her hard, groaning as I take her clit and pinch, the one action sending us both tumbling over the edge. It's like one continuous cascade of pleasure. With every squeeze of my nanny's magical pussy, rope after rope of cum fills her womb.

That thought alone sucks out what little air I have left, making me dizzy. But do I pull out? Fuck no. I meant it when I said she was mine, my actions now only solidifying that further.

I'm claiming her. Marking her in the most primal way.

As I spill into her, I can't help but cradle her against me, reveling in the feeling of my seed dripping out of her tight little hole.

"Mine. All mine." I'm murmuring against the crown of her head when we hear a door creak open.

We have about two minutes tops to get her covered up before one of the kids comes barreling in. Ripping off my shirt, I swipe up her leg and remove the traces of our mating as she tucks me back in. She's just buttoned up my pants when the pitter patter of feet enters the room.

"*Apa?*" Alex's groggy eyes assess the situation, and even though he's only ten, I know he can put two and two together if he looks closely enough.

Crumpling up my shirt and shoving it out of sight, I head toward the laundry room. "Yeah, son?"

"Where's your shirt?" I can't see him now, but I can

definitely hear the wheels turning in his head.

"Got something on it. Putting it in the laundry." I need to dispose of the cum rag, keeping it as far away from his innocent eyes as possible. Thankfully, Anaya comes to the rescue.

"Hey, bud. Why don't you go wake up your sister and ask her if she wants to help make some muffins with me?"

"Yes!" Alex's tone is cheerful as I hear his steps carrying him away from the living room and down the hall.

I'm walking back toward Anaya when her shy smile stops me in my tracks. She's breathtaking with her mussed hair and flushed skin. I'd give anything to make her look like this every damn day.

Leaning in, I press my lips to her neck, dragging them slowly up the column of flesh before stopping at the shell of her ear. "Thanks, baby."

I feel her body tense before her hands are at my chest, pushing me away. "For what?"

"For giving yourself to me. I promise I won't take you for granted."

She scoffs, her eyes narrowing into tiny slits. "I did no such thing." She points back and forth between us. "If anything, what we have is purely physical. You're an asshole, Austin. And you might be blessed between those thick thighs, but there's no way I'm trusting you with my heart."

Pain cuts right through my chest, cracking it right where I stand. But who am I kidding? I deserve it. What have I shown her thus far? Nothing but a cranky Crown.

She's given me her back, so I sidle up behind her, pressing

myself into her tight ass. "It's okay, baby. No matter what you say, I know I'm your daddy." I cup her mound and squeeze. "She knows it," I release my hold and slide my hand up between her breasts, pressing it into her heart, "but I'll work until she knows it too."

"Austin." Something akin to a choked sob falls from her lips, her body sagging into mine.

"Shhh. Baby. I got you. Daddy's got you."

I stand there soothing her for as long as possible, only stopping when tiny feet let us know of the kids' impending arrival.

With a herculean strength, I pry myself from Anaya just as the children come tumbling in.

"Muffin time!" Amanda is doing a little dance as her beaming smile hits me square in the chest. *Happy. My little girl is happy.* This is what Anaya does to our family. Injects joy where there was none to be had.

She's definitely our sunshine after the storm, and I intend on capturing every ray.

Chapter Eighteen
ANAYA

Holy mother of God. What in the world did I get myself into?

Did I really agree to being friends with benefits, minus the friends part, with Austin?

I'm rushing back to the kitchen where I left the children, my arms wrapping around my newly acquired dress as tightly as possible. As if doing so will rid myself of the sins I just committed with their father.

A deep warmth spreads from my chest up to the tip of my ears, and I know I must be the color of those strawberries on the counter. "What do we have here?"

Amanda and Alex are sitting on stools, all the supplies and then some are strewn about atop the rich butcher block workbench.

"Stuff for our muffins! There're blueberries, chocolate chips, and strawberries too!" Amanda is practically bouncing in her seat. She's so excited.

"I vote for chocolate chips," Alex chimes in, his sly grin reminding me so much of his father's.

I'm about to respond when thick fingers flex into my lower back. "I second the chocolate chips."

Austin's deep voice sounds off beside me, and it takes everything in me not to visibly react. Instead, I steel myself and shoot him a glare that dies in place when I see the warmth in his eyes. There's something there I haven't seen before, and I definitely don't hate it.

He opens his mouth to respond when there's a knock at the door; the sound making him take his hand off my body and step away. I instantly feel the loss and I hate myself for it.

Besides the fact that we're so wrong for each other, I just can't trust him. He's already let me down once, even if it was probably for the best. But that memory has stuck with me, and I'd be a fool to forget it.

I'm still reprimanding myself when Penelope walks into the kitchen. Austin must've let her in when I was deep in my self-loathing.

"Hey kiddos. What's all this?"

"Muffins!" Both Amanda and Alex answer simultaneously.

Penelope's smile lights up her face as she takes everyone

in. "Oh wow. You know what I just realized?"

"What?" Austin answers.

"You all have A-names." She points, listing each one of us out. "Amanda, Alex, Austin, and Anaya. I can't believe I never noticed that before!"

The kids are clapping as if this is the coolest news in the world.

"That's because we're the A-Squad. You know, like the Kardashian, but way cooler." Alex's face turns super serious, like he's just declared this as law.

"I love it." Austin smirks beside me, his thick fingers coasting up my side and making me shiver. Thankfully, nobody catches it and I'm able to step away before he does something else that'll visibly turn me into a pile of mush.

Needing to change the subject, I step closer to Pen. "Hey, why don't you help us with the muffins now that you're here."

"Sure you won't mind having a P in the mix?" She snorts, as if she's just said the funniest joke.

"As long as you don't put P in the batter, then I think it'll be all good." Austin cuts in, his dad joke bringing ruckus laughter from the kids.

"Ha. Ha. I guess I should've seen that coming." Pen raises a brow and shakes her head as she goes to wash her hands.

"Yeah. You really did set yourself up for that one." I chuckle, pouring the flour into a bowl.

In just under forty minutes, we're done prepping and baking, making the entire kitchen smell like a mixture of chocolate and blueberries. *It's divine.*

"Mine is going to be the yummiest," Amanda chirps, followed by Alex's protest.

"No. Everyone knows chocolate chips are superior."

"It's not a competition, guys." I'm shaking my head and smiling just as a loud pounding cuts through the room. "What in the—"

"Oh god. I think I know who that is." Pen's face turns flushed, irritation clearly painted over her features.

"I'll get it," Austin huffs, wiping his hands before storming toward the door.

The room is silent, save for the banging on wood. Whoever it is, they want inside.

"Where is she?!" Jack's booming voice cuts clear across to the kitchen.

"Calm your tits, brother. You're not seeing her like this." Austin's voice is steely in his resolve.

"I tried to keep him back, but you know Jack. There's no talking him out of something when he's put his mind to it." Jace's voice is faint, but it's clear he's here too.

Pen blows out a sigh beside me. "Ugh. I'll deal with him." She's about to walk out but turns at the last minute. "Don't go anywhere. I actually came here to talk to you regarding a favor."

Her words take me aback. *A favor? From me?* "Of course. Anything you need."

She's smiling as she exits the kitchen with my nosy self and the children in tow.

"Penelope!" Jack roars, desperation painted over his rugged features.

"I'm here, big guy. Haven't gone anywhere." She walks right up to Jack, pressing the palms of her hands to his chest as she looks up into his eyes. "You don't have to go all caveman on me. I promise I won't leave… yet."

He growls at that last part, his eyes going wild. "*Penelope,*" her name is uttered like a threat. One that Pen rolls her eyes at. "I just got you back and I don't plan on losing you again. You need to tell me whenever you're stepping out of the main house, or this is what you'll get every time."

Something flashes before Pen's eyes, her lip curling up into a sneer. "Fine. I'll tell you when I'm leaving, but that doesn't mean I'll let you stop me from doing it." She slaps Jack on the chest before turning toward the living room where we're all openly staring. "Now, if you'll release me. I need to talk to Anaya about some things."

I smile at that, turning to the kids. "What do you guys say? Feel like taking our muffins to the main house? I bet Mom would love to try your creations."

"Yes! She can be the judge," Alex bellows.

"You're toast, bubba." Amanda points her little finger into her brother's chest, the action making all of us chuckle.

"Alright. Let's get everything packed up and head over." I'm walking into the kitchen when I hear Pen huffing behind me.

"You have to let go of me, you know… *Ooof.*"

"What? Can't fault me for needing one last hug," Jack retorts.

"That wasn't a hug. That was a strangulation of my torso," Pen mutters as she comes up behind me, bee-lining it to the

Tupperware drawer.

I can't help but sigh at their banter. Despite their differences, the love they hold for one another is clear as day. No amount of snide remarks can mask it. That man would tear through heaven and hell to be by her side.

God, how amazing would it be to have that sort of connection with someone? One where you'd never be worried and waiting for the other shoe to drop.

As I package the jam into our basket, I remind myself that some things just aren't meant for me. And to be honest, it's safer that way. Can't get torn apart if you don't put yourself out there in the first place.

Austin

"You sure you don't want to head to the main house too?" I'm staring at Jack, hoping he'll go chasing after Penelope.

It's clear he's still planning on pursuing her and I'm not ready to be around that.

"Nah. It's probably better if I give her some space. You know... absence makes the heart grow fonder and all that jazz."

Jace snorts. "Well, you sure as fuck weren't giving her space, storming over here like some damn crack addict looking for his next hit."

"Whatever," Jack snarls. "That was because I didn't know she was on the property. You try losing the love of your life, only to get her back and then have her go missing again. You'd have acted the same way."

I'm groaning, rubbing a hand over my face, when Jace's booming laughter fills the room.

"Yeah. Fat chance in hell of *that* ever happening. I don't do love. Closest thing I'll ever come to having that is this camgirl on OnlyFriends." He bites his bottom lip and groans. "God created perfection with that one."

"*Christ*, Jace. Please tell me you're not watching that shit up at the house. Can't have one of the kids walking in on that." Jack's brows drop in disapproval, but Jace is either oblivious or just doesn't care.

"It's not like I don't lock the door. Besides, you can't expect me to live the life of a monk up here. There's literally no pussy for miles!"

I laugh, patting our youngest brother on his shoulder. "Don't worry. You'll be out of here soon enough and back to your glamorous lifestyle in Miami."

Jace beams as he walks toward the hall. "Counting down the hours."

"You and me both," Jack mutters.

I'm about to say something when Jace's smirk stops me cold, his hand holding up a discarded piece of lace I know all too well. For fuck's sake, my cock is still coated in the owner's juices.

"Well, well, well. What do we have here?" Jace is all smiles as Jack lets out a whoosh of air beside me, his mouth dropping open before he's muttering under his breath.

"*The fucking irony.*"

Ignoring Jack, I storm forward, ripping the tiny white fabric from Jace's hand. "Both of you, shut it. This doesn't concern you."

"Like hell it doesn't!" Jack's now laughing behind me. "You can't keep giving me shit about Pen if you're fucking the nanny."

"The *much younger* nanny." Jace has to put his two cents in, the two assholes now laughing at my expense.

I give them my back, stuffing the still damp fabric into my pocket for safekeeping. "I know how this looks, but it's not like that." Finally turning toward my brothers, I let them in on my thoughts. "This... with her... it's so much more than some old dude fucking the young nanny."

Jack snorts, "If you're old, then I'm ancient."

I raise a brow while Jace walks over and shoves at Jack's shoulder. "I wouldn't give him more ammo than necessary."

He's talking about his age difference with Pen. At Thirty-five, he's over a decade older than my stepdaughter. But in all reality, I'm no better.

Anaya is twenty-one to my thirty-two. That's a full fucking decade and a year.

"Look, I'm still not one-hundred percent with you and Pen, but I get it now. What you said in the study about having no control over who you fall for."

Jace's mouth is hanging open while a self-satisfied smirk plays on Jack's lips. "So, is she on the same page?"

Our youngest brother chortles. "Of course she is. Didn't you see the panties?"

I shake my head and throw my head back. "It's not that simple. She's still married and I'm a widower. A widower because of my own damn fault."

Even though Blanca was unfaithful, that doesn't mean I'm absolved of the role I played in her death.

Jack sighs, taking a couple of steps forward before clapping both hands on either of my shoulders. "Look. I don't know how to make this any clearer. It wasn't your fault. There were so many things in motion, and based on what we've uncovered, she wasn't exactly innocent in all this."

Jace nods. "Yeah, she'd basically wronged the cartel who off'd her. Some may even say it was a long time coming."

"Jace," I growl his name in warning. "Watch it. She's still the mother of my children."

"The adulterous mother of your children," Jack mumbles under his breath, his hands dropping to either side of him.

Focusing on him, I finally notice the lines around his eyes are deeper, probably from everything he's had to shoulder while I was gone. Sighing, I let a little bit of the resentment I'd been harboring float away. *Maybe I've been too hard on him.*

"I take it Penelope told you?"

"Yup."

"Told him what?" Jace looks between us, his brows pulled together.

Walking over to the kitchen, I pour myself a coffee, offering both brothers the same. "Blanca had been keeping a diary of sorts. Pen found it and gave it to me. Apparently, Blanca had been stepping out for some time, though she never mentioned her *beau* by name."

"By the sounds of it, he had lots of money."

Jace scoffs. "So do we. I can't believe that skanky ho. She had us all fooled."

"Watch it brother." I raise a brow, reminding him he still needs to respect her, even though she didn't do the same for the sanctity of our marriage.

"Fine. Fine. But that should at least give you a hall pass with the nanny."

"Her name's Anaya," I growl, not liking the way he's addressing the woman who's rocked me in the best way possible.

"I thought it was Monroe." Jack teases beside me.

"You two are impossible. The point is, this is between me and her. We'll tell the kids when it's time, but it won't be soon since they've recently had a lot of change."

"Then it's a done deal? Anaya feels the same way?" Jack's eyes are full of warmth, and I can tell he's coming from a place of concern.

I let out a sigh, rubbing the back of my neck as I peer out the window. "She's not exactly on board, but she's not off the train either."

Jace chuckles. "Sounds like you have your work cut out for you."

"That I do, brother. That I do." And as I say those words, I know I won't mind one second of it. Anaya is more than worth it, and I'd fight until my last breath to call her mine.

TROJAN CROWN

Chapter Nineteen
ANAYA

"About that favor…" Penelope is chewing on her bottom lip with slightly narrowed eyes. If I didn't know any better, I'd think she was nervous.

We're in Jack's study after having left the kids with Mom, both eager to spend some time with Gamma Mary.

Now that we're in here, I'm glad for the privacy. Whatever she's about to ask seems serious. Trying to ease some of her worry, I take both of her hands in mine and squeeze. "You can ask me for anything, Pen. Seriously."

"I'm pregnant." She lets it out in one fell swoop and I can't help but smile, trying not to act too unsurprised.

"Congratulations! That's amazing news, isn't it?" I'm hesitant, not sure how I'm supposed to be reacting to this information. Yes, I'd be ecstatic if I were in her shoes, but then again, I'm not privy to everything that lies behind her situation with Jack.

She shifts in place, her lips pursing as she squeezes both eyes shut.

"Jack's the dad!" She blurts out quickly, peeking at me through one eye.

"That's wonderful, Pen! He's going to be such a good father. Definitely has the protective part down pat." I chuckle, my reaction finally making Pen open both eyes and smile.

"Oh god, I can't tell you how relieved I am to have another girl in on my predicament. It's been so hard carrying this around all by myself."

Her face is all splotchy, and her breathing is coming out ragged. It's clear she still needs soothing. I pull her into a hug, rubbing slow circles down her back. "Shhh. This is a happy moment. Don't let anyone take this away from you."

"Thank you, Anaya. That means the world to me. That you're not freaking out and being all judgy."

"Never. True friends never judge." I pull back, looking into her eyes so she knows I mean it. I'd love nothing more than to be her friend.

Genuinely good people are hard to come by, and I can tell that Penelope has a good heart.

She's smiling now, her eyes all misty as her face turns pink.

"I feel the same way. And I want you to know that there's no judging on the whole you and Austin situation."

Now it's my turn to blush. "Um. That... There's... Yeah, nothing's happening there."

She purses her lips to the side, one solitary brow raising. "I'm not buying that. But anyway, just know that you won't get any opposition from me."

My throat gets tight and my chest gets heated. It's time to change the subject. "So, that favor you needed. Is it about the baby?"

Mission accomplished. As soon as I've mentioned the baby, Pen's face transforms, a light glowing from within that no amount of makeup could recreate.

"Yes! I need to give you a rundown of Jack and me first, though." She scrunches her nose and blows out a breath in annoyance. "Long story short, we were together. Now we're not together, but he wants to be."

I cut in, sensing there's more to this. "Okay, but do you want to be? Back together, that is."

Pen rolls in her lips, fighting a smile as she gives me a quick nod. "Yes. But I'm making him work for it. I need to be sure that he won't break my heart like he did in the past." She walks over to the large chesterfield and plops down, bringing a throw pillow to her lap and squeezing it tightly. "But regardless of what happens between Jack and me, I'd never cut the baby out of his life. That's where I need your help. With telling the kids. They need to know that they're going to have a nephew."

My mouth hangs open. That's a big ask. Not that I wouldn't

help, I'm just not sure I'd be the best person to break the news. "What were you thinking of doing? Did you want me to let in on their new status as auntie and uncle?"

Penelope chuckles. "Oh god no. I wouldn't do that to you. I just need you to warm them up to the idea first. You know, like dropping hints at a new baby between Jack and me. Try to gauge what their take would be on it."

I let out a deep sigh, feeling a weight lift from my shoulders. "That I can definitely do. Count me in."

Pen claps her hands together, a wide smile gracing her face. "Awesome. Let me know what kind of feedback you get from them as soon as you have it. They've been through so much; I don't want to risk this news impacting what little progress they've made." Her face turns somber, something dark flashing before her eyes. "How's Amanda? Is she still having her nightmares?"

I walk over, lowering myself onto the leather sofa beside her. "Yes, but not as frequently as when I first got here. I think she's doing better. There's definitely hope."

Pen's eyes close, her mouth slightly parting as she sucks in a ragged breath. She looks lost in a moment—one I wouldn't wish on my worst enemy.

Grabbing hold of her hand and placing it between mine, I try to impart as much comfort as possible. "Whatever it is you've gone through, it's all in the past now. You've survived it and you're stronger for it. It didn't end you. You're here. You've got this. And you know why?"

Pen keeps her eyes closed, a tear rolling down her cheek,

but she answers. "Why?"

"You've got this because you're a survivor, and that spirit will carry you through whatever lies ahead. People like us never give up. We fight until our very last breath."

Pen's eyes open at that, her trembling lips turning up into a hopeful smile. "God, Anaya. Thank you."

"Any time," I whisper back as she wraps me into a tight embrace, this moment between us embedding itself into my memory because of what she says next.

"You've got the mom role down pretty good. Sure you don't want to be my step mommy?" She's cackling as my entire body has gone stock-still. "Oh my god. You should look at your face."

She's pulled away from me now, her eyes dancing over my surely pale features. "Um…"

"I was kidding, Anaya. Sort of." She bursts into hysterical laughter again. "I mean. Technically, Austin and I aren't related at all anymore, so that term would only apply to the kids."

I'm still reeling, unable to form words. What she said caught me so off guard. I'm not ready to be anyone's stepmom, am I? Dear god. What am I saying? Austin and I aren't a thing, and we'll never be a thing, so this shouldn't even be a question.

Finally regaining some of my composure, I shake my head and break myself free of Pen's hold. "Girl, no. Don't even joke like that. I'm still married. Although I'm hoping that won't be the case for long. But despite that, I can't just jump into another relationship right after. And one with my employer? Yeah, no."

"Look at you rambling and all nervous." Pen is giving me

side-eye, her lips rolling in and fighting a smile.

I'm about to give her a piece of my mind when the study door opens and Mom stands under the frame, the look on her face turning my body into ice.

"Ray is here." Mom's words hang in the air like an ominous cloud, neither of us knowing what to say until Pen jumps in.

"Is Ray the soon-to-be ex?" I nod in response before Pen continues. "Right. Well, I'll take the kids so you can handle business. Holler at the men if you need anything."

She's disappearing down the hall toward the children when Mom grabs my wrist. "Give me a moment. I need to grab the shotgun and call the foreman."

"Why the foreman?"

"Child, if I call Austin, he'll shoot the man right where he stands."

My eyes go wide at her statement. "What? Why?"

Mom scoffs. "You'd have to be blind not to notice, Anaya. That man is clearly protective of you, and don't go fooling yourself into thinking it's just because you're his nanny."

My mouth is opening and closing like a flailing fish. She's wrong. She must be. What Austin and I have is purely physical.

There's a pounding off in the distance, the sound pulling me from my thoughts. "Ray. He's going to break down the door." Stepping into the hallway, I speak over my shoulder. "Go get the shotgun and be at the ready."

"On it." Mom responds as I walk toward my ex, my stomach churning every step of the way.

"There she is. My beautiful wife." Ray's words have bile rising in my throat.

"I'm not your wife. Not for long, anyway," I mutter under my breath as I walk down the steps and onto the gravel. "What are you doing, Ray? I thought I made it clear the last time you were here. We're over. There's nothing to discuss."

His eyes narrow, darkness filling them before it's gone and a placid expression settling over his face. "That's only because I rushed you. I pressured you and you reacted hastily. If I'd given you more time, you wouldn't have felt cornered." He steps closer, his hand reaching up to brush a strand of hair out of my face. "You never did like ultimatums."

I hate that he knows anything about me, but I can't deny that what he's saying is true. At least the part about ultimatums. "I may not like the way you rushed me, but the conclusion would have been the same, regardless. You cheated on me, Ray. That's not something I could ever get past."

The man I thought I once loved drops to his knees, his arms wrapping around my legs like I'm his lifeline. Gone is the alpha I fell for and in his place is this pitiful excuse for a man. "One time, Anaya. It was just one time. One moment of weakness. She meant nothing, and if I could take it all back, I would. I'd never hurt you the way I did. I'm so fucking sorry. Please believe me."

He's squeezing me tightly, pleading that I take his words as truth. Even if they were, would I want to go back with him? The fraction of time I've spent with Austin has shown me the potential of what could be. That a relationship could be explosive, hot, and all consuming.

These are things I never once felt with Ray. And to be honest, he was the first man that had made me his world. I found safety in that, albeit false. I felt safe in the idea that he would never want to leave me, just like my dad had. This one facet of our relationship was the main driving source of why we were together, and now that it's shattered, I don't think I could ever fall back on whatever it was, because it sure as shit wasn't love.

"I don't know what to tell you, Ray. I don't want to be with you anymore. Even if I accept what you did and forgive you, things could never go back to the way they were."

My words have Ray shooting back up to his feet, his hands going to either of my biceps. "Don't say that, beautiful. You were made for me. Let me prove it to you? Don't our years of marriage deserve at least that?"

I rear my head back, my mind and heart conflicting with the guilt he's just dropped at my feet. "Even if I wanted to give you another chance, Ray, how would I do that? I'm in the middle of a job, nannying for the Crown family. I'm not in a position to move back home, even if I wanted to, which I don't."

Ray's lips turn up into a sly smile. "Don't worry, darling. I thought you'd need a little more groveling before you'd take me back, so I made some arrangements."

I'm blinking, surprised by what he's just said. "Arrangements?"

"Yes. I'm staying at the ranch."

"What?!" I'm stunned, choking back a plethora of choice words. "How did you even do that? Mom handles all the booking, and she *never* would have allowed that."

"I used an alias." He's smirking, his fingers digging deeper into my flesh. "Just think about it. I'll still be giving you some space. You don't need to stay in the cabin with me, but I'll be close by so you can let me win you back. And if, after all that, you still don't want to be with me, then I promise I'll let you go. No matter how much it breaks me."

Silence stretches between us, my heart pounding with the reality that he's going to be here for the foreseeable future. *God, why is this happening?*

I open my mouth to respond when a loud booming voice cuts into our moment.

"Hands off!" Turning my head, I see Austin getting off an ATV, the Polaris quickly approaching behind him.

Great. The cavalry's here. Let's just hope Mom was wrong about Austin shooting Ray. As much as I don't like him, I still don't want him dead, and I definitely don't want Austin getting in trouble because of it.

Chapter Twenty
AUSTIN

"**H**ands off!" I roar into the space between us. With every step I take, my ears ring and my heart threatens to beat out of my chest. This guy needs to drop his fucking hold on my girl STAT, or shit's about to get real ugly.

Dark eyes turn to mine, but he does nothing to remove himself from Anaya. *Asshole.*

"Now, why would I do that? She's *my* wife."

His words are like a blow to the head. I knew who he was as soon as Sam called it in, but seeing him here in the flesh—*holding what's mine*—has me feeling positively murderous.

"Ray." Anaya wiggles out of his hold, and lucky for him, he lets her. "Meet Austin. Austin, this is Ray."

"Her husband." He beams, though Anaya's face sours.

"I wish I could say it was my pleasure, but it's not. What are you doing on our property?" My lips peel back in a snarl.

"I'm your guest." The asshole wears a self-satisfied smirk, and it takes everything in me not to beat it off his face.

Needing confirmation of this, I turn to Anaya's mother, incredulous that she would allow such a thing. "Mary?"

She'd been hanging by the doorway when I arrived, but she's working her way toward us as my brothers and Sam offload from their vehicles. "Yes, it's true. He'd used an alias to book his cabin."

Her eyes are apologetic, but even if what she's saying is true, this fucker can't stay. "Then I guess we better issue a full refund, because he sure as hell isn't staying here."

My chest is rising and falling rapidly when Anaya's small hand falls on it, bringing me some sort of calm, at least until her words crush me where I stand.

"Austin, he'll only be here for a little while. He just needs closure, and I suppose maybe I do too. I owe us at least that much." She's speaking, but her words won't sink in. It's like I'm frozen in horror, trying to will what she's saying away. "If it's okay with you, I'd like for him to stay. I promise to not let it affect my time with the kids."

I'm blinking. Staring. Shocked. How could she want this man here? After what he did to her? And then to say she won't let it affect her time with the kids… that means she'll be seeing him at night, when Amanda and Alex are asleep.

God. My stomach pitches at the thought of them together, his filthy hands all over her delicate skin, and I just about rip my hair out.

A strong hand lands on my shoulder and I see that it's Jack, his eyes full of concern before they turn to Penelope. "Yes. If it doesn't affect your time with the kids, then it's fine that he stays."

Jack's fingers dig into my shoulder, knowing that I'm wholeheartedly objecting to this bullshit, but he's agreeing to it anyway. Even though I know where he's coming from, the only thing making me keep my mouth shut is that Anaya requested it herself.

For him. The dick bag who cheated on her.

Ray's eyes have flitted down to where Anaya's hand is still perched, and I can't help but preen at that small victory. *That's right, fucker. She might still be married to you, but I'm the man she's freely touching.*

Unable to hold back, I wrap an arm around Anaya's waist and bring her small frame to mine, whispering into her ear, "If he crosses a line, even once, he's out on his ass. Understood?"

Anaya shivers in my hold, her neck flushing red at my open display in front of the others. But ask me if I fucking care. She finally nods, whispering a soft *yes* into my chest.

I run my nose along the shell of her ear. "Yes what, baby?"

She pulls her head back and gasps, her intense blue eyes focusing on mine as her whole body trembles.

I'm thinking I've asked too much of her when she surprises

the hell out of me. Anaya grabs me by the collar and brings me down to her height, her lips by my ear. "Yes, *Daddy*."

It's barely audible, but the words still reach me, heading straight for my cock. Jesus, this is all so wrong. I'm getting visibly hard right in front of Anaya's husband. Before I can fully process that, my nanny is pushing me away and turning toward the steps.

"Ray, mom will have someone show you to your cabin. As for me, I have a job to do." Her long blond hair is swaying as she walks back toward the main house and away from her bumbling husband.

"But, but… when will I see you?"

She's just reached the door when she turns to him. "If it's not too late, then maybe I'll stop by when the kids are asleep."

And with that threadbare promise, she's off, leaving me hard and aching in her wake. She's a little spitfire, my girl, and even though she can probably hold her own, there's no way I'm letting her go see him without some sort of protection.

"Sam, please take Mr. Garcia to the cabin next to ours." I turn toward my two brothers and gesture toward the house. "Family meeting."

I don't have to say more, my brothers just nod and follow me into Jack's office. After my declaration at the cabin, they can probably sense what I'm feeling. This situation is all kinds of fucked up, and it needs to be fixed immediately.

"How could you?" I pin Jack to the wall as soon as Jace closes the door behind us.

"Easy, brother. You heard Anaya. She wanted him to stay here."

"I don't know what you're worried about, Austin. The way she was blushing in your arms, you'd think she was your wife instead of his." Jace snickers as he pours three rocks glasses. "I'm surprised the fucker didn't start throwing punches with how you were touching her."

I release my brother, but not before shoving him away. "Yeah. Well, I still don't like it. He shouldn't be here."

Jace hands me a glass. "Don't get your panties in a wad. Based on what she said, it's just for closure, anyway."

I raise the amber liquid to my lips and swallow it in one go. "I still don't trust him. She'll be in his cabin at night. That's not safe. We need to turn on surveillance and post close enough to intervene in case anything happens."

Jack goes to sit behind his desk, turning on his computer in the process. "Doesn't that seem a little excessive to you? I mean, the transgression that caused their breakup. Was it violent?"

"No. But that doesn't mean it can't escalate to that here. Mary greeted him with a shotgun, for fuck's sake."

"Yeah. Well, that's still none of our business." Jack raises a brow, begging me to argue, and of course I do.

"It's *my* business because she's *mine*!" I growl, declaring ownership even though I have no right to.

Jack sighs. "Look, Anaya asked if it was okay. It's something she clearly needs if she's willing to voice it in front of everyone."

Jack's words make sense, but I don't like them one bit. "I see what you're saying, but I'm not letting her go unprotected. I can't. Ray is being put in a cabin next to ours. This should let me keep a close eye, and if that fucker so much as sneezes funny, he's out of here."

"Fine, but you risk her getting angry. You're straight up violating her privacy, and so far, other than a hunch you have, there's nothing to warrant it. Nothing's come back from the men of WRATH, has it?"

My eyes narrow. "No. But again, that doesn't mean there's nothing there."

"Just let Austin do his thing, Jack. It's his own funeral if she kicks him to the curb."

Jack shakes his head and sighs. "They'd have to be something first, in order to kick him anywhere. And from the sounds of it, that wasn't a done deal."

I'm huffing my way to the door before I swing it open. "Yeah, how about you let me worry about that. Seems to me like you've done enough, agreeing to this bullshit."

I don't even let Jack respond, slamming the door behind me as I step into the hall and nearly run Mary down.

"Mr. Crown." She's averting her eyes, knowing full well she's in deep shit with me.

"Mary. Why?" I stand there, unwilling to back off or elaborate. I made it clear she was to call me if this ever happened again, but she didn't. She called the foreman.

"I..." She finally looks up, defiance filling her steely eyes.

"I didn't think it was prudent. Not with the way you look at my daughter."

I'm taken aback by her words. *God. Am I that obvious?* "Explain."

"I thought it was best if I called Sam. He wouldn't have the need to inflict bodily harm on Ray the way you were about to, had my daughter not stopped you."

Wow. Just wow. Is that what happened? My mind flits back to when Anaya had laid her hand on my chest.

Yup. There's no doubt that I was on a one-way path toward kicking Ray's ass. Still reeling from this, I stumble past the house manager. "Fine. But next time, call me anyway. Whatever the consequences, they're mine to deal with."

I'm in a fog, heading back toward my cabin. I need time to think. This is all too much and all too fast.

Am I letting my feelings for the nanny cloud my judgment? She's still married and I'm still fucked up from everything that's happened. Maybe it's best if I give her a little space.

Chapter Twenty-One
ANAYA

"There you are." Ray's voice sends bile crawling up my throat, my reaction to him now a visceral one.

"Ray, I'm busy. Now is not a good time." I'm outside the barn, watching the kids take their riding lessons. Technically, I could spare a couple of minutes of talking since the children are otherwise occupied, but knowing Ray, a few minutes could easily turn heated and that's not something I want Amanda or Alex to witness.

"I figured you'd say that, but I promise I'll make it quick. Turns out they put me in the cabin right next to yours, less than a hundred feet away."

My brows shoot up, shocked as hell that Austin would allow that. "Okay. I'm not sure what you want me to say to that."

"I want you to say that you'll come have dinner with me after the kids are asleep. Maybe we can get started on our own." He waggles his brows and I just about throw up on the spot.

Gasping for air, I brace myself on the fence corralling the horses. "Excuse me? I'm not sure what gave you the impression that we are in any sort of position to be procreating together, but newsflash, we're not. I'm not getting back with you, and the only reason I'm even okay with you staying here is so we can both get closure. It's the least I could do after two years of marriage."

Ray's eyes narrow, his nostrils flaring from anger. "Anaya, you owe me more than *closure*. And with the way your *boss* was holding you, I'd say we're more than even now." There he is, the alphahole I originally fell for. Too bad for him, I can now differentiate between an alphahole and an alpharoll, and I much prefer the latter. "Look, I just want you to come to dinner tonight. We can talk, and if it makes you feel better, I promise to keep my hands to myself... for now."

A sly grin spreads across his face, the sight making my skin crawl. I turn away, unable to stomach his smile. It all feels so surreal, like what we shared these past two years was fake and the veil I'd been under has finally been lifted, allowing me to see the real man that lay beneath.

Despite this revelation, I cave, coming to terms with the

fact that I'll have to face him eventually. Mom's words ring true in my head. I can't keep running away, and even if it's just to end things, this needs to happen.

"Fine. But it's just dinner, and there will definitely be no touching," I answer Ray but keep my eyes trained on the kids, unwilling to give him any more of my time until tonight.

"Thank you, baby. I promise you won't regret it." Out of my periphery I see him quickly turn to leave, probably knowing that his lingering would result in my taking back my promise of dinner—something I almost did as soon as he called me *baby*.

My stomach turns at his term of endearment, the one that I'd gotten so used to hearing from Austin. I'm not even sure he realized the slip up, but that didn't stop me from soaking it up every time it fell from his lips.

I know I shouldn't compare the two men. It isn't fair to either of them, but I can't help it. It's like my entire life I'd been craving Coke, only to get a sip and have it be the generic brand with Ray. The can *says* cola, but the taste is far from the real thing.

Now that I've actually tasted what real dominance and support are with Austin, it's hard for me to go back to the way things were. Where Ray exerted his "guidance" with unfettered control over my finances, friendships, and even what I wore, Austin showed me that a true *Daddy* only took control when it was in his girl's best interest.

My core clenches at the promise of his spanking, never letting me think I was anything less than perfect. *God, that was so hot.*

And even though I can't be with him, for more reasons than I care to admit, it doesn't mean that I'll settle for less. I'd rather abstain for the rest of my life than subject myself to the likes of Ray. Even so, a promise is a promise, and I gave him my word.

I mentally brace myself for the argument we'll be having tonight. But I know that the only way out is through, and despite how unsavory the journey getting there will be, I will make it to the very end and be free of that man once and for all.

I know I'm running late as I'm tiptoeing out of Amanda's room, but I just can't seem to care. It's been such a day between Ray's unexpected visit and all the newness of my pseudo relationship with Austin that I just want to dive into my bed and sleep, not addressing any of it until tomorrow.

Apparently, fate has other plans.

I've just closed the door to the bedroom when two firm hands fall to my waist. *Austin.* The scent of sandalwood and something that's all him envelops me. I want nothing more than to fall back into him, but I can't.

What we had was just physical, and now that Ray is here, I'm not comfortable with even that much. Not because I want to go back with Ray, but because it just doesn't feel right, being with another man while my husband is a stone's throw away.

"Talk to me, baby. What's going on in that pretty head of yours?" Austin murmurs into my hair, the softness in his voice melting me on the spot.

Needing to nip this in the bud, I turn to face him but he fails to drop his hold. "We can't do this, Austin."

His eyes narrow, but he doesn't back off. No, instead he pulls me in tighter.

"Do what? This?" Austin grabs hold of my chin, tilting my face up to his before his tongue laps at the seam of my mouth. A full body shudder wracks me as I gasp, the opening an invitation for him to do more, even if my mind isn't in agreement with my body.

His tongue invades, caressing my own with a hungry embrace. *Heaven.* His mouth on mine feels like sheer heaven.

I'm mewling as his feet walk me back into the wall, his hands desperately roaming my body. Austin pulls back enough to lick a trail up the column of my neck, punctuating his assault with a nibble of my ear. "Or do you mean this?"

"Austin." I'm going for a warning, but his name comes out sounding more like a plea.

"What, Anaya? What does my baby need?"

Damn. It's so hard to think when he's calling me baby, his hands and mouth owning every inch of me.

Him. That's what I need. To feel him inside me, stretching me until I shatter, all of my troubles gone and forgotten.

But not only is that wrong, it's irresponsible.

Reaching up a hand, I trace the line of Austin's sharp jaw. "I'm not going to lie. I need you." A deep rumble comes from Austin's chest as something long and hard twitches against my stomach. "But that doesn't mean I can have you."

Austin lifts me, his strong hands falling to my ass as my

legs wrap around him, bringing his hard length directly to my heat. "Who says you can't have me? Tell me and I'll set them straight."

His eyes are wild, full of need and determination, and I know I'm about to shatter both. "I do. I say I can't have you."

"But why? We both want this." His brows are pushing down as he grinds down on me, the tip of his cock nudging my clit and making my head fall back.

"*Jesus.*" I roll my hips, unable to resist his hard length. *Just one little rub up and down.*

My action is enough of a green light for Austin, an animalistic growl coming from him as he carries me down the hall and into his bedroom.

I fucked up. I know I did. That swivel of my hips was a clear invitation.

But could you fault me? This man is like the finest dessert. It's like trying to keep yourself from a piece of chocolate when you're on a diet. It's damn near impossible.

Austin closes the door with his foot before he takes me to his bed, ready and willing to do whatever he needs of me. *God, does that make me a horrible person? What kind of woman readily fucks another man while her husband waits for her?*

"Whatever thoughts you have running around in your head, stop them right now. Don't let them into our bed."

Our bed. Why does that sound so good?

With a predatory gleam in his eyes, Austin flings me onto the mattress, my body landing right in the center.

"We really shouldn't," I whisper into the dimly lit room,

but there's no fight in my words—not when he's crawling toward me, staring at me like I've hung the moon.

"We should, and we will. You're mine, and I don't plan on letting you forget it." Austin's hand finds the hem of my dress, slowly lifting the cotton fabric and exposing my core. "Jesus, you're soaked."

He lowers his face, dragging the tip of his nose over my drenched slit, the coarse fabric of my panties making me mewl out in a needy plea for more.

I'm about to push him away when a rumble has me looking down into Austin's possessive gaze. "Your scent gets my cock so fucking hard, baby. I could live and die between these thighs."

How? How am I supposed to deny him access to my body when he says things like that?

"Austin." I want to say more, tell him all the reasons we could never be, but no words follow.

No matter how much I try to deny this thing between us, it's futile. Our bodies are drawn together, like an unspeakable tether tightening with each passing second and every inhale.

Austin climbs up my body until his eyes are on mine, flitting back and forth, his breath hitching. "I know, baby. I know. I feel it too."

"What's going on? What is this between us?" I whisper into his lips, his minty breath pulling me in and making me want a taste.

Austin doesn't disappoint, his hot tongue dragging a lazy stroke across my bottom lip and making me shudder before he answers, "It's fate, Anaya. You were made for me. You're mine and no piece of paper or scrap of gold can ever say otherwise."

Just then, he takes my hand in his, twisting the lone gold band free from my ring finger and flinging it across the room until it's as far away from us as possible.

I'm gasping, my mouth hanging open as I take in what he's just done. I'm not attached to the wedding band, and at this point I'd only been wearing it out of sheer habit rather than sentiment—*but still*.

Taking my jaw in his hand, he raises a brow. "That's right, baby. Make no mistake, you belong to me and no other." He's nudging my thighs wider, his hand possessively cupping my sex. "This pussy is mine and I won't stop fucking it until you're screaming my name loud enough for Ray to hear."

My core clenches in his hold, the sheer sinfulness of his words threatening to make me come on the spot.

"*Christ*, baby. You like that, don't you? Having your Daddy fuck you while your husband listens." He's nipping at my bottom lip, sucking it hard before releasing it with a pop. "Yes, the thought of him hearing you moan my name makes you drip with want."

I'm panting, his words turning me on more than they have any right to. I'm so lost in him that his fingers catch me by surprise, making me yelp when he's inserting three of them at a time, pumping and pressing into that spongy wall as my vision fades to black. "Oh, fuck."

"So. Damn. Wet." Austin crawls down my body, his lips biting at my nipples over the dress and soaking the material until the dusky color peeks through. "Fucking perfect, Anaya. My dirty little girl."

It's the last thing I hear before his mouth is assaulting my clit, his tongue flicking the tight little bundle of nerves so hard my back is arching off the bed. "Oh, god. *Austin.*"

He's making obscene sounds, his mouth eating me with abandon as his hips violently fuck the mattress. *Lord, he wants me as badly as I want him.* That realization makes my walls pulse around his thick fingers, still busy, drawing out every single ounce of pleasure my body has to give.

Noises I don't recognize are being pulled from my throat, my head thrashing left to right as I try to understand the sensations washing over me. Never in my life has my body felt like this, like a million sparks of light have taken residence in my body, popping off like Pop Rocks all at once.

Austin takes my clit between his teeth, applying the slightest bit of pressure, and I detonate, exploding so hard I feel myself gush as an unintelligible string of words leave my mouth. *Holy Jesus. I've never done that before. Come so hard I actually squirted.*

"What—what are you doing to me?" I'm breathing heavily, each word coming out on a ragged pant.

Austin's deep chuckle has me shivering and my nipples tightening even harder. "Showing you who you belong to, baby." He sits me up before his hands reverently go to my face, his touch so at odds with his next words. "But first, you need to be punished."

"What? Why?" I'm sputtering as his large hand goes to my

throat and tightens, feeling the thick swallow I've taken upon hearing his words.

"I specifically remember you having to scream my name as you came, but you didn't. Seems to me like you need reminding."

My mouth parts on a gasp as he flips me over, placing me on all fours as he trails a big hand up the back of my thigh. "Hands on the rails, baby girl."

In a lust filled daze, I do what he says, my core already pulsing with excitement at what's coming next. I've never been manhandled like this, and I love it. Like really—*really*—love it.

Despite my curves, I feel so small and delicate in his hold, his strong muscles flexing as he picks me up and throws me around. It's fucking hot, and I'm already wanting more.

"Good girl." Austin's praise pulls me from my thoughts, the cold air hitting my freshly exposed skin as he lifts my dress up and over my ass, letting the fabric bunch at my waist. A feral growl rumbles behind me and I can't help but look back.

My breath catches at what I see. Austin's emerald eyes are a tempest of emotions, want and possession dancing in them in a searing gaze as he hones in on my core. "No other, Anaya. This little cunt will have no other."

A whimper tumbles from my lips at his declaration. To be claimed like this would scare most girls off, but not me. I want this. I want him. Even if it's just physically.

I go to touch him but he growls, "*Hands*."

Austin issues a quick slap to my swollen clit, making my hands fly back to the headboard. Oh god. Why does that feel *so* good? My tingling little nub received a burst of pleasure from that bite of pain, and I can't help but push my hips back, wanting more.

"Next time you do that, I won't let you come." He runs a knuckle between my folds, nudging the bundle of nerves with his next words. "Now be a good little girl and grind on Daddy's hand. Use me like a toy. I want to feel your juices dripping down my fingers."

Oh god, this filthy man has me biting my lip as I press back into him, using him like I used to hump my teddy bear when I was a little girl.

Shame washes over me as heat fills my cheeks, the memory of my swollen needy pussy pressing against the teddy bear's nose, grinding on it and pressing my little clit on the hard plastic until the sensation exploded into relief. *The act was shameful then, and it's sure as fuck shameful now.*

I'm married, my husband a mere hundred feet away, and what am I doing? Grinding on my employer's hand like it's my own personal sex toy. It's wrong. This is all so wrong, but it feels so good it's bringing me to the edge of bliss once more.

I feel a second climax approaching, the tell-tell darkness shrouding my vision, when his husky voice issues a command. "My name, Anaya. Say it."

His hand retreats, and I whimper, only to have my body shake when his palm quickly slaps my core again. "Austin!" His name leaves my mouth on a broken sob. He's driving me to the point of madness, taking me to the edge only to pull me back at the very last minute with that biting sting.

"That's right, baby. It's *my* name on your lips." He's brought his knuckle back to my slit, rubbing round and round my swollen clit. Over and over, he plays this game until I'm shaking, tears streaming down my face as my body begs for release.

"Please, Austin. I need you."

The sound of his guttural roar mixes with the ripping of fabric as Austin tears my dress right down the middle, the white cotton falling to either side of me on the bed and leaving me completely exposed. There's no warning. All I feel is the stretch of fullness as Austin impales his massive cock between my folds, the sensation of him in me feeling righter than anything in my entire life ever has.

This, right here and now, is where I want to be.

I know this is wrong, but right now, as his hard length slides in and out of me, his balls slapping against my sensitive clit, I give no fucks. I'll willingly drown under this sea of pleasure and sin if it means I can have him, just this once.

TROJAN CROWN

Chapter Twenty-Two
AUSTIN

Jesus fucking Christ. I've died and gone to heaven. My fingers dig into Anaya's wide hips, the vision itself making my balls draw up with the need to fill her, mark her and make her take my seed. Filling this pussy with my cum and putting those birthing hips to use are now my driving force.

I don't recognize the sounds that are coming out of me. My chest rumbling as I violently thrust into her warm and willing body. It's like the primitive man in me has finally emerged, ready to take and claim.

Both of my kids were happy surprises, but with Anaya, I'm

not taking any chances. I want it all with her, and that includes as many babies as she'll give me.

As if reading my thoughts, my girl's walls flutter around me, my name moaned with every slide forward. "That's right, baby. Who does this pussy belong to?"

"You. Only you."

"*Fuck yes.*" I pull my hand back and slap her plump ass. "Goddamn, Anaya. You own me. You own this fucking cock."

As the words slip from my lips, I know they're nothing but the truth. I'm hers just as much as she is mine. She may not have my name yet, but all of that will get sorted in time.

Delicious sounds have my gaze dropping, my eyes falling to where we're connected and making my cock throb inside her.

I lick my lips, watching her puffy folds stretch around my girth, all glistening with her arousal. It's too much, the vision so fucking hot it makes me release a rogue rope of cum into her womb. *Jesus. I'm not going to last much longer.*

Snaking my hand around Anaya's front, I bring her up so her back is flush against my chest, both hands now cupping and kneading her full breasts. "These tits, baby. They're perfect."

I nuzzle against her neck, biting and sucking the tender flesh as my fingers pinch and tweak her erect nipples. *Oh fuck.* I swear I see God when her walls clamp down on me, making it clear she likes a little bit of pain.

"Do you like this?" I tweak her nipples again and she flutters around my cock, a soft whimper falling from her mouth. "Answer me, baby. Do you like it when Daddy pinches your little nipples?"

Anaya mewls as she clenches down hard, her walls milking me and making my eyes roll back. "*Fuck.* I'll take that as a yes."

Leaning back on my heels, I keep my hands tightly affixed to her breasts. "Bounce on me, baby. Fuck Daddy's cock while he plays with your pretty little tits."

She moans something unintelligible, her head falling back onto my shoulder and giving me a clear sight down her front. *Perfection.* I know I've thought it before, but it's the goddamn truth. Her body was made for me. My own personal little fuck toy.

And as if her heart and soul weren't enough, God made her a kinky little thing, her body a wonderland of pleasure to enjoy. Just then, visions of Ray taking her infiltrate my mind and nothing but blind rage consumes me, making me pound harder into Anaya from below.

"*Mine,*" I growl, letting a possessive hand wrap around my girl's neck, needing to claim her in every way possible. "Say it, Anaya. Scream so loud it makes your throat burn. Let that piece of shit know who you belong to."

Applying more pressure to her throat, I fuck into her hard, every thrust sending her body bouncing up in the air, only to be stopped by my collard hold.

Over and over, her ass slams into my lap, turning the tight globes a pretty shade of pink. I'm transfixed by this sight, lost in the beauty of how well we fit, when her words bring me to the edge—making my balls draw up and my back tighten.

"I'm yours, Daddy. All yours."

"*Fuuuuuuck.*" That one word is like the key to both of our

release. As her pussy contracts around my cock, I in turn flood her from within, releasing rope after rope of cum in what is the hardest climax of my life.

Even though I'd asked her to scream my name, she called me her daddy, a role much bigger than that of just a lover.

Daddy. That one word runs so much deeper than a kink. It's ownership, protection, and devotion all rolled into one.

I know it. She knows it. And it's clearly what we both want and need. With my hand still firmly affixed to her throat, I bring her back onto my chest, my lips pressing to the back of her head. "You're perfect, baby. Perfect and all mine."

She's silent, simply trembling in my hold as our chests rapidly rise and fall from our exertion. I'm about to ask her what she's thinking when a muffled vibration sounds off, my eyes following it and falling to the jeans I'd discarded on the floor.

The sound stops, then starts again, and as much as I don't want to, I pull Anaya's warm body from my lap, lowering her down onto the mattress before going to pick up my cell.

I tap the button to answer with unnecessary force, growling as I bring the phone to my ear before answering. "Hello."

"Need you at the main house, brother. The men of WRATH have an answer for us on *el Jefe* and his men."

My hackles rise at Jack's words, my entire body going rigid in anticipation of battle. "Be there in five."

I don't wait for him to answer. *He's probably making the rounds and calling all the brothers.* Instead, I head to the bed and to my woman who's lying there, deep concern etched over her features.

"Is everything okay?" Anaya is moving to cover herself with a pillow, but I'm not having it. Just as I did in her room before, I grab her wrist and stop her.

"No, baby. Not when you hide yourself from me." My eyes rake over her delectable body, appreciating every curvy inch.

She's blushing, but she's no longer trying to cover herself. "I'm serious, Austin. Who was that? Was it about Ray?"

I growl, my heavy body pinning her small one to the bed as I grab and raise both hands above her head. "Listen to me and listen to me good. You will never speak another man's name in our bed. Understood?"

She's blinking up at me, her edible mouth parted in surprise. A beat passes and I think she's going to deny me, but she nods, her breath coming out shaky as she answers in a soft whisper, "*Okay.*"

"Good girl." I give her a chaste but hard kiss before peeling myself from her body—one of the hardest things I've ever had to do. "I have to go see my brothers, but I'll be back soon. Don't leave this room."

Her brows furrow as she partially sits up, her palms pressing against the bed. "But I was supposed to meet R— Umm, I have plans. Plans that won't take long. Besides, shouldn't I be staying in my room? What if the kids come looking for me? Oh god, the kids… They must've heard us!"

Her face is a deep red, clearly embarrassed, but she needn't be.

"This room is soundproofed. All the master bedrooms in the cabins are. It's one of their touted features." As much as I would've liked that soon-to-be ex of hers hearing her scream my name, I knew it was probably better he didn't. Not yet, at least. I run a hand along her curves, sinking my fingers into her hips possessively. "And as far as your *meeting*. Cancel it."

Anaya's mouth is hanging open, her wide eyes glaring at me. "I can't just cancel. I gave him my word."

My stomach churns as my heart threatens to beat out of my chest. "Listen to me, Anaya. You're mine, and I take care of what's mine. Unfortunately, there's a meeting with my brothers right now and I can't run the surveillance on our guest's cabin like I originally wanted to. Which means you won't be as safe."

Anaya sits upright, her legs swinging over to the side of the bed. "You were going to spy on me?!"

"Surveil. Not Spy."

She shoves at my shoulder, but I fail to move. This is something I'm not willing to compromise on.

"It is *so* not the same thing."

"It is, and the answer is still no. You're not going, not until I'm able to give you a gun or taser or something. Anything to keep you safe when you're out of range and next to a wild card." I pull her onto my lap, cradling her head to my chest. "You're too fucking precious for me to lose, Anaya. I won't survive it."

I feel her body melt into mine and I hope that somehow I've gotten through to her. Maybe I'm just being jealous—a possessive man over what's his—but the thought of her at Ray's cabin just feels wrong.

She sighs into me. "Fine. But just for tonight and just until you can get me some sort of protection. I don't think he'd do anything, but it's smart not to go in blind."

"That's my girl. Making Daddy proud." I'm teasing, but not. I love this little game we play, and I'm not ready to give it up.

Unfortunately for me, Anaya might not feel the same. She's groaning, burying her face into my chest. "Oh god. I can't believe we did that."

Pulling back enough to take her face in my hands, I level her with a narrowed glare. "Did what, Anaya? Claim each other? Give each other what the other needed?" My eyes are wild, bouncing back and forth between hers. "There's nothing wrong with what we did. Yes, we may be a little jagged inside. Broken because of what we've survived, but those broken bits call to one another, recognizing their other half and making them whole. I won't be ashamed of caring for you, giving you what you need. And I sure as fuck won't let anyone shame you. Not even yourself. Understood?"

Seconds tick by as I see the wetness pool in my girl's eyes. I know she's seen her share of heartache, and I vow right then to never be the one to add to it. It's now my job to protect her, keep her safe from harm, and that means away from Ray. At least until I can set up better parameters for their meeting.

Pressing my fingers to the underside of her chin, I tilt her face toward mine. "Answer me, baby. I need to know you understand."

Anaya sniffles, blinking away a single tear, but she nods. "I understand."

Her words bring me a sense of peace I needed in order to

function the rest of the night. And without wanting to, I lower her onto the bed, pulling the heavy down comforter over her naked body.

"God, you're beautiful." It was more so whispered to myself, but the accolade has her blushing all the same. "Stay just like this, baby. I'll be back soon. Promise."

Lowering myself, I press a kiss to her forehead, lingering just for a second. She smells of sex, sweat, and her; the combination a heady drug I don't want to leave, but I know that if I don't pry myself away now, I never will.

With one last glance, I rise from the bed and walk out the door, needing to get this meeting over with as soon as possible. Now that I have Anaya in my bed, revenge seems like nothing but an afterthought and something that could wait. Too bad for me, the other Crown brothers don't feel the same.

TROJAN CROWN

Chapter Twenty-Three
AUSTIN

"**I**'m here," I mutter into the room where all my brothers sit waiting. Shocked to see Hunter in person, I whip around and point. "How in the hell did you get here so fast? Weren't you up the mountain?"

"Nah. I had some business to take care of down valley when Jack called." Hunter's face is stoic, not giving anything away. I'm about to pry him for more info on this business of his when Jack cuts in.

"Sit, brother. Our call is about to start."

Sure enough, Jack's computer chimes. He pushes some buttons and the TV in the corner turns on, the webcam on it pointed back toward the room making us all visible.

"Good. Everyone's there." Aiden, the former navy seal, is on the left side of the screen and Cárdenas is on the right. *This is interesting.* I thought it was just a meeting with the men of WRATH securities, but I guess it's a family reunion too. "Cárdenas, can you hear us clearly?"

"Yes." The one word comes out thick with accent, punctuated with a raised brow.

"Let's get down to business, then. Gentlemen, I've asked for you to be here because of a new revelation Don Cárdenas has provided. As previously mentioned in other calls, this is a secure communication and cannot be traced or hacked, so feel free to say whatever it is that needs to be said."

Cárdenas purses his lips to the side, his eyes slightly narrowing. Yeah. I'm betting he's not too keen on sharing all of his nitty gritty with us, despite Aiden's reassurance. "It has come to my attention that you've been looking for the members of Las Cruces, but you will not find them. They have been… *detained* and will be unavailable for the foreseeable future."

My chest tightens at this information and the missed opportunity for revenge. "Cárdenas, with all due respect, this was my business. You had no right to *detain* them."

Cárdenas' eyes find me in the room, his nostrils flaring at my response. "Austin Crown, my condolences for your loss."

His words have bile churning in my stomach. I should be distraught, mourning the loss of my wife, but instead my dick is coated in another woman's juices—a woman I can't wait to get back to. After a second, I respond with as much composure as I can muster. "Thank you. But that's not the only wronged I was seeking justice for."

He must see something in my eyes because the cartel boss throws his head back in a throaty chuckle. "I see our Blanca was still up to her same antics. But no worries, friend. If it's blood you're after, why don't you come pay us a visit? I've got plenty to help you quench that thirst."

My brows shoot up at his words. Does he have the rival cartel detained? I thought that was a euphemism for murdered. To say that it piqued my interest would be putting it mildly.

Even though we've both been with the same woman, I sense a sort of camaraderie with this man. Maybe it's the fact that we've both seen death up front, and even caused it, though I'm sure his tally is much higher than mine, but I trust him. "I'd like that. Let me know when I could come down for a visit."

Jack bristles behind his desk, no doubt unhappy with my travel plans, but he says nothing in opposition. "I'll be down there within the next couple of days, Daniel. Maybe I can bring Austin with me, and we can all give the detained a visit."

Well, well, well. It seems like my big brother might have a little blood lust himself.

Daniel Cárdenas nods, his eyes scanning the room. "Yes, that'll be fine, but we need to make sure my daughter is protected when you're both gone. I take it the rest of the brothers will stay behind as well as some of the WRATH team?"

Aiden cuts in. "Yes. We're almost done with bulking up surveillance around the property, and as soon as we've finished, we'll be leaving a few team members behind to help with added security."

Good. I like the sounds of that. With Ray lurking about, I wonder if I can add a directive to keep him away from my girl. "Aiden, we'll also need extra security around the kids and Anaya."

Aiden nods once. "The nanny, right?"

My cheek twitches at her title. Yes, she's the nanny. The nanny I'm fucking. But she's so much more than just that. Instead of going into all that in front of everyone, including a cartel boss who thinks I'm still mourning my dead wife, I simply nod, unable to say more for fear of it all spilling out at once in an undying declaration of love for the much younger nanny.

"Okay. We can definitely set that up. Your cabin and the neighboring one are the last ones to get the upgraded security systems installed, but we should have it done by the time you fly out."

God, the thought of leaving Anaya and the kids behind is sheer torture, but this is something that must be done. There's no telling how long the rival cartel has left. Not when they're being detained by Daniel. His men are more brutal than the Las Cruces with their decapitation.

I shudder at the rumors I've heard. Instead of simply severing the heads, they go with a Colombian necktie. Come to think of it, I'm not sure which is worse. Either way, they don't have long before any chance of us getting our answers is gone.

With a resigned sigh I get myself ready for the conversation with Anaya. I know she won't be happy about this, but she'll just have to understand. Just like I'm letting her have closure with Ray despite my hating it, she too will have to let me put this thing with Las Cruces to rest.

The sooner that's all done and over with, the sooner we can move on with our lives and step toward our forever as a family.

Anaya

God, why does he have to smell so good?

I roll my head to the side, pressing it into the pillow that smells of everything sinful and delicious, making it harder to get out of his bed, even though I know I have to. My phone is in my room and Ray has been waiting for a dinner visit that will never come.

Despite my not wanting to break my word, Austin is right. I can't go into Ray's cabin unprepared. He's never hurt me, but the look in his eyes the last time he paid me a visit was bone chilling.

Mentally giving myself one last push, I peel the covers off and head toward Austin's dresser, needing at least a shirt of his to cover up before heading outside.

My eyes land on the tattered dress he tore into two. *Damn, that was hot.* My nipples harden into points at the memory of him taking my body and making it his, the evidence of his release still dripping down my leg.

Even now, thoroughly used, I'm still hungry for more. The way he held me, the way he owned me, it was everything I never knew I needed. He's my *daddy* in all the right ways, taking care of me and putting me in my place when I need to.

Yes, I'd originally been embarrassed by what I was craving from him, but the way he explained it to me while he held me to his chest—it all made sense. And if I were being truly honest with myself, it's what I'd always been searching for. That's why I went to Ray so willingly, forgetting the only friend I'd ever had and moving clear across the country with him. Too bad for me, he was just an imposter. Not really an alpha at all, just a damn cheater with his own set of issues.

I'm tiptoeing into the hallway, grateful as all hell that Austin's room is soundproofed and that the kids didn't hear all the noise we'd been making. *They'd probably be scarred for life.*

Unfortunately, I'm not sure my room has the same feature, so I quickly snag my phone from the dresser and head back into the living room so as not to wake the kids with my conversation. I could probably get away with texting Ray, but my guilt has me pressing the call button instead. It's the least I could do after giving him my word and failing him. I'm not him, and going back on a promise is not something I'm used to.

Bringing a throw pillow to my chest, I clutch it for dear life as the line rings and rings before Ray finally answers. "Anaya?"

"Ray. Hi. Umm"

"Are you on your way?" He sounds irritated, not making what I'm about to say any easier.

"About that. I can't go tonight. Austin had some family business come up, so he had to step out. I need to watch the kids so I can't leave the cabin."

There's a pause before he finally answers. "So, aside from the kids, you're alone?"

Oh, God. Why did I admit Austin isn't here? "Yes, but technically no. The ranch hands and WRATH members are still on the property. All just a call away should I need them. You can call them too if you need to. Their number should be in the drawer under the house phone. All the cabins come with the property phonebook."

I'm rambling and I know it's giving my nerves away, but I just don't care. The last thing I want him thinking is that he can come over here when Austin isn't home.

"No, Anaya. I don't need *security*. But I don't like that you're all alone, despite all those people being a phone call away. I'm the closest to you. Why don't you just let me come over and keep you company until Austin gets back. That way we can have our much needed conversation and you and the kids stay safe with me. It's a win-win."

He's persistent. I'll give him that much. "I don't think that's a good idea, Ray. If they were my kids, I wouldn't feel comfortable with another full-grown man in the house, one I hadn't fully vetted myself. It really isn't professional of me to do that either."

"Fine. I can see that, but I don't like it." Ray blows out into the phone. "I just miss you, baby. I don't like spending more time away from you than necessary. Any idea when you'll be able to stop nannying for them?"

My stomach flips, unhappy with what he's saying. "I might

have a break tomorrow, but I'm not sure.

"That's good, but not what I meant. You don't have to work, Anaya. You've never had to. Our home might be modest, but I've always provided for you. There's no need to do all of this, caring for other kids when you should be caring for our own."

Straight up bile crawls up my throat. "No, Ray. You and I won't be having children."

"Why not? You're not on birth control. We could get started tonight if you wanted to."

Oh god! What have I done! I'm *not* on birth control and Austin and I have been having unprotected sex. This is something I should have stopped from the very first time, but now it's been twice that he's come inside me with nothing to prevent a pregnancy.

My chest is heaving rapidly, my breath coming out fast and shallow.

"Anaya? Are you okay? I'm coming over." Ray's panicked voice has me snapping the fuck out of my mini panic attack.

"No! No. I'm fine. I thought I saw a mouse. Freaked me out, but turns out it was just a shadow from the tree outside."

"Hmm." He doesn't seem like he believes me, and I can't have that.

"Honestly, I'm fine now. I should probably get going. I'll call you tomorrow about what time to meet up."

"Anaya, please. Please don't shut me out just yet. I know I messed up, but I love you. I promised you forever because there's no one in this world I'd rather live life with than you."

His words cut me deep, inching the gap of guilt a little wider. Should I be giving him another chance? Am I hanging onto his infidelity too tightly? He said it was only one time. Just the once with that woman. God, I'm a fucking hypocrite. Here I am, still coming off the high Austin's fingers and cock provided. I've slept with him twice. Doesn't that make us even now?

"I'll think about it, Ray. I promise." Giving him my word, I click the line closed, needing to end the call before my mind is too far gone and I'm left a puddle of guilt and insecurities.

Unable to sleep with all the craziness going on in my head, I head to the kitchen for some late-night comfort food. Maybe some of mom's hot chocolate will do the trick.

But just as I'm about to turn into the kitchen, a small book catches my eye, the moon illuminating its cover and calling me to it. It's what Austin had thrown against the wall right before he took me for the very first time.

"Did that make you feel better?" I questioned.
His forest green eyes land on me, his pupils
growing by the second as they travel down my body.
"No. But hearing your voice did."

It wasn't my imagination. He liked what he saw. He liked it enough to take and let my body soothe whatever ache this book caused.

Picking it up, I open it to where a feather lies inside. *Oh wow, it's a journal.* I know I probably shouldn't be reading this, but my curiosity gets the best of me. I never said I was a saint, and I already know I'm nosy as hell.

Maybe just one little glance will take my mind off this

major decision hanging over my head. I don't want to think about giving Ray another chance. Not when I've just discovered bliss with another man.

Resolved to put my responsibilities aside for just a moment, I dive into this book of untold secrets, letting it drag me away from my own problems and delve into those of the irresistible cranky Crown.

TROJAN CROWN

Chapter Twenty-Four
AUSTIN

It's been a long night, and after ironing out the logistics of our trip, the only thing I want to do is crawl into bed with my woman and maybe take her for another round. Having her on me, next to me and under can't come soon enough.

I'm like a kid on Christmas morning, opening the door to our bedroom only to come to a screeching halt when I see she's not where I left her. A rumble starts deep in my chest, wondering where in the hell Anaya's gone to. *She wouldn't leave the kids alone, would she?*

Flashes of her in Ray's arms invade my mind, and I just

about go blind. That fucker can't have her. He had his chance and blew it. She's mine now.

I'm storming into Anaya's room next only to find the bed empty, the sight sending another flash of rage flowing through me and triggering my instinct to chase her down. *Oh where oh where has my baby girl gone?*

A chair scraping in the kitchen has me heading that way, the sound bringing me some semblance of peace—one that won't be whole until I have eyes on Anaya.

Sure enough, I see her blonde hair sway as she whips around from the pantry; her face caught in a state of surprise. "Oh my god. You startled me!" She whisper-hisses, pressing her palm to her chest. She's clad in nothing but my shirt, the sight making me drool on the spot.

"Just me, sweetheart." I walk up to her, encircling my arms around her small waist and bringing her toward me. "It's late. What are you doing out of bed?"

She's looking up at me through full lashes, her blue eyes almost clear from the moonlight. "I couldn't sleep. Besides, I can't stay in your room. What if the kids wake up?"

I run a hand up her back, splaying my fingers at the base of her neck and into her hair, digging the tips in possessively. "*Our* bed, Anaya. And we're always up before they are. There's no need to tell them until you're ready."

It's true, Amanda and Alex both love to sleep in—one of the few traits they took from their mother. They sleep like the dead and good luck trying to get them up before they're good and ready.

Still, Anaya doesn't seem sure. Not having any of that, I pick her up bridal style and carry her back to bed. "Come on, baby. It's late and I want to get some more of this body before we tuck in for the night."

I'm laying her down on the bed when she starts with her feeble attempt at protesting. "Austin, we aren't a thing. This is just physical and I'm not sure it should happen more than it already has."

"Is that why you're wearing my clothes? Because that sure as hell makes you look like mine." My eyes soak her in as I pull off the shirt I'm wearing, throwing it to the side.

"Aust—" Anaya's words die on her pretty mouth, her pink tongue poking out as she licks her lips and stares me up and down. "God, how are you even real?"

I chuckle, my laugh breaking her from her thoughts. "Baby, that's how I feel about you. You're like a goddamn angel sent to drive me insane."

Her warm hand trails down my chest, her pale skin such a contrast to all the ink I've acquired over the years. "Why green? It's all black except for the splashes of color, each and every one of them green."

I take in a deep breath, never having really told anyone this truth. "I'm the only Crown brother with green eyes. Growing up, I was teased for it. Told that I was adopted, that I wasn't really a Crown. When I turned eighteen, my parents told me the truth. I was, in fact, adopted. I'd been dropped off at the steps of my father's firm at the time. Nobody knew who'd done it. Since my dad was the first one to arrive at work that morning, he was the first one to find me. Called my mom in a panic and, well, here I am. A Crown."

Anaya's palms are flat on my chest, her eyes looking at me with so much sadness. "Oh god, Austin. I didn't know."

"It's not something we advertise." I wink, giving her a cheeky smirk to lighten the mood. "But when I'd been dropped off, I had nothing to my name save for a green blanket and onesie. Pair that with the color of my eyes, and they were the only tangible things that I had tying me to my biological parents. The color just stuck, and I tried to tie it into me anywhere I could."

"Your art. It's like you're embedding more of them into you, into your life."

I nod as I lower my body onto hers until my lips are a mere breath away. "But it's all pointless now. I see that family is what you make of it. Like you and the kids, you're more of a mother to them than Blanca ever was. Sure, she gave birth to them, but I never once saw her rocking Amanda the way you do when she has nightmares."

Anaya's face twists, something flashing behind those icy blue eyes. "Don't. Please don't."

"Don't what, baby? Tell you how amazing you are?" I lick at the seam of her mouth, swallowing her moan when she gives me entry.

She tastes of everything right in this world, and I know I want to live and die with this woman by my side. My cock swells as our tongues dance, the push and pull of our kiss making me pump my hips into hers. As much as I want to take her again, I need to make sure she's okay. I wasn't exactly gentle with her, and I've already come inside her twice today.

"Are you sore?" I let a hand trail down between us, my palm splaying possessively at her core.

She's panting, her hooded gaze looking up at me with a mixture of adoration and something else I can't pin. "A little."

Groaning, I let my head fall to the crook of her neck, inhaling deeply before sucking on the tender flesh and releasing it with a pop. "I'm not going to lie. My dick wants inside that magical pussy of yours, but I'm not going to risk hurting it. She's my baby too, and I have to make sure she's okay."

I've pulled back just enough to see Anaya's cocked brow. "Well, since this is our last time and all, I figured I should get a taste. In for a penny, in for a pound. Right?"

I'm chuckling as I let her roll me onto my back. "Baby, I don't know what you're going on about, but this is definitely not our last time."

Her eyes shoot up to me, the intensity in them almost sobering my heated state. "I mean it, Austin. This is our last time. I'm your nanny, nothing more."

I'm about to argue that her actions prove different, but I'm silenced by her mouth sliding onto my bulbous head. As soon as those lips wrapped around the tip, I was a goner. All coherent thoughts left my body, never to be seen again. *Holy Jesus.* She's sucking in all ten inches, taking me in until my cock hits the warm wet walls of her throat. And as if I hadn't already died and gone to heaven, this woman swallows, taking my throbbing shaft into her tight channel and making a spurt of cum squeeze down her throat.

Yup. She's insane if she thinks I'm letting her go after this. Never in my life have I received head this good. Pair it with her magical cunt and heart of gold? Yeah, it's safe to say she'll be bearing my name in no time.

"God, baby. You're so fucking perfect. So perfect and mine." My eyes are taking her in as she gags on my length, her eyes watering from the effort. Despite my size, she's humming in approval, her hips pumping into the mattress in an effort to seek relief. Needing to rectify this situation, I dig my fingers into her hair and pull her off my cock before twirling her around, reverse cowgirl.

"Give me that pretty pussy." I lift her ass in the air, issuing a quick slap to her swollen lips before sliding a finger through her drenched slit. "Let Daddy lick it and make it feel better."

Anaya mewls, shoving her heat back into my waiting mouth. Needing no further invitation, I lap at her wetness, reveling in its taste. "Mmmph, baby. Your taste makes me so fucking hard."

As if in agreement, my dick bobs up, slapping Anaya's face and making her moan. *She liked it.* Before I can say anything else, she's wrapping a hand around my shaft and taking me in her mouth, the action making me hiss out in pleasure.

"Goddamnit. You suck Daddy's cock so good, baby." My hands fall to her ass, kneading the juicy globes as I pump my hips into her wet hole. "That's right, just like that, baby. Let Daddy fuck that pretty mouth."

She moans around my length; the vibrations sending a jolt

of pleasure down to my balls. Everything she does feels so damn good. I need to make her feel the same, because leaving her without pleasure isn't an option.

With my hold on her ass, I bring her juicy folds to my face, lapping up her essence and reveling in every single drop. She tastes of honey and sin, everything my soul requires. And right then, I know I'll never get enough.

Needing more of her, I impale her with my tongue, letting my thumb circle the tight ring of muscles at her rear.

Anaya gasps, my cock instantly missing her warmth. "*Austin.*"

"What, baby? Do you not like this?"

She looks back at me from her position on all fours, the blush on her face making me want to flip her over and fuck her raw. "Nobody has ever been back there. Technically, I've only ever been with one other man."

I growl, not liking the mention of anyone else while she's in our bed. Before I can think of it, my hand is rearing and giving her ass an open palmed slap. "What did I say, Anaya?"

Her eyes flash in a mixture of surprise and heat. "I'm sorry, Daddy. Let me make it up to you."

She turns around, giving me a view of her gorgeous tits as she straddles me, her hands going to my chest and pushing me back down onto the bed.

I cock a brow, my dick ready and waiting for whatever she has in mind. "And how exactly are you planning on making it up to me?"

She's biting her bottom lip, her eyes dancing with greedy

mirth as she grabs a hold of my shaft, running the tip of my cock up and down her drenched slit and making me groan. "Let me make you feel good. Don't you want your little girl's tight pussy?"

Oh shit. I almost nut on the spot, her dirty words threatening to take me over the edge. "God, baby. There's nothing I want more, but I don't want to hurt you."

Her head rolls back as she impales herself with just the head, sliding on and off the tip and squeezing every last ounce of self-restraint I possess. She's mewling, "But it hurts so good, Daddy. Let me have it. Let me have your big cock."

Fuuuuuuck. I'm gone. Lost in the heat of this woman.

With both hands digging tightly onto her hips, I shove her down, hard. "Take it, baby. Take Daddy's cock. It's all yours."

And God, does this woman take. She rides me like a woman possessed, grinding down hard with every push and milking me hard with every pull. It's some sort of miracle I don't spill into her.

Knowing how my girl likes her tits played with, I raise up and take one into my mouth while I palm the other, kneading the plump flesh and groaning when she clamps down on me harder. "Baby, you keep doing that and Daddy's going to fill you before you're ready."

Her eyes hood as she licks her lips. "But that's so naughty, Daddy. You could get me pregnant."

Fucking hell. She likes that, her pupils blowing out and giving her dark and dirty wants away. Unable to hold back any longer, I flip her onto her back and give her one hard thrust.

"Does my baby want that? Daddy filling her up and making her his?"

Anaya whimpers, her eyes shutting as she nods, giving me all the permission I need. "Open your eyes, Anaya. There's no shame in what you want. You're mine and I'm yours." I swivel my hips into her before retreating and slamming back in. "I'll always give you what you need, baby girl."

And if I'm being honest with myself, this is something I need too. To tie myself to this woman for all eternity, having a bond between us that no earthly being could ever shatter.

Creating life isn't a decision that should be taken lightly, but with this woman I want it all, and I know deep in my soul that there's no other person who I'd rather share this with.

For fuck's sake, she's already amazing with Alex and Amanda. And as I continue to thrust into her, her nails clawing down my back as she pants and moans, I know that growing our brood is the only thing that makes sense.

"Daddy. Please. I *need* it." Anaya digs her heels into my ass, clamping down her walls around me and holding me in place as she rubs her clit on my root.

Roaring, I lower my mouth to her chest, sucking on a full breast before biting down onto her milky flesh. Unable to hold on any longer, I let go, giving my girl what she wants and finally letting myself shoot rope after rope of hot cum into her womb.

Like a warning shot, my release triggers her own, and Anaya lets out the most glorious sounds that have ever graced my ears. As my girl revels in her climax, my cock twitches inside her, my entire body spasming from the most intense orgasm of my life.

I pull back just enough so that I can see the beauty lying beneath me, and as a soft smile falls on those plump lips, I know there's no going back.

Yeah. This girl is mine, and there isn't a soul on this earth who can say otherwise.

TROJAN CROWN

Chapter Twenty-Five
ANAYA

I should be floating on a cloud of bliss, having more orgasms than I ever thought possible in a twenty-four-hour period, *but I'm not.*

Guilt wracks me as I think back to what we just did. I let him come inside me—*again.* Not only did I let him, but I wanted it. I wanted to tie myself to him. Bind us together despite everything I've read in that damn journal.

I groan, wishing I could turn back time and stop myself from reading the thing.

I was only a quarter of the way through when Austin came home, and I had to quickly stash the book in the pantry so as not to get caught red-handed.

It's obvious his late wife had been cheating on him and I'm thinking that's why he was so angry the first time he took me up against a wall.

Is that all this is to him? A way of getting her back even after death?

If it were, then his words of adoration wouldn't make a lick of sense.

My mind is lost, trying to make logic from the mush in my head when the kids come running into the kitchen.

"Alex took my dolly!" Amanda is screeching at the top of her lungs.

"I needed it for my experiment. Consider it a sacrifice for the greater good," Alex snickers.

I run my hands down the front of my apron, turning to face them. "Kids, you know the rules. You can't take things that don't belong to you without asking."

A ball of lead forms in my stomach, the hypocrisy of my words not lost on me. I did no such thing when taking Blanca's journal and reading it for myself.

Alex sighs, "Fine, but now your doll won't be famous for being the first one ever to fly on my special aircraft."

"I don't care. They're stupid anyway." Amanda rips the doll from her brother's hand.

"Language," Austin admonishes as he strolls into the kitchen in all his morning glory.

My mouth goes dry as I take him in. He looks edible with his mussed hair and pajama pants so low they expose that deep v that leads down to that monster cock of his. Lucky for me, he's yet to put on a shirt, his broad chest decorated with art that only serves to accentuate his defined muscles.

"Anaya?" Amanda's small hand is tugging at my apron, breaking me from my spell.

"Yes, sweetheart?"

"Can you fix her? Alex ruined her hair with this goo." She's pouting, looking down at her doll covered in slime.

Turning toward Alex, he simply shrugs. "It made her aerodynamic. Her crazy hair before had been slowing down my speed."

Austin places a hand on his son's shoulder. "Alex, what have I said about messing with your sister's things?"

"I know. I know. Anaya already told us. No taking things that don't belong to us without asking first."

God, hearing it from his little mouth makes me cringe, the guilt seeping in deeper and making me feel worse than I already do.

Not only am I a cheater like Ray, but now I'm a cheater like Blanca too. I'm no better than those two, which begs to question, should I be trying harder with Ray? Am I not the same as him now?

I vowed to love him through thick and thin—isn't that what this is? The thin?

I'm turned back to the sink, rinsing the doll's hair when Austin comes up behind me, pressing his hips into my ass, that delicious length of him pulsing between my cheeks and seeking entry despite the layers of clothing.

"Morning, baby. Why'd you let me sleep in?" He's caged me in, both hands at either side of me on the counter as he whispers into the crook of my neck. As if that weren't enough, he runs his nose along the sensitive flesh and inhales deeply, the action making me shiver all over.

"Austin. The kids," I whisper, trying to turn and break his hold, but he's not allowing it.

"They're back in the living room. And so what if they see? The more I think about it, the surer I am that this is where you belong, and I'm not talking about you just being the nanny."

His words give me pause. He might be sure, but I'm not. He's already been through so much, the last thing he needs is playing house with yet another cheater.

"Is she clean yet?" Amanda comes bounding back in and Austin finally releases me, but not before quickly grinding against my ass, the action making me bite back a moan.

Despite my reservation, I'm only human and that man makes my lady bits sing. Every. Single. Time.

"Sure is." I hand the doll back to Amanda. "Though she's a little soaked." *Much like my panties.*

"That's okay. I'll just pretend she's been at the creek with all of her friends." Amanda holds the doll up, twirling her around before she runs back out of the kitchen.

As soon as she's cleared the archway, Austin's hand issues a quick slap to my ass. "Give me ten minutes and then we're taking the kids over to your mom. We have training to go over."

My eyes shoot up. "Training?"

"Yes. We talked about this yesterday. There's no way I'm

letting you near a wild card without some form of protection."

"Ah. Okay, I remember."

He gives me a blinding smile before swiftly pressing his lips to mine; the action catching me by surprise. Austin pulls back, chuckling as he walks out of the kitchen as if what he just did was no big deal. "Get used to it, baby girl. Now that I've had you, I don't see myself letting you go."

I'm left standing there, gaping after him, wishing that what he said was true. But there's so much more to our dynamic than mere want. There are duties and promises that were made, not to mention a conscience that's driving me insane. I could be pregnant now, for goodness' sake, and the father wouldn't be the man I'm legally tied to.

With a groan, I bury my face in my hands and pray that I'm guided to where and what I'm supposed to be. Because as things stand, I have no damn clue.

"You ready?" Austin's hunter green eyes are staring me down as we stand in front of a miniature armory.

"Wow. Are all of these yours?"

"They belong to the family. Years ago, when Jack started the ranch, we all put in a substantial investment amount, knowing that this would be where we would bring our families when we eventually retired. Part of that was making sure this place was safe, and part of that safety is lying here before you."

My brows raise. "Well, I can safely say you'd be able to

defend a small army with all of this."

Austin gives me a soft smile. "Don't worry, baby girl. You don't need to learn how to use all of this." He takes my hand and slides a ring onto my ring finger, his eyes turning molten before his eyes go back down to the rounded metal and flipping open what looked to be a small medallion. "This is a safety ring. If you ever find yourself in trouble, simply press this and I'll come find you. Wherever you are."

I swallow thickly, trying not to read into the fact that he placed it right where my wedding band used to go.

"Do you understand me, Anaya?" His intense eyes are back on mine, waiting for my acknowledgment.

"Yes. I push, you come."

Austin smiles at that. "That's an oversimplified way of saying it, but yes. You hold the power to make me come. Whenever, wherever."

The double entendre isn't missed, making my body turn heated. It's too much that I have to look away, only saying a quick 'thank you.'

Austin clears his throat and turns to the table in front of us. "Okay. As far as active protection, you'll need to take a taser and this gun of pepper spray." He takes out a pink gun looking thing, but it's holding a tube. "All you have to do is unlatch the safety, point, and shoot. Make sure to direct it at the assailant's face. As soon as you've hit your target, run. Don't stop. Don't look back. Just run."

"Got it. Unlock safety, point, shoot, and run."

"Good girl." Austin pulls me in by the waist, his lips falling to the top of my head and pressing a kiss there.

It's no surprise now that his praise melts me. I live for it, but I sure as hell don't deserve it. I'm far from good. Even being here in his arms like this is wrong.

Pressing both hands to his chest, I push off and he lets me. "Is that all?"

Austin's brows press together. "No, there are some evasive maneuvers I'd like to teach you in case you ever get into a situation where your assailant is on you." His face turns stormy, a myriad of emotions playing out behind his eyes. "But first there's something I need to tell you."

My stomach drops, and as much as I'd been telling myself this could never be, the thought of him telling me this to my face makes me want to die. If there ever was a come to Jesus moment over my feelings about Austin, this is it. It's clear as day that I want him for more than just a night. *I want him for the long run.*

"I need to head back to Mexico with Jack." His eyes are laser focused on mine, trying to read my emotions—my emotions that have now hit an all-time low.

I'm sputtering. A million questions wanting to come out all at once. "But—but, what about the kids? You just got back. Is it safe? How long will you be?"

"Shhh, baby. It's going to be okay. Everything is going to be okay." Austin rubs his hands up and down my arms as he brings me close to him once more. "It's only for a couple of days, and it's as safe as it's ever going to be. We're visiting Pen's biological father, needing to handle some family business. Think of it as our version of closure." He's raising a brow now, probably thinking of my closure with Ray.

Yes, I know I'm in no position to demand anything from him, but I still worry. And as if reading my mind, Austin smooths a hand over the back of my head, speaking past my silence.

"Baby, I promise it's nothing you need to worry yourself over. Jace, Hunter, and Matt will stay on the property, and we'll also be leaving behind one of WRATH's best security team."

I nod, letting my head fall to Austin's chest and accepting the comfort he's giving me. Even though he's saying it's safe, I can't help but worry. I know I can't have him, not really, but that doesn't mean that my heart won't shatter if something were to happen to this incredible man. And the kids… God, the kids. They're not going to take this well.

"How long until you're back." I tilt my head, looking up at him.

"Just a couple of days. And I'll video chat every night. I promise." His eyes are staring into mine, trying to impart his truth, but it doesn't feel like enough. I need more. I need him here.

It's selfish. I know it is. He's not even mine to have. I belong to another, and I've gone way past being even, stepping into all new territory with my infidelity. Some might even argue that it's an outright affair. But as his strong arms hold me, his chest rising and falling on mine, ask me if I care.

I don't. Not when his scent envelops me and the beating of his heart is in rhythm with my own. I might not get to keep him, but I'll let myself enjoy him while I can.

TROJAN CROWN

Chapter Twenty-Six
AUSTIN

It's early morning, almost twenty-four hours since we left Colorado and I'm already jonesing to be back home with my woman and kids. Time can't move fast enough as I exit the interrogation room without so much as a drop of new information.

It turned out that Cárdenas had been holding *el Jefe* and most of his leadership, killing all the rest. And the only reason he's kept these fuckers alive for this long is because they have something he wants.

Unfortunately for me, I don't know how much longer he's planning on keeping them alive, and I'm nowhere near getting the details I need.

Jack grunts beside me. He's in the same foul mood, and I can't really blame him. "At this rate, brother, it doesn't look like we'll be getting answers."

I shake my head and sigh. "We have to keep trying. Only they know what went belly up with Dad and I'm betting it's tied to what they thought I was hiding. They wanted it bad enough that they were willing to kill for it."

Jack raises a brow. "They're a lethal cartel. It doesn't take much to make them go all machete happy."

"Were, brother. Past tense. After Daniel's through with them, there won't be anything left but a memory."

Jack opens his mouth to say something, but we're interrupted by Ernesto, one of WRATH's security detail. "Austin. We've got Mary on the line for you."

My brows push together, wondering why Mary is the one calling. If something happened at home with the kids, then it should be Anaya making the call, shouldn't it? *Oh fuck.* Unless something happened to my girl.

With quick fingers, I take the phone from Ernesto's hand. "Talk to me, Mary. Is Anaya okay?"

A strangled sound comes across the line and my stomach knots, unwilling to accept any bad news when it comes to this girl.

"Mary. Answer me."

"She's *fine,* Austin. She just had to go back home, is all."

I stop breathing, the room starts tilting, and I swear I see double. "What the fuck do you mean, she had to go back home?"

Her words make little sense. Anaya wouldn't leave the kids like that. She'd grown so attached to them and I'd even dare say grown to love them.

"I'm sorry, Austin. But she said this was something she had to do. She didn't want to leave the children, but she said they were in good hands with me, and that things had to be this way."

My mouth is hanging open, unable to make words. Taking my silence as incredulity, Mary tries to explain further.

"She said she had to do it while you were away, that she wouldn't be strong enough to do it if you were here."

That is the only thing that makes sense, because there is no way in hell that I'd let her leave. Over my dead fucking body.

"Did Anaya say why she had to go *home*?" That last word has to be dragged from my lips, tasting of rancid, decaying flesh. Her only home should be with me, not wherever the hell she's gone off to.

"She said she owed it to her marriage."

She's with Ray.

Mary's words replay in my head, splitting me in two—the one half being the man who would chase Anaya to the ends of the earth and the other the one who would send it all to hell, letting it all burn down around him as he clung to the only thing that mattered, his children.

I want to hurl this phone against a wall, watching it splinter into a million tiny pieces, but I can't. I have vengeance to seek and two children to care for. Losing myself in this anger for yet another woman who couldn't stick around. First my mother, then Blanca, and now her. They're all the same. *Fuck them all.*

"Austin, I didn't mean to upset you. I just wanted you to know since I'm the one caring for the kids now. It's your right to know any changes when it comes to them."

Her being so candid gives me pause. "You're so close to the vest about things considering your daughter's personal life. Why tell me all this now?"

There's a beat of silence before she finally answers on a long sigh. "Because even though she's my daughter, she was your nanny, and this is a conversation she should've had with you. I support her in everything she does, but I can recognize when she does wrong, and leaving you like this is wrong."

Leaving *me* like this, not the kids. Interesting choice of words, but I can't let myself linger on them. Not for a woman who left me for another. One who's already proven himself unworthy of her love.

Shaking my head, I vow to not spend another second thinking of the woman who turned my world upside down in such a short time. She's clearly made her choice and I'm no fool to go chasing after wasted dreams of happily ever after. If she wants that asshole Ray, then she can have him.

"Thank you, Mary. I'll see you when I get home. Please give the kids a hug and a kiss for me."

"Will do," she answers as I hit the button, ending the call and needing to put as much space between me and this new development as possible.

A hand claps on my shoulder, and I turn to see Jack wincing. "Sounds like you can use a drink. Good thing we're due a break."

I nod. "Sure. A drink sounds good."

"Come. Let's head to Daniel's office. That's where he keeps the good shit."

"If by the good shit you mean the stuff that will numb my soul, then I'm down."

"*Ooof.* The nanny really did a number on you, didn't she?"

"You have no idea, brother. No fucking clue."

I slowly lower my rocks glass, savoring the tang of Cárdenas' tequila. "What do you mean?"

Daniel raises a brow. "I'm surprised you didn't know. *El Jefe's* brother was your dad's primary contact."

His words have my heart threatening to beat out of my chest, my ears ringing with this new revelation. I'm about to ask him for more when Jack beats me to it.

"How are you so sure it was him?" Jack is skeptical that we could miss such a big detail in our recon, and I don't blame him.

"I could see why you wouldn't catch that. They look nothing alike. While *el Jefe* is all tattoos and rough edges, his brother Raul is nothing but sophistication and smooth edges." Daniel signals to one of his men before continuing. "We hadn't seen it at first either, and the only reason we ended up finding out is because one of my men lived in Tecate where the two brothers grew up."

"Wow, so anyone on the outside looking in would think that

Dad was just having a regular business meeting. Just another cut-throat businessman." Jack rubs at his stubble while I'm still at a loss for words.

Daniel chuckles, but there's nothing light about the look on his face. "You got the cut-throat part right. Raul is one of the deadliest men in all of Mexico."

This piques my interest. "Oh? How so?"

The cartel Don takes a sip of his drink, his eyes misting over. "There's only one man that's ever been able to make a dent to his body. In his early teens, when he was still green in the family business, one of his father's men tried to kill him and his brother. I guess that shit was really the beginning. What triggered the killer in him because the man who took him on was left nothing but piles of shredded flesh... and Raul? All he ever got was a nick to his upper lip."

Daniel's words have my body stilling. "Where is he now? Raul? He wasn't among the detained below."

I'm sitting there, praying that by some miracle he's one of the dead. That this is why he's not here on this compound.

"No. He's not here." Daniel takes another sip of his drink as the man he motioned earlier hands him an envelope. "Raul is a slippery fucker. A ghost. Only seen when he wants to be seen."

"So, is Raul the only one you haven't been able to track down?" Jack asks, oblivious to the horror show running through my head.

I'm about to ask if Daniel has any more information on Raul when the Don throws down the open file, pictures spreading out across the mahogany table. *Motherfucker.* There, right in front of us in black and white, lay photos of our father with *el Jefe's* brother.

As I stare at the photos, my heart stops beating, and all air is sucked from my lungs, all while Jack releases a string of curse words.

"I take it you two have met Raul before?" Daniel looks between us, his brows furrowed.

"*Fuck*!" I push off the table, my chair toppling over before I pace in front of the two men. "Yes, we've fucking met him."

Daniel is still confused, his eyes shifting back and forth between Jack and me when Jack finally decides to clue him in, because lord knows I can't voice the words.

"Daniel, Raul is the nanny's husband. He's been at the ranch."

Chapter Twenty Seven
ANAYA

ast night…

The clock mocks me, the seconds hand ticking by and increasing my anxiety with every shuffle forward. I've been able to put off meeting with Ray because of Austin leaving, using the excuse of getting the kids ready for his departure. But that was earlier today, and as the sun sets, I know my time has run out.

I told Ray that Mom could watch the kids while I went over to his cabin to talk, so he'll be expecting me any minute. Bedtime has come and gone, the kids eking out every bit of sun Colorado summers have to offer, and mom is in the guest room watching one of her *novelas*.

She's got this, so I know I could leave right now, but I'm not ready.

Doing everything I can to stall, I decide to get my bag in order, making sure to have my Mace gun and taser with me. I'm closing it up when my eyes land on the pantry door. *The journal.*

I pull out Blanca's diary from its hiding place, needing the distraction, even if for just a moment. *Who knows, maybe I could gain some insight from one cheater to another.*

I go to open it when a picture of Blanca falls out, and I freeze. It's innocuous, a photo of a smiling woman, the pendant she's wearing, one that shouldn't give anyone pause—but it does me.

I swallow the lump in my throat and pick up the offending image, bringing it closer to me for inspection.

Sure enough, it's the same jagged piece of gold I own, the outline leading down to a solitary yellow diamond. The jagged line outlined in the precious metal is an exact replica of the scar running across Ray's upper lip. The piece is custom, designed to remind the wearer of their beloved's mouth.

Was he lying? Did this just happen to match the scar along Ray's cheating mouth? *Cheating.* The one word reverberates inside my head.

Oh god. What if Ray had been cheating… with Blanca?! Is he the mystery man in her journal? It can't be. Her man had been flying her all around the world. Meanwhile, I'd been relegated to a tiny one-bedroom home.

Picking up the picture once more, I storm out of Austin's

cabin and head toward Ray. None of this makes any sense, but I need answers and I need them now.

Thankfully, it doesn't take me long to reach him—the one good thing of having him as a neighbor. I'm about to knock on the door when it swings open, a smiling Ray beaming down at me as if I held the secret to eternal life and were about to share it.

Scowling at him, I rush past him and into the cabin. "What the hell is this, Ray?!"

I throw the picture at him, but he catches it with swift hands. He takes one look at the photo and the smile he'd been holding for me vanishes. Instead, the coolness that replaces it is enough to chill the entire room.

My stomach churns and I go to clutch my bag, only to realize it isn't there. *Shit.* I left in such haste that I left behind my only forms of self defense.

A deep sense of dread blankets me as Ray closes and locks the cabin door behind him. When his head rests on the wood, giving me his back for the slightest moment, I have to ask myself—*should I run?*

"This isn't how I pictured tonight going." Ray's voice has taken on an edge I've never witnessed before. It's as if he's a completely different person from the meek imposter who groveled at my feet, begging for forgiveness.

When he turns to face me, the look in his eyes is enough to summon any and all demons hiding in the dark. It's evil. Nothing but sheer evil emanating from his glare.

I stumble, taking a step back and gathering all the courage

I possess. "What's going on Ray? How does Blanca have my pendant?"

His eyes narrow as he steps forward, walking me until my back has hit a wall and his arms are caging me in. "Stupid girl. That's not your pendant. I commissioned it long ago. Long before you came into the picture. Yours was but a mere replica of the original."

I'm blinking, unable to form words. Was he cheating on Blanca with me? Am I the other woman? "But we're married. We exchanged vows."

My eyes are dancing back and forth between his, searching for answers I doubt he'll ever share. Ray throws his head back and cackles, the action exposing his sinewy neck and vibrating flesh. "Ray exchanged vows and promises of forever, but I'm not Ray. He isn't real. Just a character, one of my many, created to serve a purpose."

My breathing is erratic, my body unable to process everything he's throwing at me. Two years. Two years of my life I've given to this man, only to find out that it was all a lie. Not a moment of it was true.

"*Why?*" The one word comes out squeaky, and I'm surprised that it came out at all.

Ray's eyes land back on mine, a brief flash of pity dancing before them before his mask of indifference is back in place. "Don't take it personal, doll. It's just business. I needed to keep tabs on the Crown family, and having multiple sources of contact is the best way to go about it."

My jaw drops. His words now making sense. "Oh my god.

You married me for my access to this family! You slept with Blanca for the same. Shit, if Pen were of age, you would've fucked her too, wouldn't you?!"

I'm shaking, my body vibrating with rage when Ray's hand slaps me across my face. "Snap out of it, Anaya. I don't need a hysterical woman on top of everything else. We've got shit to do, and the faster you come to terms with it, the quicker we can get on with them."

The sting of his palm has my breathing slowing, making me realize that violence is not out of the question for this psychopath. I need to buy my time, find a way out of this so I can let Austin and the brothers know what's really going on.

Ray shakes his head, all while tsk'ing and raising a brow at me. "I see those wheels turning, Anaya, and that just won't do."

He grabs me by the nape, making me wince and him cackle. "If you think that's uncomfortable, just wait for what I have in store."

"I rather not, thank you." Even in this dire moment, I can't help but sass. It's in my blood.

"There's that little spitfire I married. Too bad she'd left me sometime after our first move."

His words have my eyes narrowing. "If I disappeared inside myself, it's because you left me every chance you got. You made me feel like I wasn't enough to keep you home, but I now see that it was all a lie. You never wanted me in the first place. I was just a means to an end."

Ray shakes his head, the corner of his mouth tilting up in a smirk. "Don't be too hard on yourself, Anaya. You were a lot of fun in the beginning and at least you were low maintenance. Unlike Blanca. She required trips to Europe and time away from the family. But you, doll, you were the easy one." He's walking us down a narrowed hall and toward the only soundproofed room in the home.

Oh god. This isn't good.

"What are we doing, Ray?" My voice cracks, unable to hide my growing fear.

"I had an elaborate plan, but seeing as how your man is now in Mexico, things have taken a rather unexpected but pleasant turn."

My brows push together, too many things coming together at once. "You know about Austin and where he is?"

Ray pushes me onto the bed, his hand flying to the nightstand and pulling out some rope. *Oh, hell no.* Without thinking, I'm flying off the bed and running toward the door, screaming at the top of my lungs. "Heeeeeellllllll—"

I wasn't even able to make it past the foot of the bed when Ray's hands are latching onto my biceps, swinging my body around like a rag doll and throwing me on the bed.

"I see you're not going to make this easy." He's grabbing me by the jaw now, his fingers digging into my flesh so hard I can't help but whimper. "Be good and I won't strike you. But make no mistake, if you step out of line, I will whip you, and it won't be that daddy shit you play with Austin."

What the fuck? How in the hell could he know that?

Ray smirks while retrieving the rope he'd dropped. "I bugged his cabin. You think I'm an amateur?"

"But why? Why go through all that?" I'm missing the big picture, unable to see past the years of deceit and hurt. "What information were you after?"

He's taking my hands and feet and tying them to the bedpost, making sure I can't make another run for it. "You don't need to worry about that. Right now, all you need to do is help me get Penelope to my cabin."

I scoff, even as he finishes tying up my leg. "I will do no such thing. Torture me all you want; I will not drag another person into your sick and twisted web."

Ray shrugs, pulling out a phone and typing something I can't see. "Fine. I'll just blow up Cárdenas' villa. Jack and Austin included."

A garbled scream rips from my throat in protest, the action only making Ray look up from his phone for a split second. He's still typing away at the damn thing, and I'm wondering if he's delivering the orders that will end Austin's life.

I can't let that happen. I won't. "Fine. I'll help you get Pen here if you show me proof you can do what you say. Otherwise, it's a no go."

Oh god. I hope he buys my bluff.

Ray sighs, looking bored at my request. I'm thinking he's not going to answer when he turns and walks toward his dresser, pulling off the laptop that's been left open.

The closer he brings it the clearer the picture gets. It looks to be surveillance footage of a gorgeous villa by the sea. Oh wow. Is that Cárdenas' home?

My eyes are scanning the property when I see them,

gasping as Jack emerges from one of the doors with Austin quickly trailing behind him.

"There. You've seen them." Ray walks back to the dresser and places the laptop down ever so gently. "Now let's call Penelope."

"No. Just because you have eyes on them doesn't mean you can blow them up. If I'm risking Pen's life, then I need to see proof you can do what you say."

Ray's brows shoot up, an amused smile playing on his lips. "Keep your eyes on the screen, kitten." He takes out his phone, tapping the screen.

Not two seconds later, a small fire emerges right at the edge of the property, sending a group of men running toward it. "*Holy shit.*"

My jaw is still hanging open when Ray is pressing the cabin phone to my ear. "It's ringing. Make it believable or the entire villa goes up in flames."

"Hello, Mr. Garcia?" Pen's voice cuts through the line, making guilt settle deep in my chest.

"Penelope, hey. This is Anaya. I know it's late, but Ray and I have had some wine and I don't feel comfortable with either of us riding out to the main house. I'd baked a cake earlier and meant to bring it with me to Ray's cabin for dinner, but forgot. If it's not too much trouble, would you mind driving it over?"

Ray's head looks like it's about to pop-off, his eyes practically bugging out of their sockets.

"Oh my god! I'm so sorry! I totally took a huge piece of the cake earlier. I didn't know it was for your dinner."

"Don't worry about it, Pen. Just bring over what's left." I'm going to hell for this. Making a pregnant woman feel guilty for eating chocolate cake. That and roping her in on whatever Ray has planned.

"Of course! So damn sorry. I'll bring you a bottle of Jack's favorite wine to make up for it." Shuffling sounds come across the line. "Okay. Be there soon."

The line goes dead and I'm left staring at Ray's intense glare. "You stupid cunt. That could've gone horribly wrong. She could've sent Matt or Jace. Then where would we be?"

Free or dead. Seeing the state Ray is in, he'd probably murder me and flee before he'd let any of the Crown brothers reach me.

As guilt weighs heavy in my heart, I know that I've at least bought everyone some time. And as soon as Pen gets here, we can start hatching a plan on how to get away from Ray and alert the guys.

Two heads are better than one, and whatever it is that Ray wants us for, he seems to need us alive… *for now.*

Chapter Twenty-Eight
ANAYA

"Let go of me, you fucking asshole!" Pen is struggling against Ray's hold but freezes upon seeing me tied up to the bed, her face going pale and her bottom lip quivering.

"I'm so sorry, Pen. Please forgive me!" I'm praying that she doesn't hate me for this… if we live at all.

"Why?" The one word is whispered, but it's enough to make me feel the eight-thousand-pound weight of guilt it leaves behind.

"Because she's smart." Ray pushes Pen down onto a chair, his hands making quick work of the rope he's left behind for himself. "And if you're smart, you'll also do as I say."

"Like hell I will!" Pen flails, trying to buck herself from her chair.

Ray grunts but doesn't stop constraining her hands. "Anaya, be a doll and tell your friend what happens if she doesn't cooperate."

"The guys." My words come out on a choked sob, the weight of my tone making Pen still in her chair.

"Jack?" Her eyes are wide open, her throat bobbing up and down on a swallow.

I nod, the only movement I'm allowed because of these damn ropes. "He has eyes on them in Mexico and has rigged the whole place to blow with them in it if we don't comply." My eyes shift to the man behind her, his towering frame now moving to her feet. "What I don't understand is the why? What are you trying to get from them, Ray? Is it money? You sure seem to have a ton of it if you were flying Blanca to Ibiza."

Ray's eyes shoot up to mine, probably surprised that I had that bit of information thanks to Blanca's journal.

"My mom? You were with my mom?"

Shit! I didn't even think about Blanca being Pen's mom. Way to put my foot in my mouth. I've caused this girl enough grief without having to drudge up more painful memories for her. "I'm so sorry, Pen."

I've spoken, but it's as if she didn't hear me. She just keeps staring at Ray. "You. You're the one she was cheating on Austin with?"

Ray sneers. "You say that like it's not an upgrade. I can

assure you, little girl, I was more of a man than your stepfather ever was to her."

I snort at that. "You've got to be kidding me, right?"

Pen shoots me a worried glance, shaking her head as if to say, *shut the fuck up!* I suppose she's right. I shouldn't be antagonizing the psychopath, especially in our current predicament—but I couldn't help it. He's delusional if he thinks he's a better lay than Austin.

Thankfully, Penelope has a better head on her shoulders, and she steers the conversation in the right direction. "If it's not the money you want, then what is it?"

Ray's narrowed gaze leaves me and focuses back on Pen. "That is none of your business and irrelevant right now. All you need to do is worry about what cover story you're giving Mary and the other Crown brothers because, come morning, you're both coming with me."

My mouth drops open as Ray turns and exits the room, the slamming of the door echoing loudly and signaling our impending doom. We need to find a way out of this fast, or I'm afraid we won't come out of this alive.

Austin - Present time…

I'm still pacing, reeling from the revelation that Ray is Raul, brother to one of the most notorious cartel leaders in all of Mexico, when the door to Cárdenas' office flies open.

"Don Cárdenas, we have some urgent information for Mr.

Crown." One of the WRATH team members steps around Daniel's man, heading straight for Jack.

"It's Penelope. She's missing. She's not at the main house and the man we'd posted inside was found passed out in her bedroom."

"*What*?!" Jack roars, getting up with so much force that his chair goes flying back. "Where were my brothers? Where were the other men you left behind?"

"They'd been doing the rounds on the property, sir. And nobody had left except for Anaya and her husband."

A beastly sound rips from my throat upon hearing this. I knew what Mary had said was true, but at the time, I had no clue Anaya had left with a serial killer in disguise.

Jack is pulling at his hair, his eyes mad. "Did at any point Anaya make it to the main house this morning?"

"Yes. She came to drop a cake off for Penelope, but she was in and out in under ten minutes." The man answers, shifting on his feet and growing increasingly nervous. I would be too if I were him.

"And where was Ray during this drop-off?"

"In the car, sir. He was the one driving."

Jack looks like he's about to rip the guy's head off, so I step between them. "Bring me all the footage you have. I'm thinking somehow Penelope was smuggled out with Ray."

"Yes, sir. Of course, sir." The man turns on his heels, quickly exiting the room.

Turning back toward my brother, I brace my hands on his shoulders and give him a quick shake. "Pull it together, man.

This is not the time to fall apart. We need to get our girls back, and we won't be able to do that if you're a mess."

Knowing what I do now, I highly doubt Anaya went with her *husband* willingly.

Jack nods, his eyes narrowing on something behind me. "I doubt they took her by physical force. My girl would've screamed bloody murder, and after her last stint in Mexico, I made sure she had more than enough training in self-defense."

I blow out a breath, nodding in agreement with his assessment. "It had to be compliance under duress because even though she may want nothing to do with me personally, she would never leave the kids like that."

Jack's hand lands on my shoulder and squeezes. "She wouldn't leave you like that either."

God, I can only hope that his words ring true. But in all honesty, that's not what really matters right now. Even if she didn't want me, I still wouldn't want her in the arms of that psychopath.

Cárdenas, who'd been on the phone most of this time, clears his throat. "Gentlemen, it appears there are live bombs scattered throughout the perimeter of our home. One went off earlier today, tipping my men off. This means we need to move, and we need to move now."

My jaw ticks as I curse the day that prick Raul was born. "This doesn't sound like a fucking coincidence."

Cárdenas nods. "It does not. Fortunately for us, we have a system of underground tunnels and caves that'll help us get out. And unfortunately for Raul, his brother is coming with us."

As soon as Daniel reminds us of Raul's brother, everything clicks into place. "That fucker wants to barter release, doesn't he?"

"That's what I would do," Jack answers.

"He has my daughter, and both of your women. I'd say that's what he's going for. But if he hurts so much as a hair on my girl's head, that *pendejo* will pay with much more than just his brother's life."

"Agreed." All the ways I can torture this motherfucker start popping up in my head, and the only reason my train of thought stops is because the man from earlier walks in holding a laptop.

"We found the footage, Mr. Crown." He places the laptop on the large wooden table and hits play.

As soon as he does, I can see Ray getting out of the car to help Anaya with a large piece of luggage, one that presumably holds Penelope.

Jack unleashes a strangled groan. "My babies. The fucker took my babies."

God, my poor brother. At least I have the benefit of seeing that Anaya is still okay. For all we know, my stepdaughter could be dead inside that luggage.

Cárdenas has been deathly silent, but a quick glance over my shoulder lets me know he's seen the footage and has come to the same conclusion as us.

"*Ese hijo de puta muere hoy!*" *That son of a bitch dies today.* The cartel Don roars, making the windows rattle and his men line up for battle. "Ramon, prepare the vehicles. We're leaving immediately. Antonio, get us eyes on the prize. We need to cut him off wherever he's headed. I don't care who you have to call or work with to make it happen. Just do it."

A fleeting sense of peace settles over me knowing we have a powerful underlord on our side. But it quickly vanishes, knowing life is fucked up and there are no guarantees. We may have a venerable king calling the shots, but it doesn't detract that we're dealing with a cold-hearted killer who's between a rock and a hard place.

"We need to play our cards right if we want to get our girls back. Raul is unpredictable and there's no telling what he'll do once he finds out we've moved his brother."

Daniel nods. "That's why we need to let him make contact first. He needs to think he's still in charge of this situation. That his messed up plan is still underway."

I stare at the laptop screen, my eyes focused on Anaya's hand. The ring is missing. *Fuck.* My girl can't call for help even if she wanted to.

Jack speaks, but it's muffled by the roaring in my head. "Agreed. Hopefully, that gives us enough time to track them down."

"Don't worry. My men will make that happen or it will be their head on a spike right next to Raul's." Daniel's voice is low and menacing, but none of his men flinch, knowing well what they've signed up for.

As we're guided out of his office and down a dark passage, all I can think about is the taste of my girl's lips and how sweet she falls apart around me, showing me the most vulnerable parts of herself. That beautiful creature is mine, and there's no way in hell I'm letting any man take her from me.

One way or another, I will find her and bring her home. Damned be anyone who stands in the way.

TROJAN CROWN

Chapter Twenty-Nine
ANAYA

"I'm about to call your daddies, so be on your best behavior and keep those mouths shut until I say so." Ray's upper lip peels back in disgust, clearly unable to let go of my special relationship with Austin, still calling him my daddy.

Rolling my eyes, I can't help but give him shit. "You're just salty because you never made me come the way he could. You were a fraud from the start. Not an alpha at all, but some sick and twisted psycho with multiple personality disorder."

"Anaya!" Pen whisper-hisses, but I don't care. It's clear this asshole wants to kill me. Might as well make it worth it on my end.

Ray stalks over to me, rearing his hand and slapping me across the face so hard my head bounces off the hotel wall. The sting should hurt, but instead it just reminds me I'm still alive. That the pain and soreness from being shoved into a trunk for hours-on-end isn't some messed up nightmare, but real life.

"If you can't be quiet on your own, then I'll make you." Ray's hand goes to my jaw while the other pulls a piece of fabric from his pocket. With a jostling of my head, he quickly gags me before shoving me back down onto the dirty hotel room floor. "Now do as you're told, or I'll cut your tongue out."

My eyes narrow into tiny slits. Who *is* this monster? He's unrecognizable. Far from the man I originally fell for. But I suppose that man was only what the creature who lurked beneath wanted me to see.

Before I can get too lost in my head, Ray takes out a satellite looking phone and presses buttons, all while a bound Pen scotches closer to me, dragging herself inch by inch, ass to feet.

"Are you okay?" She whispers, earning a raised brow from Ray.

I nod, not wanting Pen to get in trouble with this monster. It's bad enough I dragged her into this with me. I don't need Ray offing her prematurely because of me, too.

A line clicking through has us both looking toward Ray, his hand positioning the sat phone in front of him and showing off the sick grin he's donning. "Cárdenas. Good to see you, old man."

A deep voice booms from the phone. "Cut the bullshit, Raul. We know you took the girls."

I snort, unable to help it. Of course his real name is Raul. There isn't an original bone in this crazy man's body. *Raul* shoots me a raised brow in warning and I nod and roll my eyes, unwilling to let him see me cower. I've already given him so much of myself, he can't have this too.

"Fine. I'll get down to business. You have something I want and I have something you want. I say a trade is in order." Ray's tone is indifferent, as if he were talking about a bunch of sweaters instead of two human beings.

"We need to see the girls first. Make sure they're okay." Cárdenas, I presume, speaks into the line and you can hear that the words are forced. "Only then will I even entertain the idea of freeing your *brother*."

I suck in air, well, as much as the gag allows. *All this for his brother?* Nausea consumes me at the realization that we've been played.

I willingly offered myself and Pen on a platter, all to save Austin and Jack. But knowing Raul's brother was being held captive puts a whole new perspective on our situation. There's no way he would've blown up the building if his brother was in it, would he?

Penelope's body trembles next to me, and I wish I could hug her to me in comfort. I have a plan; we just need to wait until we're alone in the room with Raul's laptop bag. When he'd found my ring, he shoved it in there along with any other jewelry I had on me.

I'm not sure if he knows what it is or if he's planning to remove all identifying articles before he kills us, but if I can get a hold of it, then we might stand a chance at surviving this.

Ray's words interrupt my thoughts of escape. "You only get one proof of life, but I want the same."

There's shuffling and a long silence before Ray nods, liking what he sees on the screen. Without another word, he's flipping the phone so that the receiver is facing us, a salt and pepper man staring back at us with nothing but furious rage blazing in his eyes.

"*Papa*," Penelope gasps. So this must be her biological father then, the infamous cartel leader she'd told me about.

When our kidnapping was first underway, she was sure her dad would find us, but her hope dwindled with each passing hour. Maybe she was right to put her faith in him because if looks could kill, Ray would be long dead.

That type of determination moves mountains, and lord knows I killed any hope of Austin coming after me when I fed my mom that bullshit line about wanting to go back with my husband. I guess it's good that she's here with me. Pen is definitely worth saving, and if I'm lucky, maybe that means I'll get saved too.

"Hang tight, princess. You'll be home soon." The man on the phone speaks, his tone stern but comforting.

Despite his assurance, the look in Ray's eyes speaks of horrors to come. "I'll message you the drop-off point. No one other than yourself and my brother must show up, or both girls get it. If you're risking him, then you're risking them too."

"I gave you my word, *pendejo*. Don't try me." Cárdenas seems at wit's end with our captor, and I suppose I would be too if I were in his shoes. From what I've been told, this isn't their first run in, but I sure hope to hell that it's the last.

But Raul doesn't respond to the Don's jab, he simply goes on with his demands. "One hour. Be there or they're dead."

Cutting the line before Pen's dad can answer, the psycho whirls on us, his hand reaching for the top of my head and pulling me to standing with one hard tug that threatens to rip the hair from my skull. "Finally. I can be rid of you."

My eyes are staring into his soulless ones when Pen sputters below us. "But-but, you said you were going to trade us?"

Raul flicks his gaze below. "I did. But I never said you'd be alive when it happened."

All color drains from my face. Not out of fear for my life, but for Pen's and her unborn baby. I did this. I put her in this position, and I deserve to go. Not her.

I jerk my head, still in my husband's hold. "Ray. *Raul*. Please. Let her live. Do whatever you want with me, but let her live. She has nothing to do with this. She isn't even a part of your world."

Raul's fingers dig deeper into my scalp, tightening their hold and making me wince. "Stupid girl. Just as that child in her womb is already destined to play a part in this darkness, so was she the day she was born." With his free hand, he pulls his gun from its holster and taps it on my cheek. "She's the daughter of my enemy, and for that, she will pay."

Not if I have anything to say about it. With one swift move, I knee Raul in the balls, making him hunch over and the firearm in his hand go off.

My heart pounds in my ears, waiting for the darkness to drag me under, sure that I've been shot. But it never comes. Instead, a loud thud sounds off behind me before a string of rapid-fire words and footsteps invades the room.

It all happens so fast. More gunfire and more cursing. The room blurs as Ray drops me, my shoulder the first to make impact with the floor. *Oof.* Sharp pain blooms from my arm and through to my soul. I'm lost in the crushing sensation when a pair of muscular arms wrap around me, lifting me off the ground.

"Fuck. Baby girl." Austin's voice cuts through the haze and I'm sure I must be dreaming. "Talk to me, Anaya. Your words, baby. I need them."

Blinking, I try to assess if this is all real. Sure enough, the scent that is uniquely his envelops me as the throbbing pain in my shoulder reminds me I'm still here. Alive. Alive and in the arms of the man I love.

"*Austin,*" I gasp, my one word causing this beast of a man to smile.

"There she is." He brings me closer to his chest until his lips are pressing a kiss to the top of my head. "Let's get you home."

Yes, please. Nothing ever sounded better.

As his feet carry us out of the room and I let myself sink into his warmth, I can see that Jack is holding a crying Penelope in his arms. Thank God. I don't think I could've forgiven myself if anything ever happened to her or her baby. I just pray that everything we've been through hasn't harmed the little peanut growing inside her.

Right then, I vow to make it up to her any way I can. She's been nothing but good to me and here I come, dragging her into an evil man's grasp.

"Shh. Baby. I can practically see those wheels churning. Everything's going to be okay." He nuzzles into my hair before pressing another kiss to my head. "Daddy's got you."

And with those three little words, I melt. *Fucking melt.* Letting the stress of the past twenty-four hours wash away, finally letting sleep reach me and take me under.

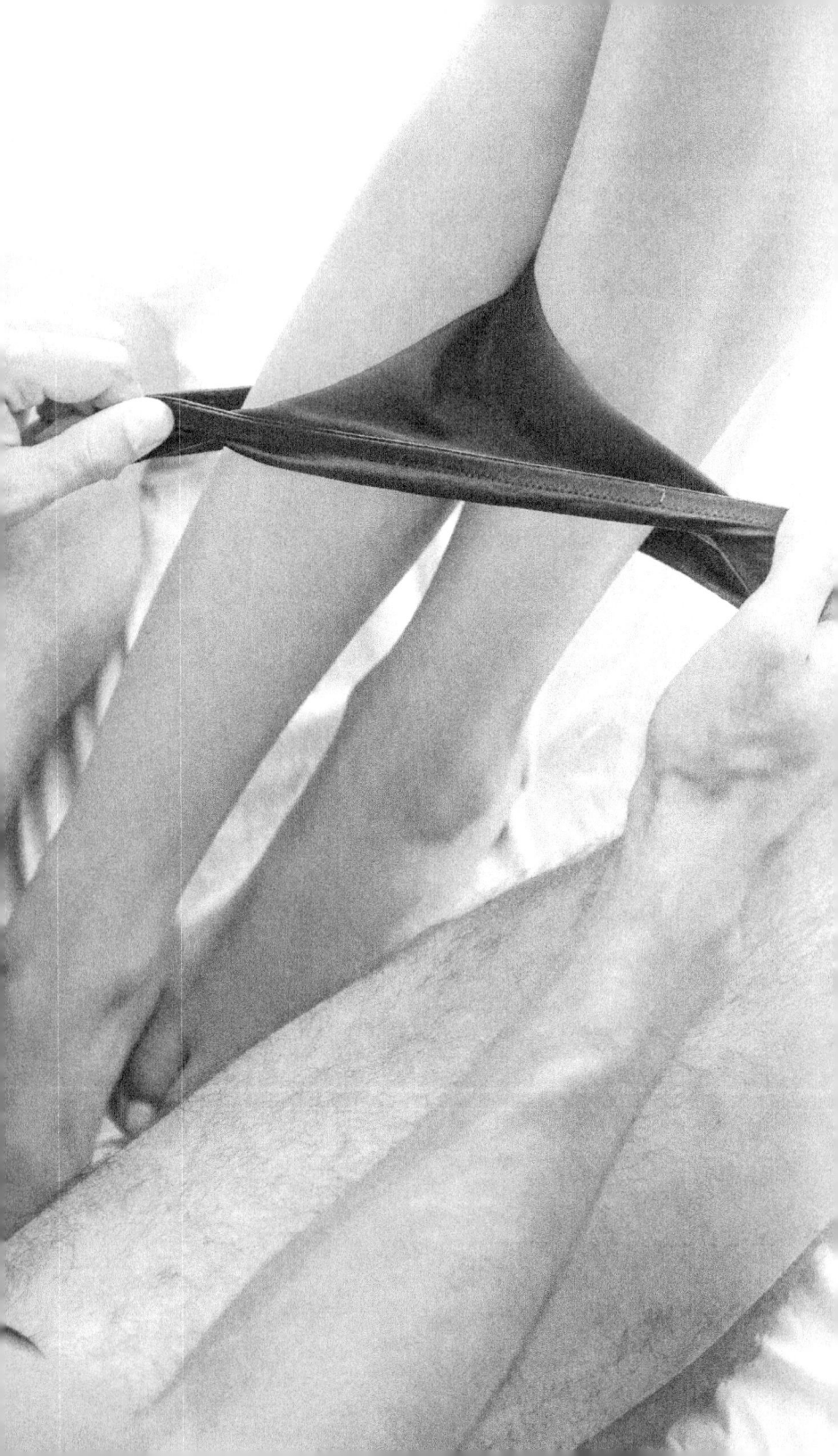

Chapter Thirty
ANAYA

Murmured words have my eyes opening and lazily assessing my surroundings. We're in a private jet, and if I'm not mistaken, it's the same one that brought me to Colorado a couple of months ago.

As I sit up, I catalog everything that transpired in such a short time frame. I left my cheating husband, fell in love with a grumpy Crown and his family, and found out that the past two years of my life were all a lie. I close my eyes again, shaking my head and letting out a long and tired sigh.

"I know. Ditto." Pen's voice has my eyes shooting up and I see she's coming out of a room in the back of the jet.

Immediately upon seeing her, guilt gnaws at my soul. "Penelope. God, I'm so sorry."

I'm about to go into a full-blown apology when her raised palm stops me. "Don't even. I already know what you're going to say, and I don't want to hear it. I've thought about this a lot, and if I were in your shoes, I would've done the same exact thing. Hell, I probably would've been even more ruthless. I mean, we *are* talking about my baby daddy."

Relief floods me at her words, but I'm not letting myself off the hook that easily. "Still, that should've been a choice that you made. Instead, I thrust you into it."

She's shaking her head, that smile of hers never leaving her lips. "Look. It's clear you're in love with Austin. That's why you did what you did. And take it from one love struck girl to another. It's all water under the bridge. Now, if you hadn't called me when my man was in danger, then we would've had problems."

Her smile finally drops, and she pins me with a poignant stare. I know what she's saying is true, because that's how I would feel had the roles been reversed. I'd rather be put in danger a million times over if it meant I had a chance at saving the man I love.

And speaking of the devil, Austin comes into the main cabin with Jack trailing behind.

"You're up." Austin's smile takes my breath away, and I've never been gladder to be alive than I am right now.

I nod, a sudden shyness taking me over. "I am."

"Good. I need a moment with my girl." Without preamble,

Austin swoops down and takes me in his arms, the pressure against my shoulder making me wince as he walks us to the rear of the jet.

We've almost reached the door when my whimper has Austin's brows pushing together and his steps faltering. "You hurt?"

"It's nothing. I just hit my shoulder when I fell earlier." I attempt a weak smile, but he's not buying it.

"We'll need to have that looked at." He continues his path toward the room Penelope just left and I see that it's a small bedroom, complete with a bed and an attached bath.

"Wow. I didn't know this was here." I'm still looking around in awe when Austin lowers me onto the bed.

"It is, and we're going to put it to good use." He peppers kisses across my face before looking down at me. "But first, we have some things to discuss."

"Oh, we do?" I'm gnawing on my lip, pretty sure what these discussions will entail.

Austin nods, his eyes losing their heat and filling with sadness. "What you told your mom about wanting to try again with *Ray*, was that real?"

I roll in my lips and suck in a deep breath through my nose. "I'm not going to lie to you and say that the guilt of cheating on Ray wasn't getting to me, that I doubted if you and I should've been doing what we were doing. But no, I never wanted to leave the way I did. I would never do that to you or the kids."

The sadness in his eyes lifts a bit, but his face doesn't return to the smiling one it had been before, and I can't stand it.

Sitting up in the bed, I take his face and cup it between my hands. "Listen to me. You are everything I never knew I needed. You understand me in a way no one ever has. Only you, Austin Crown, can fill this void inside of me and make me whole." His eyes are turning glassy, and I pray that he's really listening to what I'm saying. "Even if it would've taken me months to figure out, there's no doubt in my mind that I would always choose you. To hell with being proper and keeping my word to any other man. It would all be illusory because my heart and soul could only belong to you. You are my everything."

My big strong alpha releases a lone tear, the wetness trickling down the sharp lines of his masculine face and hitting my fingers in a reminder that I've touched him. Hopefully in the same way he has me. "Baby girl, those are the sweetest words I've ever heard. I know this may be a bit too soon, and the timing couldn't be more wrong, but I fucking love you."

I break down in front of my man, releasing all the pent up fear and anxiety I'd been holding onto since I left Colorado. "I love you too, Austin. So so much."

He pulls me into his arms, resting his lips on the crook of my neck and breathing me in. "Good, then it's settled. You're mine, and as soon as my legal team can dissolve your ties to that dickbag, then you'll bear my name."

My body tenses. Is he saying what I think he's saying? Pulling away as much as I can, I look Austin in the eyes. "Was that your way of asking me to marry you?"

Austin gives me a soft chuckle. "No, baby. I wasn't asking. I'm telling. You're mine and I'm yours, and nothing anyone can say or do is stopping this trajectory of bliss we're on."

I'm blinking away tears now, looking at the love of my life through blurry eyes. Yes, he might be overbearing and a little controlling, but I love every little bit of it because he loves me just the way I am—scars and all.

I lightly smack him on the chest. "Fine. I'm agreeing to this half-assed proposal, but only because I know I can put you in your place when needed. Remember, Austin," I lower my hand and grip his surprisingly erect cock between my fingers. "I'm the one who truly holds the power."

A deep growl reverberates from Austin's chest as his body presses into mine, lowering me onto the bed. "There's no secret there, baby girl. My mind, body, and soul are yours for the taking. Now shut up and let Daddy make you feel good."

God, yes. I want nothing more than to lose myself in him and the pleasure he provides. I'm overcome with the need to taste him, my tongue reaching out and licking a hot path up the column of his neck before sinking my teeth into the taut flesh.

"*Fuck.* Is my little baby horny? Does she need this big cock?"

Still latched on to his neck, I give him a small nod, humming as I lap at the mark I've just left him. *Mine.* This strong alpha male is all mine.

"Dammit. You're wearing too much." After having grown accustomed to my easy access dresses, Austin is struggling with my yoga pants, and I can't help but chuckle, earning me a growl from an already exasperated man. "Oh, you think this is funny?"

I'm about to tell him yes, when he flips me onto my

stomach, making me yelp. He's ripping down my pants, the cool air hitting my backside before I'm sucking in a sharp breath and his open palm is slapping my bare ass. I should be appalled, getting spanked like a child, but I love it. Dare I even say, *I need it?* Yes. I definitely need it.

Wiggling my ass in his face, I look back at him over my shoulder. "Harder, Daddy."

Austin's eyes turn molten, his nostrils flaring in response. "Oh, I'll give you harder, baby girl."

He issues a punishing blow to the other cheek, and I'm still reveling in the sharp sting when his open palm repeatedly slaps my swollen lips with fast little strikes. *One. Two. Three.*

Ohmyfuckinggod. I'm a whimpering writhing mess under his grasp, his big hands holding me up by the hips and keeping me from sliding down onto the bed.

I can't believe I almost came from that alone. And as if he knows I'm a hair's breadth away from release, Austin lets one of his calloused hands trail down to my damp slit, his thick fingers parting my folds and making him hiss.

"These juices, baby, they're enough to drive a man mad."

I'm about to babble some incoherent string of words when a hot mouth on my pussy has me moaning instead. *Lord Jesus.* Nothing, absolutely no toy or man, could have a thing on Austin's lips. They're magical.

And if his lathing up my aching core wasn't enough, my world sways as his long tongue slides inside of me, fucking me in slow rhythmic thrusts while his thumb circles my swollen clit. I'm so lost in this man, I can't help but chant. *Yes, Daddy.*

Yes, Daddy. Yes, Daddy.

Austin growls into me, his tongue continuing its assault as his thumb and forefinger end me with one final pinch to my aching bundle of nerves, and I shatter—splintering into a million tiny pieces of release as I twitch and shake beneath Austin's hold.

I'm still tingling from the explosion of pleasure when Austin flips me onto my back, my legs splaying to either side of him and leaving a cradle just for him.

A love drunk Austin is staring back down at me, his hooded eyes spelling nothing but more delicious pleasure. "Oh, I'm far from done with you, little girl."

I smile in response, ready for anything this man has in store. Feeling myself flushed, I raise a brow and bite the corner of my lip before answering. "I'd be disappointed if you were."

Austin throws his head back in a deep chuckle, the action showing off the strong column of his neck and the possessive mark I've left behind before he lowers his face back to mine. "You're a little brat, aren't you? That's okay. I'll enjoy spanking the sass out of you."

One of Austin's possessive hands goes to my ass, squeezing it before his open palm trails up my thigh and he sinks his fingers into the flesh around my knee, pushing it to the side and leaving my core completely exposed.

A growling Austin shakes his head. "Never. That's when I'll have enough of this perfect little cunt." Both of his hands are on either of my knees, holding me open as he greedily stares. "Now be a good little girl and stroke me. Show Daddy how much you want his cock."

I'm panting, turned on by his dirty words and no longer feeling any shame for this game we play. Needing to make him feel as good as he makes me feel, I take his velvet sheathed steel into my hands and pump, paying extra attention to the mushroom tip. I'm practically drooling as I watch each stroke make my man react, his chest rising and falling rapidly as I continue my pumping.

"Now, baby." Austin's words come out ragged. "Take that big dick and shove it into your tight little hole. Make Daddy feel good."

Oh god, yes. I drop one hand, guiding my hips toward his pulsing cock, the long, turgid flesh now twitching in my hold as I swipe the tip up and down my soaking slit. Wanting more, I rub my clit with his fat head, pushing the tiny pearl side to side and moaning as the slick flesh edges me closer to climax.

"Baby," Austin growls. "Stop playing with Daddy and fuck that cock."

I grin like a fool, but the smile quickly falls from my lips when Austin slams into me deep, his balls slapping against my ass as he curses up a storm.

"*Christ. That's tight,*" Austin grits through clenched teeth.

I can't answer, too caught up in the feeling of his thickness inside of me. Whoever said size doesn't matter was full of shit. Austin's dick is the perfect combination of length and girth, making me quiver and shake from the first moment he's inside of my walls.

My fingers dig into Austin's chiseled chest, the nails

trailing down in a possessive hold and leaving my mark. Mine. This man is all mine and I'm never letting go. He gives me everything I never knew I needed, and I'll do whatever I can to be the same for him. He more than deserves it.

"Come back to me, baby." Austin's hand reverently cups my cheek. "Don't get lost in that pretty head of yours."

God, how does he know me so well?

But as he slides out and slams into me hard, I know. I know that the reason we understand each other is because we were made for one another. Soulmates.

His hand that had been on my cheek now trails to my nape, positioning my head so my gaze is now forced to be on where we're connected.

"Look at that, baby. How good that tight little pussy takes Daddy's big cock."

Jesus. His words have me clamping down around his girth, soaking in the naughty nature of our intimacy. He knows just what to say, what words will trigger these dark desires inside of me. And not only does he indulge me, but he also comes alive under their spell. He's the perfect half to my whole.

"Yes, baby." Austin's mouth falls open. "Just like that. Milk Daddy's cock."

Lord! His dirty words are like a command, demanding I let him have my release. And like an obedient little girl, I let him have it, my walls tensing and releasing over and over his girth, pulling his milky cum into my womb and making my own climax extend, blending in with his and making it one tangle of pleasure and ecstasy.

As his body falls on top of mine, our heavy breathing the only sound in the otherwise silent room, I know I must've done something right in life. This sort of happily ever after is something I once thought was only possible in books. But God, how glad am I to have been wrong.

Knowing this is what my forever looks like, I'll gladly accept the error of my ways.

TROJAN CROWN

Epilogue
AUSTIN

It's been three months since we rescued Anaya from Raul's grasp, and so much has happened since then, but the best out of all of it is having finally dissolved Anaya's marriage to that lying, cheating, psychopath killer.

Oh, he's still very much alive, much to my dismay. But after we failed to pull the necessary information from him, we handed Raul over to Cárdenas and his men. They've kept him under lock and key with only daily rounds of torture to keep him company.

I'm surprised he's lasted this long, that his body hasn't given out. But then again, he is a special kind of crazy, so I guess that'd make sense. Whatever. I don't give a damn if Daniel keeps him away from me and my family.

El Jefe's brother almost cost me the love of my life, and had it not been for WRATH securities being able to trace the ring I gave Anaya—despite it not being triggered—then I'm sure I'd be singing a different tune, needing that asshole's head on a silver platter.

"You ready, brother?" Jack steps into the room as I give myself one last glance.

I'm standing in front of our full-length mirror, looking at the linen suit Anaya picked out for our special day. My girl, despite all her bravado, was ready to tie the knot as soon as we were able. And I, of course, was more than ready to officially call her mine.

Today is the day we become a family, giving the woman of my dreams and the child she carries my name, binding them to me for all of time.

She's everything I thought I wanted and more.

Like a gift I don't deserve, Anaya soothes a part of me that had long been shoved into darkness. A deep fear of rejection that I never really analyzed until she came into my life.

When she left me to go with Raul, my soul shattered, despite the walls I'd erected. But like a Trojan horse, she'd already snuck inside my heart, digging her little claws in deep and taking residence inside my soul.

It's no secret that I was destroyed by what I thought was her rejection, and I don't forgive easy, but when I saw that she'd only done it to spare my life, that she'd risked going with a man she knew was capable of death and deceit—that sort of sacrifice is eye opening. And thankfully, because she'd already laid claim to my heart, I could see. See that this woman was meant for me, my soon to be Trojan Crown, infiltrating my darkness and tearing it all down with her love.

Not only did she satisfy that basest of carnal pleasures, letting me dominate and care for her, but she showed me it was okay for me to let her love me, showing me I too was worthy of her devotion.

Letting out a slow breath, I know deep in my bones that the woman I'm marrying is my soulmate—the one person I'm supposed to spend the rest of my life with.

Turning, I see all my brothers standing behind me, all with wide smiles and clear joy in their eyes. Clapping my hands once, I beam back. "Oh, I'm beyond ready."

"All right! Let's get this party started." Jace hoots and hollers.

Matt shoots him a smirk. "You sure you want to be done with your brotherly duties so quickly? Seems to me like you'd enjoy as much time away from that baby momma of yours."

Jace grimaces, the truth of Matt's words written across his face as plain as day. "Yeah, I'm not gonna lie. She's a bit much, but what can I do? It is what it is."

I shake my head, clapping a hand on my younger brother's shoulder. "You know, just because she's having your baby doesn't mean you have to marry her."

Hunter clears his throat. "Especially when you're looking at her daughter the way you do. That's a disaster waiting to happen."

Jace pales at Hunter's words, giving away their veracity. My poor brother got a cougar pregnant—a one-night stand he's now promised forever to. Unfortunately for him, he seems to have the hots for her barely legal daughter.

"It is what it is, and today is not about me. It's about celebrating Austin and Anaya getting married." Jace pins us with his glare, and we drop it… for now.

We all love him too much to let him throw his life away by tying himself to someone he doesn't love. I know the consequences of that all too well. Blanca and I got married because of a pregnancy scare, and looking back, I don't regret it because of Amanda and Alex, but had I had the chance to just have her as the mother of my children instead of also my wife, I would've probably done things a little differently.

"Come on." Jack opens the door to my room. "Let's go watch you make Anaya a Crown."

I step out into the hall and toward my future, ready to make that woman mine. "You don't have to tell me twice."

Anaya

"You look stunning." Mom tears up as she takes me in.

I'm wearing a strapless cream-colored dress, covered in lace and flaring from the knees down. As soon as I tried it on, I knew it was the one. And if I really think about it, that's how it happened with Austin.

From the moment I saw him, I knew he was different. It was visceral, all consuming, and there was definitely no escaping that cranky Crown. But I wouldn't have it any other way. He may not be perfect, but he's perfect for me.

Never in a million years did I think that I'd find a partner in life that would understand my broken bits. Not only does he see them, but he's able to put them back together and make them whole.

"She really does." Pen sighs wistfully, her hand going up to dab at her eyes.

"Oh no. Don't you start crying too. Then I'll start crying and I'll ruin the makeup Cassie did." I'm shaking my head, ushering the girls back when the makeup artist and stylist in question slips a compact into my small bag.

Cassie has been a godsend. She's the wife of one of the owners of WRATH securities and apparently, all of them are friends with the Crown brothers so we've seen a lot of them over the past couple of months. It's been amazing getting to know them, and each one has become an instant friend.

"It's for later, when Austin messes up all of your makeup because he can't get enough of you." Cassie waggles her brows, sending Pen into a fit of giggles and my mom blushing.

The door to our room swings open and Bella, Aiden's daughter and William's wife, walks in. "The groom is in position. You ready, babe?"

"Yes." I bite my bottom lip as I stare into the full-length mirror once more. "More than ready."

I'm about to turn toward the door when a booming voice

seeps into the room. "Where is she? Where's my girl?"

Bella shrieks, "Austin! It's bad luck to see the bride before the wedding!"

She's not even done speaking when Austin barges into our room, his look one of hunger and desperation as it lands on me. "The wedding is now. I'm done waiting."

My mouth is hanging open as this neanderthal of a man swoops down and carries me bridal style. "Austin! What are you doing?"

"I'm carrying you to the altar. Isn't that obvious?" He's dead serious, and I can't help but shake my head and laugh.

As he presses my body closer to his, the cheers of our guests envelop us in their warmth and joy, and I know I wouldn't want this day any different. The way he loves me, hard and fierce, is part of the reason I'm so lost for him. Austin Crown may be far from perfect, but he's perfect for me, and I can't wait to spend the rest of my life with him by my side.

TROJAN CROWN

Thank you for taking a chance on Trojan Crown. Please consider leaving a review if you enjoyed it. Reviews are like precious gold to authors and it would mean the world to me to hear what you thought of my book baby!

MEN OF WRATH

Acts of Atonement: *A Single Dad Age Gap Romance*
Acts of Salvation: *An Age Gap Romance*
Acts of Redemption: *A Second Chance Romance*
Acts of Grace: *A Brother's Best Friend Romance*
Acts of Mercy: *A Stepbrother Romance*

CROWN BROTHERS

Filthy Crown: *A Single Dad Age Gap Romance*
Sinful Crown: *A Single Dad Age Gap Romance*
Feral Crown: *A Secret Baby Age Gap Romance*

Be sure to join my newsletter so you're updated with upcoming releases freebies. There's nothing like a fresh book hitting your inbox!

Let's stay connected. I'd love to hear what you thought of the book, what's on your TBR list, or simply how your day is going.

www.EleanorAldrick.com

Instagram
@EleanorAldrick

Goodreads
www.Goodreads.com/EleanorAldrick

Twitter
www.Twitter.com/EleanorAldrick

Facebook
www.Facebook.com/EleanorAldrick

Be sure to sign up for my newsletter where I share exclusive content. You won't want to miss out!

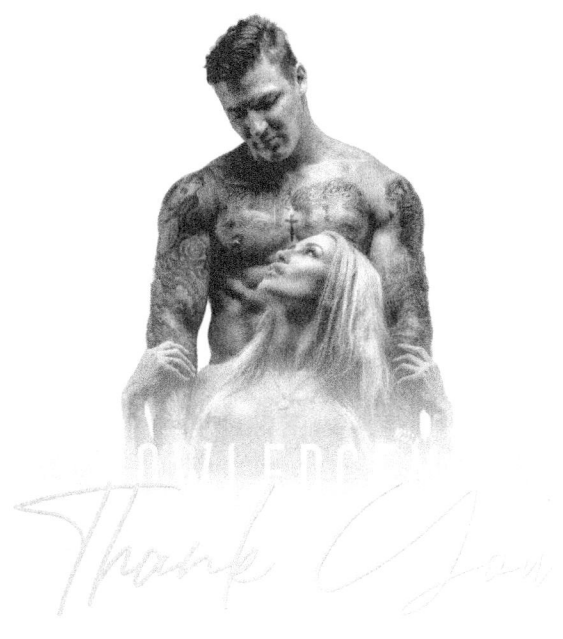

Wow. This book was especially hard to write because of the climate of time we're in. It's been an insane two years and the last couple of months have definitely been some of the hardest—but we did it. We're here at the end of book two and I couldn't be any more in love with Austin and Anaya.

This, of course, wouldn't have been possible without the friendship and support of two very special women. Lauren and Suny. You two are the icing to my cake. There's no doubt in my mind that this book wouldn't be what it is today had it not been for your love and support. I love you ladies to the moon and back.

A shoutout to the hubs is also in order because his support means the world to me. He's always eager to know how my writing is going, even though reading for pleasure isn't his jam. Shocker, right?! How did an avid reader like myself end up with someone who hasn't one fiction book to his name? I don't know, but I'm glad I did. Thanks, babe. You're my number one MVP.

    I'd also like to thank everyone in the Sinfully Seductive Squad. You ladies are amazing, pumping me up and making me just as excited when I've got no energy left. If you've written a book, then you'll probably know the phases of writing. Inevitably, there comes a point where you've read your work so many times it all starts to blur together, but you ladies have kept me going and put that spark back into my writing. It means the world to me every time you share an edit or simply let me know how much you're looking forward to the next book. I just hope you know how much I appreciate and love you.

    And last, but certainly not least, I am thankful for you, the reader. Thank you for taking a chance on my book. With so many titles out in the wild, you chose mine. I can only hope that you enjoyed the ride and that it has opened the door to a book friendship that will continue into the end of time. Seriously, from the bottom of my heart, thank you.

XOXO,

Printed in Great Britain
by Amazon